WITH OUR COMPLIMENTS

Westwood Marquis
H O T E L   A N D   G A R D E N S

930 Hilgard Avenue, Los Angeles, CA 90024
(213) 208-8765

GOLD

GOLD

Darrell Delamaide

GOLD

E. P. DUTTON   NEW YORK

PUBLISHER'S NOTE: This novel is a work of fiction.
Names, characters, places, and incidents either are
the product of the author's imagination or are used
fictitiously, and any resemblance to actual persons,
living or dead, events, or locales is entirely coincidental.

No part of this publication may be reproduced or transmitted
in any form or by any means, electronic or mechanical, including
photocopy, recording, or any information storage and retrieval
system now known or to be invented, without permission in writing
from the publisher, except by a reviewer who wishes to quote
brief passages in connection with a review written for inclusion
in a magazine, newspaper, or broadcast.

Published in the United States by E. P. Dutton,
a division of Penguin Books USA Inc.,
2 Park Avenue, New York, N.Y. 10016.

Library of Congress Cataloging-in-Publication Data

Delamaide, Darrell, 1949–
Gold / Darrell Delamaide. — 1st ed.
p.   cm.
ISBN 0-525-24771-8
I. Title.
PS3554.E4335G6   1989
813'.54—dc20   89-32061
                                  CIP

Designed by REM Studio

1   3   5   7   9   10   8   6   4   2

First Edition

To my mother

GOLD

One

I

Those goddamned anchovies again.

Drew swiveled toward the screen and tapped quickly on the keys: COM, GRA, FUT, coding the story for the commodities, grain, and futures wires. URG, priority code urgent. Bells? News tickers did away with bells years ago. Computer screens don't ring.

The quiet static of his keypunching contrasted with the roar of tension in Drew's ears. The anchovy schools off the coast of Peru had disappeared again, according to the unexpected announcement from the Ministry of Mining and Natural Resources in Lima. Drew remembered his early days as an economic journalist when the anchovies had reappeared suddenly after a two-year absence. He had been sitting quietly editing a story when the slotman started squirming and muttering about anchovies, just like Drew was doing now. So what? he thought at the time. Only afterward did the filing editor explain to him that anchovy meal is one of Peru's main exports and the leading substitute for

1

soybean meal. The Chicago commodities pits would go into contortions whenever those anchovies appeared or disappeared. Nobody knew where they went.

The second take came up on the screen. The Peruvian Ministry spokesman said nobody knew where the anchovies had gone, but gone they were: bad for Peru's exports, bad for its foreign debts. Shit, yes, he had forgotten to send it on the financial wire. He coded the second take the same as the first, adding FIN for the financial wire. He put it into the computer queue, called up the first take again, coded it for FIN, sent it out again, and sent out the second take.

Drew sat back and blinked. He should not even be sitting in the slot. It had been a long time. But MacLean had had to leave all of a sudden, and since there were only two junior copy editors on the desk, Andrew Dumesnil, managing editor of World Commodities News, found himself in the slot for the first time—he counted quickly—in six months.

Just then Tom came in. Drew tapped quickly to code the afternoon gold fixing: COM, FIN, and MET for the metals wire; QUK, quick, for the next-to-urgent priority.

"Tom, can you take over? I shouldn't even be here," Drew called over to the dapper young man. Tom, a twenty-seven-year-old Englishman, was the most seasoned editor on the desk, with five years' service. A graduate of Oxford or Cambridge—Drew could never remember which one—Tom would have been prime material for Reuters, the big British agency, but he had opted for the tiny American-owned news service instead.

The main editorial office of World Commodities News occupied a surprisingly small space on the fifth floor of the Star building in London's Fleet Street. The leased space consisted of a large room with a cubicle in one corner formed by glass and plyboard panes that stopped short of the ceiling. The central space was occupied by a round table, open on one side, with what looked like an airline cockpit in the center—a bank of screens and keyboards set in a semicircle at typewriter height. There was the chair for the filing editor, who could operate the various keyboards like an organist in a baroque church, while keeping an eye on the table surrounding him. Around the rim, like spokes on a wheel, were six computer screens and keyboards for the copy editors. Usually, like today, only two or three were

2

occupied. The entire editorial staff at WCN head office consisted of twelve persons working in shifts around the clock.

Tom stepped in the slot behind Drew. "Where's MacLean?" he asked, rolling up his sleeves.

"Toothache," Drew answered, routing the closing Frankfurt stocks.

"Toothache? More like headache. I don't know how he sits in here for eight hours a day, day after day."

Drew stood up but kept his fingers on the keyboard to code the report on the Comex opening. He straightened up. Tall at six foot two, he was well built without looking athletic. He was winning the battle so far against middle-aged paunchiness; his twice-weekly squash games kept his preference for beer from getting the upper hand over his figure. There was a softness to his features that testified to a life spent in classrooms and offices, but a lively intelligence in his eyes and animation in his face lent him a certain vigor that belied his intellectual bent. The clothes fit the man—his salary as managing editor allowed him to indulge his penchant for tailored suits and shirts. Drew picked patterns and colors that were neither sober nor flashy, corresponding to his particular notions of what was proper for a financial journalist, a man of letters living in a world of money.

"All yours," he said to Tom, stepping around the younger man and dancing quickly out of the slot.

Drew went back to his office and picked up the phone to make a call. Tom glanced at him in his glassed-in cubbyhole before scrutinizing the report of a bus contract for Daimler-Benz. Too small. Delete.

"Hello, Bart," Tom called over to the curly-headed young man on the rim. "How's things today?"

Bart turned to Tom, as though he were waking up. "Not too much going on." As far as Bart could see, not much would ever go on at a commodities news agency. He had something of the dreamer about him, as though he were a southern novelist in exile. He had joined WCN's domestic counterpart, U.S. Commodities News in Chicago, straight from the University of North Carolina. After just six months, they had dispatched him to London.

"What's all this anchovy shit?" Tom asked, scanning the printout of the outgoing copy.

3

"Soybean dealers need to know," explained Bart, turning back to his story on oil refining capacity in Europe. He'd picked up a few things on the Chicago desk. He was bright, in spite of being a dreamer.

The phone rang in the slot. "Editorial," Tom answered, cradling the receiver on his shoulder as he put on the codes for the closing Zurich stocks and sent the item off.

"Didn't you get the telex?" The voice on the other end was faint but clearly agitated. "They've blown up the mines. They've blown up the mines!"

"What mines? Who is this?" Tom said. He took hold of the receiver and pressed it closer to his ear.

"This is Van der Merwe in Johannesburg."

Tom deleted the earnings report of a small French company and pressed his finger into his other ear to hear better. "Who blew up which mines?" he asked.

"The terrorists. They've blown up the gold mines." The voice paused. "It's incredible. All of them. All the big ones on the Rand. Looks like ALF."

"Hold on." Tom looked into the cubbyhole. Drew was gesturing as he talked on the phone. "Drew," he called, "you better pick up line two in a hurry."

Drew looked at him, spoke quickly into the phone, and punched a button on his phone console.

"Are you sure? How'd you find out?" Tom could hear Drew ask through the glass.

Drew had picked up a pen and was writing furiously. "What's the source?" he interrupted. "How sure is this?" He scribbled constantly.

Tom looked at an analysis of the U.S. Agriculture Department's crop estimates that had been released earlier in Washington. He routed it into Bart's editing queue.

Drew stopped writing. He looked at the phone, jabbed the receiver cutoff, punched some buttons on the console, hung up. He strode out of the office to the telex printer, looked at the copy, and then went over to the clipboards opposite the slot to leaf quickly through the long sheets of printer paper. He went to his phone again. "Try to get me Van der Merwe in Johannesburg," he said to the switchboard operator downstairs. Then he went over to the desk.

4

"Have you seen a telex from Johannesburg?" he asked Tom.

"Don't look at me, I just got here," said Tom. "What's going on?"

Without answering, Drew went back into his cubicle and called the switchboard. "Any luck on the call to Johannesburg?" he asked into the receiver. "Keep trying, it's urgent."

"He says the ALF has blown up the big gold mines on the Rand," Drew said, coming back out. "But the line went dead. He said he heard it 'through reliable sources in the underground.' "

Tom sympathized with his superior. If it was true, the report would rock the markets like an atomic bomb. But was it true? "How in the hell would Van der Merwe get a telex out?" he asked.

South Africa had imposed a draconian news censorship eight months previously. Most foreign correspondents were sent home, and only authorized "pool" reporters were allowed to stay, each one designated to provide news for several media. They were confined to Pretoria and only allowed to report official government communiqués—on any subject. All telex traffic was carefully monitored.

"I don't know how he got it out, but he claims he did," Drew responded impatiently.

He tapped his notes in the palm of his hand, biting his lip. "Damn." He turned back into the office and sat down at the phone.

"Hello, Morgan, lucky I caught you," Drew said, when Morgan Preston picked up on the first ring. It was his direct line, and Drew was probably the only journalist who had that number. "Saw gold was steady at the fixing," Drew went on. "Quiet market, I guess." Preston was one of the five merchant bank representatives who met twice a day to "fix," or set, the price of gold. That London price became the reference point for all ingot trading around the world.

"Like a morgue," responded Preston patiently. He was a busy man; Drew Dumesnil was a busy man. He didn't call to tell him the price of gold was steady.

"Hear anything out of South Africa?" Drew asked, in what he hoped was a natural voice.

The news blackout in South Africa had made the gold market jittery at first. South Africa was still the world's biggest producer.

5

But the supply of gold bars remained steady, and the market quietly accepted that, although some unpleasant things were going on down there, one consequence of martial law was the continued steady production of gold.

"No, not really. Seems to be the same as usual." Usual round of petrol bombs, police action, scattered reports of massacres in the townships, atrocities in the white suburbs—and a steady fifty tons of gold a month. The only wild card was the Azanian Liberation Front—Azania was the "African" name for South Africa—which had split off from the African National Congress two years ago. As the front-line organization opposing white rule in South Africa, the ANC enjoyed the political support of black Africa, several European countries, and was increasingly accepted even by London and Washington. The ALF wanted action, not political support, and someone was giving them guns and explosives.

"What does the market make of this ALF activity?" Drew asked.

"Seems pretty sporadic, marginal," Preston said. "So far."

"Any reports that they've attacked business installations, like the coal conversion plants, or"—Drew paused briefly—"the gold mines?"

The journalist felt uneasy because he knew his questions would arouse Preston's curiosity.

"No. Have you heard anything?" the banker countered.

Drew ignored the question. "The gold mines, for instance; I shouldn't think they'd be too vulnerable to terrorist attack," he continued, trying to keep his tone objective. Just a hypothetical question.

"Oh, they'd be very vulnerable, if terrorists could get at them," Preston responded, to see how far he could push Drew's hypothesis.

"Vulnerable in what way?" Anxiety was creeping into Drew's voice in spite of himself.

"Well, the mines are spread out under the ground, with tiny entrances on the top." Preston exaggerated, to rub it in. "You know that, Drew. Blow up the entrances and you could pretty well sabotage the mines. But I should think our fascist friends in Pretoria would have thought of that and posted a few thousand armed guards around them."

6

"Yeah, of course. So you guys aren't too worried about South Africa keeping up its gold production?"

"Gold's trading at a hefty premium already since the township riots got serious," Preston explained cautiously. "But there's been no news to make us more worried. Drew, what have you heard?" There was an edge to the question this time.

"Look, Morgan, I've got to get back into the slot. I've been trying to reach our fellow in Johannesburg—never know what this ALF might try. I'll let you know if I get anything that might affect the market." He hung up before Preston could protest.

Shit, he cursed again. The greedy bastard was probably buying gold already. He had hated to call him, even though Preston was one of his oldest and most trustworthy sources. Information was literally gold to these people, and Drew knew his questions alone were going to start a rumor.

He rubbed his eyes. Wouldn't matter, though, if Van der Merwe's report was true. He checked with the operator; still no connection to Johannesburg. "Get me Atlanta," he said.

Atlanta was the headquarters of Sun Belt Communications, the owner of WCN. The operator was well-schooled. "Atlanta" meant not only SBC but Richard Corrello, vice-president of the News Group.

"Rich," Drew said. "Got a humdinger for you. Our man in Johannesburg says the terrorists have blown up the gold mines." He looked at his watch. Twenty minutes since his line to Van der Merwe went dead. He couldn't sit on this story if it was true.

"Are you shitting me?" Corrello, born and bred in Manhattan's mean streets, did not speak with a southern drawl. "Does anyone else have it?"

"Market's quiet. Don't think so. Line went dead while I was talking to Van der Merwe, the guy in Johannesburg."

"How reliable is this—this Van der Mer-wee?" The way Corrello pronounced the name made it sound like something children were taught to do in the bathroom.

"He's an Afrikaner, but he's been pretty straight since we've had him, going on six years. Never had any problems."

"The shit will hit the fan," Corrello said. He had come up on the newspaper side of SBC, but he knew how volatile instant screen communication had made the commodities markets. "Should we go with it?"

Drew's stomach tightened; he had known it would come down to this. "Well, we have to if it's true."

"You're going to have to call it, Drew," Corrello said. "It's a tough one, but it's all yours. You know we rely on you one hundred percent."

Drew breathed deeply. "I'm trying to get back to Van der Merwe. Lines are jammed or blocked, or something. I'll make a stab at the embassy, but I can't hold it too much longer. I'll let you know." He hung up. Tom was at the door.

"Gold's up two-forty," Tom said, turning back to the slot.

Bastard Preston. "Get me the South African embassy," Drew told the operator. Damn racists had moved the embassy out to Wimbledon for security reasons. The big building on Trafalgar Square, a monument to the glory of the British Empire, was too obvious a target for terrorists.

He drummed his fingers nervously on the desk, scanning his notes. *Extremely reliable underground sources. Went off in a series last night between 3 and 4 A.M. Maybe 80 percent of total S.A. production. ALF likely. Nobody knows. Roadblocks all around the mines in the Rand and Orange Free State.* The phone buzzed. "No answer at the embassy," the operator said.

"What do you mean, no answer? Embassies have to answer. It's only four o'clock. Keep trying." He slammed the receiver down.

"Up three-twenty from the fixing," Tom called from the slot.

Drew punched another number on the phone. "Morgan, are you buying gold?"

"I am now, like crazy," he said. "But the market was moving even while we were talking. What's up, Drew?"

"I've got an unverified—I stress, unverified—report that terrorists have hit the gold mines," Drew answered. He didn't say anything about the 80 percent.

"Bloody hell." Damn British and their bloody hells. "I'll see what I can find out," Preston said, hanging up.

II

Drew took another deep breath, put his hands flat on the desk, and stood up. He picked up his notes, walked out to the desk, and sat down at the screen next to Bart.

Tom, thin-faced, with a complexion pasty from junk food, looked up at him but kept his fingers moving on the keyboard. Drew signed into the computer system with his confidential code and opened a file; the screen went blank.

ALL, he typed. That was easy: all the wires—commodities, financial, grain, metals, oil, and news, the one that went to the newspapers. FLA: flash. It would bust into any story on any subscriber screen or printer.

UNCONFIRMED REPORTS SAY TERRORISTS HIT SOUTH AFRICAN GOLD MINES. A clumsy headline, but he had to cover his ass.

> JOHANNESBURG (WCN) — Reports that could not be immediately verified said terrorists have sabotaged some of South Africa's major gold mines. The extent of the damage and the effect on gold production was not immediately known.
> —MORE—

He looked at the screen, made sure that the "nots" were where they were supposed to be, and closed the file; the story vanished from the screen. Tom, who had been watching him closely, punched a command button in the slot. He looked at his screen and whistled.

"Send it," Drew said, on his way into the cubbyhole. "Rich," he said on the phone to Atlanta, "it's gone. Cross your fingers." He hung up and sat quietly. For one minute. Then the phone buzzed.

"Is that true?" It was Stanley Hartshorne, one of Preston's colleagues in the gold-fixing round, and a source less old and less trustworthy.

"As true as an unverified report can be," he answered. Hartshorne hung up without so much as a bloody hell.

"Up ten," Tom called in. The phone buzzed.

"Drew, you guys are nuts. That can't be true." Drew couldn't believe his ears. It was Georg Holstein, managing editor of Reuters. His German accent identified him unmistakably. Holstein

9

hung up before Drew could answer. The phone buzzed again. Drew punched an open line and told the operator not to put through any calls except from Atlanta or the South African embassy.

He went out and stood behind Tom in the slot. Gold was up 20; gold futures were up in London, New York, and Chicago; the dollar was up in London and New York. Tom ignored him, tapping the codes, routing the reports as they flashed up on his screen. Drew's phone buzzed in the cubbyhole.

"I said no calls," Drew snapped into the receiver. "South African embassy," rejoined the operator calmly. She was used to the mercurial moods of news people.

Drew looked at his watch. Seven minutes. That was quick. "You must run a correction immediately. It is absolutely not true," said a thick voice coming onto the line. No hello, no identification.

"Who's speaking, please."

"Ambassador Botha," the thick voice said. Goddamn, maybe it *was* true. The ambassador himself!

"Our source is reliable," Drew said. He almost prayed.

"Nonsense. Complete and utter rubbish. Pretoria will be issuing a statement shortly. You must correct your report immediately," the voice sputtered.

"I've been trying to reach Johannesburg for verification, but the lines are blocked," Drew said, playing for time. He wanted to see how serious they were. "I tried calling the embassy, too, but there was no answer."

"You must correct your report immediately. It is absolutely not true," the man repeated.

"I'll be happy to quote your denial. Tell me your first name and give me a number where I can call you back," Drew said. The line went dead.

The phone buzzed again. "Atlanta," said the sweet English voice.

"Are you sure of this, Drew?" Drew's stomach tightened again. Thomas Madison, chairman of SBC.

"I talked to Rich. He said it was my call. I covered us as much as possible."

"It had better be right," Madison's remark was followed by a click.

Drew was in the slot again. "Any news from Pretoria?" he asked Tom.

"Nothing yet. Gold's at four-fifty-five. That's up nearly a hundred dollars. Reuters must be going bananas." The market was shooting the moon and Reuters, the world's leading financial news agency, did not have the story.

Tom did not look around but kept his fingers playing over the keyboard. Bart sat leaning on his elbows, taking it all in. He had finished the stories in his queue and no one had thought to give him anything else to do.

"Here's something," Tom said, squinting at the screen. "French Press Association says Pretoria will have an announcement on gold mines in fifteen minutes." Drew returned to his office and tried MacLean's number. No answer.

"Some selling, now; people taking profits," Tom called out. One of the three screens in the slot was the on-line markets service, which had various "pages" of price information. Like an accomplished pianist, Tom was calling up pages for different gold markets with his left hand while coding the news stories with his right.

Drew came back to the rim and watched Tom operate in the slot. He caught Bart's eye, prompting the younger man to check his screen for new work.

Three young men sitting in a small office on Fleet Street, and they had just thrown a world financial market trading trillions of dollars into a vast and dangerous confusion. Small as it was, World Commodities News had established itself as a competitor of the big agencies, Reuters and Dow Jones, in the niche it had carved out for itself. If there had been any doubt, the churning markets reflected in the flickering screens in front of him offered ample proof of WCN's credibility.

"Drew, sit down at three," Tom said. The managing editor went to the terminal he had been at before and called up the story Tom flashed to him.

TERRORISTS DAMAGE SOUTH AFRICAN GOLD MINES

PRETORIA, Nov. 15 (FPA) — Terrorist bombings have caused an undertermined amount of damage to gold mines near Johannesburg, Johannes van Wyl, minister of Industry and Mines, said today.

Only now did Drew realize how tight the feeling had been in his chest. He breathed easier. The French Press Association was WCN's pool reporter for South Africa, responsible for distributing official communiqués to all agencies and papers in the pool. He quickly rewrote the report on the screen to lead "Confirming earlier reports," and so on. He was the only one who could write that, he thought, grimly happy. Thank God.

South Africa. Gold. It was all so appropriate. Drew recalled his long evening walks down Fox Street to the Carlton Hotel. At each street corner in downtown Johannesburg, silhouetted in the twilight, small groups of blacks would stand at the curb. They were waiting for the minibus to take them back out to Soweto, nearly half an hour away.

Drew shivered. He had gone to South Africa on assignment with the idea and hope that this country, like his own, could find a reasonably peaceful way to resolve its race problem. He sought out the businessmen, mostly Anglos, of English descent, reputed to be liberal. They railed against the stupidity of apartheid, the stubbornness of the Afrikaners—descended from Dutch, German, and Huguenot settlers—but were optimistic that good sense would prevail. One man, one vote? Well, that was going a bit far. Perhaps in a generation. . . .

He had met as well with black trade union leaders. There was a distrustful edge to their encounters with an American business journalist, but the message was clear. "Unless we have one man, one vote in two years, there'll be a bloody revolution." Rhetoric?

That had been three years ago. In the meantime, the reactionary white government in Pretoria had reinforced a system of repression that had reduced South Africa to a state of siege. A year ago, complete martial law, suspension of parliament, the summary execution of dissidents. Eight months ago, the news blackout. Revolution or not, events in South Africa had gotten very bloody. The hope of an entire subcontinent, the country was rapidly deteriorating. The intractable conflict threatened to turn it into a ruin as desolate as Lebanon. Many of those liberal Anglo businessmen had emigrated, to safety nests in the Bahamas or Argentina. The Afrikaners stayed and circled the wagons.

"They can't have another general election without black participation," a bright South African black raised in Europe had told him. He turned out to be right. Elections were suspended indefinitely.

The Cape, with its glistening white-gabled estate homes, gentle Mediterranean atmosphere. . . . Idyllic Stellenbosch, intellectual heart of the Afrikaner Republic. . . . Port Elizabeth, Johannesburg, Pretoria, Durban, Bophuthatswana, Soweto—Drew had spent nearly a month traveling around this country at the tip of Africa. The assignment from *Money Manager* had been the highlight of his brief stint as a freelance business writer. In fact, it had been his South Africa cover story for this specialized but very influential financial magazine that had brought him to the attention of Sun Belt Communications. Two months after his pessimistic story appeared, South Africa was forced to suspend all debt payments abroad and gradually seal off its economy from the rest of the world.

Landing at Heathrow after the fifteen-hour flight from Johannesburg, Drew had felt relief. His first thought was that he would never return to the country until it was called Azania. His second was just gratitude that he had not been born a black South African—or a white South African. . . .

Drew signed off his screen and told Tom to turn around any further Pretoria reports at top priority.

His phone buzzed. "Drew, are you holding back? How bad is the damage?" It was Morgan Preston, swollen fat with his gold profits and greedy for more. Drew bit his tongue.

"I really can't say more until I get the details from my man, and I can't reach him right now."

"Maybe we should have lunch tomorrow," Preston countered, sparring.

"Sure, sure," Drew said. He needed to know what was going on in the market.

"One o'clock, Savoy Grill?"

Drew assented, rang off, and punched another line to call MacLean again. Still no answer.

Preston wasn't the worst of the lot. Drew had known him nearly twelve years. Freshly arrived in the forbidding headquarters of the *Financial Times* on Cannon Street, one of the few American journalists hired by that venerable British paper in the days before it started publishing in the States, Drew's first assignment had been to cover the precious metals beat. His three years with a wire service in Zurich had made him familiar with the gold markets. Drew had known Preston by reputation even before coming to London, as the rising star at Morgenthorpe & Co. Accustomed as Drew had been to the dissimulations of Zurich's urbane and cynical gold chiefs, he was surprised, meeting Preston for the first time; the British merchant banker was straight, friendly, almost human. The same age as Drew, Preston had already been chief trader then; now he was managing partner for the merchant bank's trading activities.

III

He had to find that telex. Drew searched more carefully through the clipboard file and examined each piece of paper in the wastebasket, which had not been emptied yet. No original, no copy. Had it even arrived?

He had to talk to MacLean. As far as he knew, the Canadian lived alone. But he didn't really know the fiftyish deskman too well. There were rumors that he had been chased out of Canada because of trade union activities, but he had a solid reputation on Fleet Street. He'd been with WCN since its inception six years ago. He was always civil in the office but never went beyond polite superficialities.

MacLean's sudden departure this afternoon had been out of character, but Drew had not paid much attention to it at the time. The slotman was ostentatiously punctilious, as though defying anyone to find fault in his discharge of his duties. Except for today, with his curious need to see a dentist immediately.

"Comex and IMM are going through the roof," Tom said, referring to the New York Commodities Exchange and the International Monetary Market, the two main markets in gold futures. "There's rumors that the market will be closed early."

Drew came into the slot and started calling up pages on the market screen. The dollar was up 30 pfennigs against the deutsche mark.

"Central banks intervening?" Drew asked.

"Haven't seen anything," Tom replied.

Market operators were liquidating assets in European currencies to buy dollars so they could buy gold. Four fifths of all

14

gold transactions were denominated in dollars. The U.S. Federal Reserve, the American central bank, and the European central banks should be selling dollars against the market trend to keep the American currency from rising too quickly. "Disorderly market conditions" was their quiet term for the mayhem in the foreign exchange markets that accompanied these billion-dollar waves of speculation.

It was the simplest market rule. Whatever reduces supply will raise the price, presuming demand remains the same. If frost hits the orange crop in Florida, the price of frozen orange juice goes up. If terrorists bomb South Africa's gold mines, the price of gold goes up.

But gold was a funny animal. It wasn't like orange juice or coffee or cocoa. You don't eat gold for breakfast. Industry uses gold, but that demand is steady and predictable; it doesn't account for the fluctuations in the gold price. The greatest economist of the century, John Maynard Keynes, had labeled gold "a barbarous relic," but the centuries of greed clinging to the yellow metal maintained its role in finance. Even the central banks, which had officially eradicated gold from the world monetary system, still stacked ingots in their vaults.

New York stocks were up. Political uncertainty abroad always drew money into U.S. shares. Bonds were off, as the flow of money into the dollar pushed interest rates down. The market was like one big heaving beast trying to swallow the huge morsel Drew had just rammed down its throat.

He called Sam Peters downstairs. "Hey, great beat, Drew," the chief of sales said when he answered the phone. "Thirty-seven minutes, and what a whopper. You broke the story."

In the arcane world of wire services, careers were made on a two-minute beat. If you got the news ahead of the competition, your salesmen had something to sell. They kept logs and listed all the stories with beats. Of course, so did the opposition, and their lists had the stories missing from your list.

A beat of just minutes had been important when only newspapers subscribed to wire services. A newspaper up against a deadline needs to rely on getting the breaking news as soon as possible. At any time, some newspaper somewhere is having a deadline, which gave rise to the old saw that wire service reporters have a deadline every minute.

The growth of financial news in the past two decades and

15

the new demands of trading-room screen services magnified this premium on speed. The size and volatility of the markets meant that a trader with a sixty-second head start could make millions. Drew wondered how much Preston had made from acting on his questions.

"Thanks, Sam. It was a hard call, but we got it right."

"You sure as hell did. I'm already calling some of the big traders who haven't bought us yet. They can't afford to be without us now." The salesman's enthusiasm was infectious. Drew felt better.

"Look, Sam, I'm going to have to stay on top of this, so I was wondering if I could take a rain check on our lunch tomorrow."

"Sure, sure, no problem. That'll give me more time to sign up customers," Sam said. "But let's get together soon, and I'll buy the champagne."

Champagne. One man's poison is another's champagne. Those forlorn silhouetted figures in downtown Johannesburg flashed through Drew's mind.

"Right, real soon," Drew said. He hung up and punched the switchboard number. "Are you still trying Johannesburg?" he asked the operator.

"Oh, yes, Mr. Dumesnil, Shirley left a note and I'm carrying on," a voice with a slight Irish accent answered. The new girl was on the switchboard.

Drew returned to the slot and peered over Tom's shoulder into the screen. The dollar was up 45 pfennings as CLOSING FRANKFURT FOREIGN EXCHANGE flashed across. He doubted if Frankfurt was closing down this evening. They headed the table "closing" only because it was the end of the business day. The currency markets never closed. The center of activity just followed the sun around the globe—London, New York, Tokyo, Singapore, Hong Kong, Bahrain, Zurich, Frankfurt.

"Still no sign of intervention?" he asked Tom.

"Brown said he'd be filing a reaction story soon."

Hank Brown, the Frankfurt correspondent, was all right. Lots of enthusiasm. Of course, when you're twenty-three you live on enthusiasm. Drew cast a sidelong glance at Bart, who appeared to be daydreaming.

"Bart, why don't you call around and put together a little reaction story from London too."

16

"Sure thing," the young man said, picking up the receiver in front of him.

"Here comes Brown's piece now," Tom said.

BUNDESBANK INTERVENES HEAVILY IN MARKET

FRANKFURT [WCN] — The West German central bank sold as much as 500 million dlrs in late trading to counter the dollar's sharp rise in currency markets after the report of sabotage in South Africa's gold mines, according to dealers here.

—MORE—

"Looks clean, send it out," Drew said.

"Drew," called Bart, hanging up the phone, "is there anything there about closing down currency trading? Butchard said there's a rumor the Fed will announce suspension of trading this afternoon."

Half a billion dollars in an hour. Not even the Bundesbank, which had the biggest currency reserves of any central bank, could sustain that type of intervention for very long.

"Makes sense," he said. Sense? The currency markets hadn't been shut down since the early 1970s, when traders failed to keep up with the new phenomenon of floating exchange rates. He felt a brief flash of fear. Were the authorities going to be able to handle this market?

With a bound, he was at his phone, putting through a call to Chicago. "Bob," he said to Bob Johnson, his counterpart at U.S. Commodities News in Chicago, "I got a rumor here the Fed may shut down currency markets this afternoon."

"We'll get on it."

The Fed had been on an unsteady course since Peter Wagner had been forced out by the administration two years earlier. Wagner, a colossus intellectually and physically, had held a firm hand on the markets in the first half of the decade. His successor, Hugh Roberts, was widely perceived as being under the sway of whichever administration authority had the upper hand in the constant debate over economic policy. But it was the Federal Reserve Bank of New York, still under Wagner appointee Mark Halden, that would have the decisive say on currency markets. Drew had met Halden at a couple of European conferences, but there would be no chance of getting through to him now. Better to let Chicago handle it.

17

"Any more on this rumor?" Drew asked.

"Seems pretty widespread," Bart said over his shoulder as he punched out another number on the phone.

Maybe the Bank of England was calling around to the big British clearing banks to calm the market. Geoffrey Butchard at the Norfolk didn't pay attention to just any rumor.

"Better lead with it," Drew said, getting a nod from Bart as he listened to the phone.

Bart swiveled around to face his screen and began typing on the keyboard, keeping the phone receiver cradled on his shoulder.

"Fed has called a press conference," said Tom, who was keeping at it like the pro he was.

"Want me to spell you?" Drew offered. Tom had been in the slot more than two hours without a break, which meant as many as one hundred fifty decisions on news items.

"No, I'm all right."

In the movies, now would be the time the editor sent the copy boy out for coffee and sandwiches. But copy boys had long since disappeared from newsrooms, along with keypunchers, proofreaders, and news assistants. Through the miracle of computers, journalists had taken over all these functions. In his cynical moments, Drew sometimes wondered how much longer journalists themselves would be in the newsroom.

Bart had found someone to confirm that the Bank of England was telling people to take it easy. It went into the second take; the first was already out.

"This is getting big," Tom said. Drew grunted, and Tom and Bart giggled. "I mean really big," Tom went on. "Looks like they might shut down the Big Board. Forty million shares in the past hour." Drew remembered the time, little more than a decade ago, when forty million was a record for the *day*. "The Dow's up, but trading is very erratic and mixed," Tom summarized, from the reports flashing across his screen.

Margin calls, Drew realized. As the price of gold went up, a lot of buyers on margin had to put in more cash. They effectively borrowed on top of a small down payment in cash to meet the full price of their holdings. But that down payment was a percentage of the price, so as the price went up, the amount of the down payment went up too, and the investors had to pay in more cash. To get the cash, they were probably moving money out of stocks.

"Margin calls," confirmed Tom, reading from the screen.

It was just after 1 P.M. in New York, and the hastily summoned press conference was convening at the New York Fed. "Bronson and Cotts are with Halden," called out Tom, punching furiously at the keyboard. The presidents of the New York Stock Exchange and the New York Commodities Exchange were with the New York Fed chief for the meeting with the press. That could only mean one thing: they were going to close all the markets. Drew couldn't whistle too well, so what emerged was more like "whooey." He had never seen that before.

U.S. AUTHORITIES CLOSE FINANCIAL MARKETS. The headline flashed across the screen. Drew, standing again behind Tom, let him do the obvious codes: ALL, FLA. He felt certain all their European customers were still in their offices this evening.

NEW YORK (USCN) — U.S. authorities announced that all major financial markets in the country are suspending operations immediately because of "disturbances in the gold market."

The announcement was made by Mark Halden, president of the Federal Reserve Bank of New York, Harold Bronson, president of the New York Stock Exchange, and John Cotts, president of the Commodities Exchange. They said the suspension extended to all major stock and commodities exchanges in the country.

—MORE—

Drew was at terminal 3. He wondered if Corrello had expected this much shit to hit the fan. The second take came up on his screen.

U.S. FINANCIAL MARKETS -2-

Halden said the Group of Ten central banks had agreed to suspend all currency trading pending a meeting tomorrow at the Bank for International Settlements in Basel, Switzerland.

The U.S. markets affected are the New York Stock Exchange, the American Stock Exchange, the Philadelphia Stock Exchange, the Pacific Stock Exchange, the National Association of Securities Dealers over-the-counter market, the New York Commodities Exchange, the Mercantile Exchange, the Chicago Board of Trade, the

International Monetary Market, and most other stock and commodities exchanges.

—MORE—

Drew switched the story back to Tom and dashed for his buzzing phone. "That's right, Meg, it's all yours," he told the Geneva correspondent on the phone. She would be on the doorstep of the BIS at eight o'clock the next morning to cover the central bankers' meeting in Basel.

Halden said the suspension was only to give the market some "breathing space" to assess the impact of developments in South Africa. Markets would be reopened in a day or two, once the authorities had reestablished "an orderly trading environment."

Drew had felt a tingling at the back of his neck since the headline first came onto the screen. This must be what it's like in a nuclear power plant when a meltdown starts, he thought. Had they shut down the reactor in time?

"Tokyo's declaring a bank holiday," Tom called out, routing the story to Bart.

Something was nagging in the back of Drew's mind. He went into the office and rang MacLean's number. It was nearly 7 P.M. No answer. Where in the hell was MacLean?

TWO

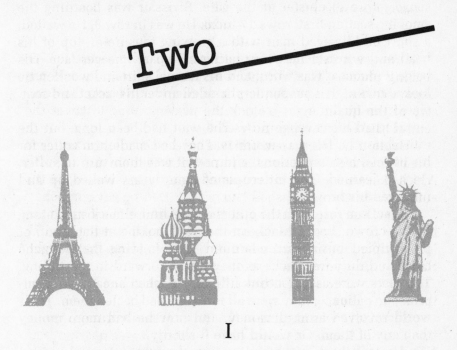

I

MacLean sat quietly at gate A-22 in Heathrow, waiting to board flight SR303 to Geneva. It was an effort of will for him not to fidget, but fear was stronger than nervousness.

He had not expected success on such a grand scale. For years he had waited for an opportunity like this one. He had nurtured his clandestine contact to Fürglin, both of them feeling a certain exasperation in their mutual loathing. But they were patient in their greed, awaiting the right opportunity.

There was an expectant buzz in the waiting room as the attendant escorted an elderly lady through the gate to board first. MacLean kept his seat and held his green boarding card ready. A small smile momentarily lit his face. He had bought an economy class ticket so as not to draw any attention to himself. But he could have afforded first class and would be able to afford first class from now on. Two and a half million dollars gave him more than enough to smile about! The figure danced in his head. Too small to merit much attention in a WCN news story, it was a fortune that would sustain him in style in Rio.

MacLean watched calmly, steeling his will, as waiting passengers rose to cluster at the gate. Swissair was boarding the smoking section first, rows 17 to 28. He was in row 8. He waited, a short middle-aged man with a growing tonsure on top of his head and a mustache punctuating his spare, meager face. His beige trenchcoat was worn, and his flannel shirt and woollen tie looked quaint. His suspenders, hidden under his jacket and coat, were even quainter.

He had his revenge now. The wait had been long, but the satisfaction he felt was worth it. They had made him suffer for his beliefs, his convictions, and now it was their turn to suffer. He had learned. The bitterness of many years welled up and furrowed his brow.

MacLean rose with the others and let himself be jostled along by the crowd. Fools, MacLean thought, looking at the group of preoccupied businessmen around him, holding their attaché cases and duty-free sacks as they thrust forward in the throng. The seats were assigned but still they pushed ahead. No discipline, no patience; they were all fools. He had beaten them. Their world revolved around money, and now he had more money than any of them. Or would have it shortly.

He took back his boarding pass from the stewardess and walked down the ramp to the plane. Tomorrow he would go to the address in Geneva that Fürglin had given him and pick up the money. Then he would fly to Rio via Milan, to further hide his tracks.

He had called Fürglin from the pay phone two blocks from the office. The Swiss had listened quietly and said nothing for a full minute. "This is it, then." It was half an assertion, half a question. They had planned it too long for there to be any misunderstanding. Fürglin hung up, and MacLean went to his flat to pack a small suitcase. He didn't have much to take—or to leave behind.

He sat in 8-D, on the aisle, not even removing his coat, after putting his bag in the overhead luggage rack. The newspapers of course had nothing yet. Most of these pompous asses probably didn't even know what was going on, MacLean thought, snorting in spite of himself.

The plan with Fürglin had grown slowly. MacLean had met the Swiss trader at one of the rare press receptions the journalist had attended. Usually he avoided such affairs; he hated to stand there, cocktail in hand, watching those wolves in pinstripes slinking around, on the make. His flannel shirt and brown sport coat made him stand out amid the blue and gray of business suits. Nor did he have that sleek, manicured look of expensive haircuts and health club fitness. Most of the hungry-eyed crowd sidestepped him, as they would dog droppings on the pavement.

Not Fürglin. Falstaffian in his dimensions, the trader had approached him with a big smile that had only a trace of condescension in it. He had spoken to him as an equal, registering no surprise when MacLean disclosed he was a journalist. Fürglin was, in fact, very interested in MacLean's work. A couple of weeks later, Fürglin invited him to lunch. He wanted to maintain contact, perhaps exchange tips from time to time. MacLean realized that Fürglin had a design in all this, a design that dovetailed nicely with his own half-formed notions of revenge.

The stewardess came by checking seat belts. She smiled at MacLean when he looked up, but the Canadian was lost in his thoughts and didn't respond.

They had hounded him out of Canada, the capitalists. A trade union activist, he was branded as an agitator; there was hardly a worse evil in their narrow nineteenth-century minds. First there had been the intolerable harassment at work, then the punctured tires and broken windows, and then the near-accident. His efforts had met with indifference among the soft, spoiled university graduates in the newsroom. They saw *him* as the anachronism, even though they were the ones caught up in this primitive system of exploitation.

The sudden thrust of acceleration interrupted his bitter reverie. He peered past his neighbor to see the receding airport lights below as the 737 climbed. The bell chimed, liberating smokers from their uncustomary restraint.

Fürglin and he had met regularly over the years, in an out-of-the-way Italian restaurant off Moorgate. Their talk had been veiled at first, but then increasingly open. MacLean learned more about how markets function, and Fürglin learned how and where WCN got its news. They refined their plot, sketched scenarios, outlined the opportunities. It was no small killing they wanted. They wanted a major market move, and Fürglin wanted a half hour's head start. He spoke vaguely of "friends" who would back him when the time came, magnifying the take.

MacLean took the plastic tray that was handed to him, even

though he wasn't hungry. He didn't want to draw attention to himself. He flipped up the lid, noticing that Swissair still used stainless steel tableware, not plastic. He snorted again. Rich bastards.

MacLean had recognized his chance as soon as he saw it. It was a routine day, and he was so accustomed to the pulse of the slot that the flow of news was almost a narcotic for him. The telex from South Africa shattered the routine.

PRODUMESNIL, EXMERWE.

How did he get a telex out of Johannesburg?

TERRORISTS HAVE BLOWN UP GOLD MINES. COULD AFFECT 80 PCT RPT 80 PCT PRODUCTION. UNDERGROUND SOURCES SAY ALF RESPONSIBLE. SERIES OF EXPLOSIONS OVERNIGHT. MORE LATER.

MacLean had immediately torn off the message, including the copy. He looked up to see Drew, sitting in his office, talking animatedly on the phone. MacLean held the message on his lap, below the desk. Bart was absorbed in his screen; Tom would not arrive for nearly an hour.

MacLean read the telex again. He folded it and put it into the pockets of his khaki pants. He picked up the phone and punched out his home number. As the phone rang in the empty flat, MacLean addressed his dentist, saying that he had to see him immediately. Then he called Drew over, pleading his aching tooth, and left to call Fürglin. He left no trace of the telex, with its news that would shake the markets.

"Tomato juice," MacLean said in response to the stewardess's question. The flight originated in London; it was perfectly normal to speak English. He didn't order champagne. That might be remembered.

He had called Fürglin again afterward. The trader and his "friends" had bought massively in gold futures and heavily in the spot market. When the news came across the wires, prices in both markets shot up. As the full import of the move became evident, Fürglin started selling and had liquidated most of his positions before the market gridlocked. He was exhilarated on the phone; they had nearly tripled their money in less than two hours. He didn't tell MacLean how much that represented in absolute terms; the journalist had no idea who these friends were or how much money was involved. Whether it had been $10 million or $100 million, though, it was now three times as much.

24

MacLean's price had been agreed on beforehand, a fixed amount that would enable him to live in comfort for the rest of his life. He was forty-six, and his notions of comfort were modest enough.

MacLean closed the lid on his food, which was untouched. He settled back into the seat. In less than an hour, he would be in Geneva.

II

Spring transformed the hillside in Pretoria. The vivid splashes of red, yellow, violet, and white against the green lawn created a heady gaiety in the balmy air. Crowning the terraced flowerbeds, the Union Buildings all but blazed in the sun, their ochre stone sharply etched against the blue sky. The graceful columns opening up to the town below had an almost Olympian aspect.

Oleg Abrassimov was impervious to the color and the weather. The tinted windows of his Mercedes limousine were shut, and he looked neither left nor right as his chauffeur wound up the twisting road. They drove past the bronze Voortrekker's monument and up behind the wings of the building. Du Plessis was waiting on the pavement as the limousine crunched to a stop.

The Russian looked incongruous as he stepped out of the black car. Palm leaves rustled softly in the spring breeze, but the stern gray face of the Soviet official presented an icy front to nature's allure. Dressed only in a sober gray suit in the mild temperature, he seemed to miss his heavy overcoat and broad-rimmed black hat. After all, it was November and it should be cold.

Abrassimov walked with du Plessis and his two aides around the pillared half-circle and into the courtyard of the east wing. Du Plessis led them up the wide stone staircase, explaining that the office was just on the first floor.

The half-closed shutters kept the high-ceilinged room dim, but that suited Abrassimov better than the bright sunlight outside. Du Plessis indicated one of the worn leather armchairs at the table opposite the desk.

"My colleague from Foreign Affairs was kind enough to loan us his office," began du Plessis, taking the second chair. The two aides, one very young and the other somewhat older than du Plessis, sat discreetly to one side in straight-backed chairs. "We thought it would attract less attention to meet up here."

Abrassimov said nothing. He had met Andreis du Plessis just once before, at the Soviet embassy in London. A plain, trim man in his early forties, du Plessis exuded sobriety.

These were sober days for the director general of the South African Finance Ministry. More than ever, the country depended on gold. South Africa owed its wealth to the rich deposits encircling Johannesburg. The white rulers had exploited the natural resources and the cheap black labor to create a standard of living unparalleled on the African continent and equal to that of the wealthiest Western countries—for the whites. But generations of ruthless oppression had caught up with them. Economic development had compelled them to bring more blacks into the cities, to pay them higher wages, to train them. And now the blacks were no longer willing to play the proletariat; they wanted a greater share of the wealth.

Pretoria's intransigence in the face of this demand had isolated the country. An economic and financial boycott had crippled South African industry and threatened the basis of that comfortable world the whites so much wanted to keep.

The only exception was gold. Nobody boycotted gold. Middlemen with massive sources of finance bought and sold gold regardless of political resolutions or financial withdrawal. There was no right or wrong, moral or ethical, when it came to the dull yellow metal yielded by the bowels of the Rand.

So now gold was everything for South Africa. It alone could finance the premium prices for the clandestine imports desperately needed to maintain a skeletal industry and basic consumer requirements.

Du Plessis was not a fanatic. Trim, with thinning hair, wire-rimmed glasses suiting his bureaucratic mien, and a Huguenot chin, the veteran number-two had been a familiar and widely respected figure in international financial circles. Before South Africa suspended its debt payments in 1985 and then imposed martial law, he had been invited regularly to business conferences, a peer discussing the course of world finance. But he was also an Afrikaner. The time for debates, for equivocation, was past.

If that meant dealing now with the Soviet Union, this is what he would do. White South Africans had little choice. The existence that gave Afrikaners their identity was imperiled. For decades, they had dutifully discharged the geopolitical role assigned to them—guarding the strategic sea lanes around the Cape of Good Hope and forming a bulwark against communism in the African subcontinent. And now they had been abandoned. Washington had yielded to short-term political pressures and undermined their very existence.

A black girl brought in a tray with tea: British influence even in this Afrikaner stronghold, thought Abrassimov fleetingly.

South Africa was the world's largest producer of gold, and the Soviet Union the second largest. Soviet production trailed South Africa's considerably, but not as considerably as Western experts thought. New discoveries in the Siberian tundra had been kept quiet, as well as the new mining technologies that enabled them to exploit the rich ore. For years the Soviets had stockpiled a sizable portion of their production, borrowing on the over-liquid Western financial markets instead of selling their gold at depressed prices. The West's successful fight against inflation had halted the flight into gold, and the price stagnated at less than half the peak it reached after the oil shocks.

The news of the terrorist strike in South Africa had changed all that overnight, reflected the deputy chairman of Vnesheconombank, the foreign trade bank of the Soviet Union. Now they could feed their stockpiles of gold to the panic-stricken market at triple yesterday's price. He had come to discuss with du Plessis how long this price would hold.

The improved situation gave him a deep secret satisfaction. He had been through a torturous hell for eighteen months after a crooked British trader at the Soviet bank in Zurich had defrauded the bank of millions on the gold futures market. The losses had wiped out the bank's capital and forced Vnesheconombank to take over the unit, transforming it into a branch. Abrassimov's career, and, he suspected, his life, had been on the line when he went to Zurich to sort out the mess. The Zurich manager had committed suicide. But now Abrassimov was going to claw back some satisfaction from those markets.

As the two men talked in the first-floor office, Michael Mijosa crept from flowerbed to flowerbed along the driveway, digging up weeds as he went along. The black gardener had seen the Russian drive up and meet du Plessis. His information had been correct.

Michael Mijosa had not looked up. He was invisible; it was his function. He had tended the Government Building grounds for more than fifteen years. For the past twelve he had been active in the underground. The Xhosa was one of thousands of members of the Azanian Liberation Front.

That evening, at home in Alexandra, he would report to his ALF commander. The Russian had come, as they said he would. Now ALF could proceed to the final phase of their agreement with the Russians.

III

Mark Halden sat down at his desk with a groan: 7:30 A.M. The president of the New York Fed had slept only four hours at the Princeton Club, his usual refuge when he worked too late to go home to Long Island. He had talked an hour ago to Hugh Roberts in Basel, just before the Fed chairman went back into conference with the Group of Ten central bank governors. Concern of course was great, but no one seemed panicky at the moment.

It was a group of men inured to panic after the shocks of the past few years. They had teetered so long at the edge of the cliff without falling off that they began to think the law of gravity didn't hold anymore.

Halden sighed. Maybe they were right. Maybe some genius was about to come up with a new theory of economics that made sense of all this mess, a new physics for finance affirming that what went up must no longer come down. In the meantime, though, Halden knew he would continue to experience bouts of profound anxiety. His own studies, including a year at the London School of Economics while he was working on his dissertation, had been progressive enough at the time, but still imbued with classic precepts. Precepts like "You cannot make something out of nothing," and "What goes up must come down." Simple precepts.

He shook off his pensiveness; he had work to do. The President's statement from the White House the previous evening had been a typical virtuoso performance. The former television announcer told his television audience not to worry, the authorities had everything under control. The markets would remain closed for one day but would probably open again on Thursday. There was no need to panic, the President said. It was just a temporary market imbalance that would be straightened out very soon.

The authorities had everything under control. Halden shifted in his seat. True enough for the moment, but could they continue to cope?

Halden scrutinized the one-page memo on his desk. Poor Carol! The memo's author, his chief international economist, probably didn't get out of the building at all last night.

The chronology started with "1538gmt." (News agencies timed off in Greenwich mean time, five hours ahead of New York, where it would be 10:38 A.M.)

> 1538gmt: Reuters, *Dow Jones*, WCN report London afternoon
>   gold fixing. Price is steady at $347 an ounce.
> 1600gmt: Reuters metals wire shows gold at $363, already
>   a strong gain.
> 1618gmt: WCN *flash cites unconfirmed reports that terrorists*
>   *have sabotaged South African gold mines.*
> 1655gmt: Reuters reports Pretoria's confirmation of sabo-
>   tage.
> 1700gmt: Reuters shows gold price at $620.

Halden studied the memo. They would have to find out from WCN what their source was. If it had not been for that flash, Pretoria could have delayed the news a good deal longer and given the central banks time to get ready. Halden had inquired yesterday afternoon at the State Department whether Pretoria had given them any notice. Of course they had not, or Halden would have heard of it right away. The president of the New York Fed was responsible for the markets.

The Federal Reserve Bank of New York, with its thick slate-gray walls and barred windows, loomed up like a fortress in the financial district of lower Manhattan. It was the biggest of the twelve Federal Reserve Banks, which, ostensibly under the control of the Federal Reserve Board of Governors in Washington, constituted America's central bank. The New York Fed had always been the executive arm of the Board, carrying out the operations decided each week by the Federal Open Markets Committee to control interest rates and money supply growth. New York also was responsible for intervening in foreign exchange markets in concert with other central banks to manage the rate of the dollar against other currencies. This task had increased enormously in significance since the historic decision in September 1985 when the United States reversed its earlier opposition to "managing" what were supposed to be free-floating exchange rates.

But that was not all. The New York Fed was responsible for supervising the banks in its jurisdiction, which included seven of the nine biggest banks in the country. And the stock, bond, futures, government securities, and commodities markets that made their home in New York. And all the brokerage houses, investment banks, and dealers who operated in these markets. Propelled by the revolution in communications and the worldwide liberalization of financial markets, developments in New York had quickly outpaced the Fed's ability to keep up with them.

The phone remained blissfully quiet. Halden had asked his secretary to come in at eight, so he would at least have that formidable line of defense again. After the press conference yesterday, he had called in the heads of the commercial banks, brokerage houses, and investment banks for separate meetings. He wanted to get a picture of the markets and what was happening in the wake of the gold news. It was daunting. The sudden announcement had disrupted the balance the Fed had tried to maintain in the markets. The central bank had put out so many fires in the past few years, from Peruvian default to massive fraud in government securities trading. Who would have expected gold to shut down the markets? The massive flows of capital set in motion by news of the gold mine sabotage had simply been too big for the fragile structure of world finance to support.

Then the quick flight to Washington, the briefings at Treasury, the meeting in the White House. Halden had been one of

30

the men with the President before his broadcast. He let Hugh Roberts do the talking, though. After the President's speech, Roberts had boarded an Air Force jet for Basel, and Halden returned to New York for meetings with aides that lasted till 2 A.M. No chance to get back out to Long Island, but it was not the first time Halden had spent the night in town.

Carol Connors was standing in front of his desk. Halden blinked. Evidently she had made it home. The tall brunette in front of him looked as fresh as though she were just coming back from vacation. Her muted lavender suit and pink blouse brought a welcome dash of color to the somber November morning.

Not for the first time, Halden was a bit in awe at the woman he had promoted to chief of her section. The Fed had been relatively liberal in its hiring practices, particularly in the economics department. Carol's place at the Fed had been firmly established by the time Halden came to New York: Princeton undergrad—Halden had noted with favor—Columbia School of International Affairs, followed by a doctorate and seven years of steadily increasing responsibility. A striking, graceful woman, Carol certainly did not fit any stereotypes about backroom drudges. Yet she had toiled long hard hours on tasks that often seemed thankless. With time, however, their accumulated impact had given her a solid reputation within the bank.

The first reports she had prepared for Halden, on London's Big Bang, the massive deregulation of the London stock market and its impact on dollar flows, had been brilliant. Halden had assigned her increasingly to the problems of the debt crisis. Not content with her written reports, he had conferred with her more often, asked her to sit in on top-level meetings, and even had her take part in the negotiations leading up to sessions with the Latin American ministers.

Six months ago, Halden had made Carol the top international person in the economics department, a heady responsibility for a thirty-four-year-old, man or woman. It was a tribute to her professionalism and long years at the bank that, whatever murmurings there had been about her age, there were none about her sex—not even the usual innuendos about how she might have won Halden's attention.

"State didn't have anything for us." Carol's question was really a statement.

"No. Nothing. Just what you read in the newspapers. Pretoria still has given no details about the extent of the damage," Halden replied.

"There's not much in the papers," she said.

Halden grunted. A three-line banner headline in the *Times* and reams of reporting that had pushed everything else off the front page but, yes, not really much in it for them.

"The market started to move even before the WCN flash," Carol continued. She had talked at length with the trading department in preparing her chronology. "We're trying to track it down. London, obviously, but there may be a Middle East connection."

Halden reflected a moment. "Do you know the WCN people?" he asked the economist.

"It's a professional operation. They get the most out of what resources are allotted to them," Carol answered. "It's SBC, and you know their reputation for running a tight ship. The man in London responsible for the story is their managing editor, an Andrew Dumesnil." As usual, Carol had done her research.

Hearing the journalist's name, Halden recalled a tall young man, thoughtful-looking, well dressed for a reporter. "I think I've run across him someplace. Was he with the FT before?"

Carol shrugged. "He's been in this job three years."

Halden paid attention to journalists. He made a point of stopping to talk with them when they chased him coming out of conferences. He would even sit with them in the bar of the Hotel Euler on those occasions when he went to the monthly BIS meetings in Basel. They sometimes had interesting gossip about his counterparts in Europe.

Halden had a vague recollection of Dumesnil. It must have been during the older man's brief stint at Treasury, as assistant secretary for international affairs. That post was almost a sine qua non to get anywhere in the Fed nowadays; more evidence of how tightly knit world finance had become.

He always seemed to be going to Paris in those days. It was a favorite venue for the regular meetings of the so-called deputies of the Group of Ten countries, the number twos from the finance ministries and central banks of the ten largest industrial countries. There were the meetings of the Paris Club, where the same group of governments rescheduled their bilateral loans to Third World countries; the ministerial meeting of the Organization for

Economic Cooperation and Development, which was headquartered in Paris; the Fontainebleau summit. The city's luxury hotels, three-star restaurants, and passion for divertissement exerted an apparently irresistible attraction for the men who managed the world's money.

They were not personally wealthy, these men, but they controlled countless billions of official reserves and had the responsibility in the end for all the money in the world. A little foie gras, champagne, and a discreet visit to the Crazy Horse Saloon certainly was not too much to ask under those circumstances.

Halden was no pinchpenny—his family had money, in fact. But he had wondered at times whether so many meetings were really necessary.

He recalled Dumesnil now. An American working for the *Financial Times*, the legendary British business paper printed on pink stock. Halden would often hold a background briefing at the modest quarters of the U.S. delegation to the OECD in rue Franqueville, a more neutral location than the embassy on avenue Gabriel. Dumesnil would always attend, hanging back a bit, letting others get their questions in first. Then he would pinpoint an issue with a question that seemed obvious once he asked it, but that no one else had thought of. It was quite a talent. Halden wondered if he was always that good.

"We'll have to find out where they got the news from," he said aloud. Carol only nodded; as usual, she had anticipated Halden's curiosity. "I've got a call in to the Bank of England's press people. We'll have some more information about WCN and Dumesnil as soon as they get back from lunch."

Halden looked at Carol and nodded with a smile. "All right, then, let's get down to the dealing room and see if we can get things sorted out."

IV

Carol walked up to her third-floor apartment. No doorman or elevator for her. And the apartment was small, one bedroom, scarcely six hundred square feet. She made a good salary at the Fed, but Gramercy Park was expensive.

She patiently found the keys for all three locks. Less patiently, Tiger began reprimanding her for arriving home late once again. She deposited the bulging briefcase—the real kind that lawyers use—in the hallway and attended first to the cat.

Then she poured herself a glass of white Zinfandel and went into the darkened living room, sinking into the sofa and kicking off her shoes. She sat in semidarkness, with only the light from the kitchen, separated from the living room by a high bar.

Carol sipped her wine, waiting for the mental numbness to pass. She realized she was exhausted but did not think about it. She never thought about it; she only thought about what she wanted to do.

She had always known what she wanted to do. But she never thought much about why.

Back in high school, in Plainview, New Jersey, she already had set her goals. When other pretty girls—Carol always knew she was pretty—had become cheerleaders or drum majorettes, Carol had studied, studied hard. She achieved the highest grade point in her class, became valedictorian, and won a scholarship to Princeton. Again, she studied hard, graduating magna cum laude in economics.

Then came Columbia, the master's degree in International Affairs and the doctorate. Banks had begun scouring the Ivy League graduate schools for bright young men and women to spearhead their burgeoning international business. Carol had been invited to four second interviews, and some heady salary figures had been waved at her.

But she didn't hesitate in choosing the Fed. She knew it was drone work, compiling and analyzing dry statistics. Not the glamour of jet planes, exotic capitals, and luxury hotels that lured so many of her classmates into banking, not even the promise of six-digit salaries that enticed others into Wall Street. She wanted to be at the center of power, and the Fed was the center of power.

Then there was Rick. They had been at Princeton together. He went to Columbia Law School. He took a job with a big corporate law firm. They got married.

It had been easy, easier even than not getting married. And it had worked out fine. She liked Rick. Their relationship in bed was uneven, but Rick was bright and appreciated what she was doing.

34

They had friends, many, like themselves, professional couples. They had less and less time for these friends as work made increasing demands. Then they had less and less time for each other. Then Rick wanted children.

Carol said no.

She would never forget the confrontation in the kitchen. It was a sultry July night. The apartment on Central Park West was air-conditioned, but the unrelenting heat and humidity of a Manhattan summer had put everyone on edge. Rick was already upset that they were not in the Hamptons. An emergency at the Fed had sabotaged their plans for a long weekend with two other couples.

Carol had pleaded with Rick to go without her, but he was too proud to be odd man out.

By Sunday night Carol still had several thick files spread out over the kitchen table. The large apartment had a study, but that belonged by silent consent to Rick.

Rick stood in the kitchen door. He had been fidgeting all day long.

"Any ideas for supper?"

Carol, immersed in the intricacies of an adjustment in the European currency snake, did not look up. "I'm not very hungry right now," she said, preoccupied.

"You know, in most households in this country, the woman takes care of meals," Rick said in even, exasperated tones.

Carol looked up, concentrated on what he was saying a moment, and then laughed in a quick burst. "Rick," she chided, "your liberal mask is slipping."

He turned abruptly away from the door.

"Look, if you're hungry, why don't you just run down to Antonio's and get a pizza?" she called after him.

"And if I'm bored, and if I'm lonely?" He was at the door again.

A look of mock concern came into Carol's face. "Oh, poor baby, feeling ignored." The air grew very tense. Carol tried to defuse the situation. "Come on, Rick, the Europeans don't throw the currency markets into an uproar every weekend. I've got work to do."

"What would they do if you were on maternity leave?"

"I'm not, and"—she leered at him—"as you of all people know, there's no imminent danger of that."

"It's not my fault we're having problems; you should know that. It's this thing about having children."

Carol took off the glasses she wore when she had to read a lot of photocopied documents.

"We've spent many hours discussing this, Rick, and we'll spend many more, but now is not the time."

Rick came over very deliberately to the table, turned a chair around, and straddled it, holding the chairback like a shield between them.

"We have to resolve this thing. What the hell are we doing together, man and wife, if we can't talk about having fucking children? We've been married for six years."

Carol looked at him quietly. It was a familiar ritual. She would explain to him that at thirty-two—their birthdays were only two months apart—they still had plenty of time. He would say it was not going to get any easier the older they got, nor would her career be any easier to interrupt.

She glanced at her watch. Halden was expecting her phone call at eight, and she still had stacks of paper to plow through.

"Rick," she said, putting her glasses back on, "go to hell."

Twelve months later, they were divorced.

That was a year and a half ago. And that was how long she'd been living in her Gramercy Park apartment, where she had the whole kitchen table to herself.

She switched on the lamp next to her, set down her drink, and got up to put a Sibelius symphony on the record player.

Three

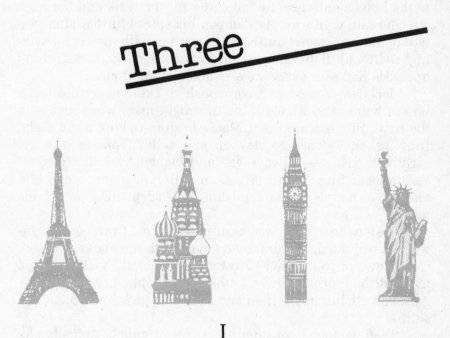

I

Rain always made Drew think of Paris. The French capital seemed to glow with some inner warmth when it rained. Gray skies softened the city's pastel tones further, but glistening water reflected light to give the streets a sparkling brilliance. London wasn't the same. The gritty, haphazard city seemed just a little grittier in the rain, even more sullen.

Paris had taken on a dreamlike quality in Drew's mind. For him, it represented Christine. The warmth and depth of that long relationship merged in his memory with the city's own deeply erotic attraction. They had lived together five years, mostly in Paris. The strains of the last months were resolved when the *Financial Times* posted Drew to Zurich. But that time, that place, that tender recollection remained the emotional pulse in Drew's life. Rain reminded him of Paris, but so did sun, snow, sleet, and fog. Paris and Christine filled his thoughts in quiet moments: waiting on the tube platform, queuing for a film, or, as now, piloting his way automatically through the rain along the crowded pavement from Fleet Street to the Savoy.

As he turned from the Strand into the cavernous lane leading to the hotel's entrance, he felt better for the walk and the fresh air. The rain could hardly dampen his spirits further after yesterday. He had stayed until 4 A.M., waiting with the young overnight editor until the Japanese markets opened—or, rather, didn't open. He had sent everyone else home at midnight.

MacLean seemed to have vanished. Drew never did reach him at home, and Richard, the overnight man, woke him with the news this morning that MacLean didn't show up at eight. Drew asked Richard to stay on and called Tom to take the early shift. He was always getting pinched by SBC's deliberate understaffing. Worse, MacLean's disappearance made him uneasy, although he kept pushing his suspicions out of his mind.

Preston, for once, was waiting for him. Drew smiled inwardly. Not much for him to do today, with the markets closed.

"How are you, Drew?" Preston said when the maître d'hôtel ushered the journalist over to the corner table. Preston, distinguished with his graying hair and navy blue pinstripes, remained sitting.

"Well enough, considering," Drew replied. Actually, he didn't feel too bad, except for this problem with MacLean.

"You're looking good," said Preston, prolonging the preliminaries. Drew was alerted. Preston usually plunged into the matter at hand, and there was a lot of matter at hand today.

"We've known each other quite a while," Preston began. "You're as straight as they come. It's not something I could say for all of your colleagues."

Drew felt a sudden queasiness. The stories one heard swirled through his head: the German real estate correspondent who had made 3 million marks buying property in areas before he wrote about them and then selling at a high markup; the Euromarket writer who regularly participated in the orgies thrown by the Oldham group in the Barbican; the celebrated case of the *Wall Street Journal* reporter who tipped off his boyfriend about the stocks treated in his influential column.

"What are you driving at, Morgan?" Drew asked. He might as well face it now.

"Someone was in the market buying right after the fixing." Preston fixed Drew with his gray eyes. "They were buying here,

38

and in Zurich, and in Frankfurt, and apparently in New York. Everywhere, in short. They were buying a lot."

Drew examined his menu carefully, but when the waiter came he ordered smoked salmon.

"How well do you know your people?" resumed Preston.

Drew studied the banker. "Okay, I'll level with you. We've had a fellow missing since yesterday afternoon." He didn't mention the lost telex.

"Could he have held the news back?"

"He was the filing editor."

Preston cleared his throat and adjusted his napkin. "So that was it," he said. "They must have made a fortune."

The waiter brought their salads, and then the wine Preston had ordered. Drew scanned the room, filled with dark-suited men in twos and threes. The bright pastels of the dining room's decor contrasted with the gray, wet spectacle visible through the vaulted windows.

"I suppose I'll have to find him," said Drew, after they had eaten in silence for a bit.

"Not much to be done now, I should think," said Preston.

Drew changed the subject. "Anything going on today?"

"Surprisingly enough, yes. There was considerable profit-taking just before the Fed press conference, but there's been a strong demand and sufficient selling to meet it. Of course, that's all spot, because the futures markets are closed, and the lack of a fixing has dampened trading." Spot was the cash market for immediate delivery and consisted of dealers buying and selling over the phone. The futures market was trading in contracts for future delivery and took place on an exchange, like Comex or IMM.

Drew said nothing. He usually found silence more effective than questions for extracting information.

"Kuwait seems active," Preston added, after a pause. "They're spreading the orders around, but there seems to be a lot of activity emanating from there."

"What's next, do you think?"

Preston looked thoughtful, as though the obvious question had provoked him to a sudden new idea. "It's amazing when you think about it," he began. "Time and again in the past ten—twelve years we've seemed very near the brink. Every time we've pulled back." He cut a bite from his slab of beef in quick, deft movements. "I think we will this time, too."

"Markets will reopen tomorrow, then, none the worse for wear?"

"There'll be the usual grumblings about better surveillance, tougher controls, and all that," Preston said. "But I think life will go on just like before." He sipped the wine. "After all, South Africa's been on the brink for some time. This thing yesterday just caught the market at a wobbly moment."

Wobbly, thought Drew to himself. When hasn't the market been wobbly in recent years? He didn't push the matter with Preston, who had already demonstrated a longer-term view than Drew had ever heard from him before.

When the bill came and Preston examined it closely, it reassured Drew that the gold trader took the figure so seriously. He sometimes feared that million-dollar deals cut off these market operators from the real world, where real people sweated and suffered for infinitesimal fractions of the amounts these dealers transacted.

II

Back at the office, Drew talked to Meg Hanrahan, the Geneva correspondent who had gone up to Basel to cover the central bankers' meeting there. He could picture the pressroom in the futuristic headquarters of the Bank for International Settlements, which looked like a nuclear power plant and was known locally as the Tower of Basel. It was something of a glorified men's club for the central bankers. The BIS, in fact, maintained a full-fledged sports club outside of Basel.

As usual, Meg recounted, the Europeans were balking at the Americans' presumption that everything depended on stabilizing the dollar. The world had operated on a de facto dollar monetary system since World War II. Following the war, the United States accounted for more than half of all production in the non-Communist world. There didn't seem to be any alternative to the dollar. But in the eighties, the U.S. share of the world economy shrank to less than a quarter, while Washington seemed increasingly irresponsible in the management of its financial affairs. Monetary conferences had developed a routine of plaintive, sometimes whining Europeans, with Americans cast in the role of the heavies.

Washington would get its way again, of course. Whatever the Europeans might think, four fifths of all world trade and finance was transacted in dollars, and nothing could work without a stable U.S. currency.

"How much are they putting in the kitty?" Drew asked his reporter.

"The Europeans are putting up the whole reserves of the EMF," Meg said—the European Monetary Fund, with a good $50 billion in reserves. "The Fed will match it, and the Japanese will pitch in with twenty billion." Would that be enough? "The understanding seems to be that the Fed will double its amount if necessary," Meg continued, not waiting to be asked.

Quite a war chest. But they would need it if the market started to stampede again and the central banks intervened to smooth out trading.

"Will it be finished this evening?" Drew asked.

"Has to be. They want everything to open on time tomorrow," replied the young woman. Her voice had the energy of controlled excitement; she was clearly enjoying herself.

"Give us a three-take backgrounder now—and keep on it," he added superfluously. Meg would write her piece on the portable computer she took everywhere with her and transmit it over the phone into the agency's main computer. Then the slotman could flash it around the world.

David Sangrat called. "I need to see you. My driver will pick you up at five," he said, hanging up before Drew could respond.

Sangrat was one of those ubiquitous middlemen who populated international finance in the wake of the oil shock. His chief distinction was his longevity; a Lebanese Christian, he had proved more resilient than most in keeping up with the shifting fortunes of his Middle East clients.

He had not said please in making his request, but Drew would certainly go. He owed Sangrat too much over the years, and the Lebanese kept very accurate accounts. The older a journalist got, it seemed, the more obligations he accumulated.

Drew had always thought that journalism was a profession

41

for young people. Cynicism was well known to be an occupational hazard, but it was not so well known that the first object of that cynicism was the profession itself. Drew had seen too many tired, bitter reporters to wish himself a lifelong career in journalism.

The responsibility and authority of his job as managing editor might have changed his attitude, but he was finding instead that it just brought a new dimension to his cynicism. Sun Belt Communications was a darling of the stock market. Tom Madison's tight control of costs and his decentralized management had resulted in an almost uninterrupted chain of quarterly earnings increases. But an accountant like Madison was too calculating. He maintained the quality of his newspapers and agencies just high enough to keep market share, but there was no commitment to traditional journalistic values. SBC awarded generous bonuses to top managers for good performance, but performance was measured in terms of pennies saved. The goal was not a top-quality product but a higher number on the bottom line. Don't look for the best reporters, look for the cheapest who can get the job done.

Drew was lucky. At thirty-eight, he had made the transition into editorial management. As a reporter he would have been facing a rapidly diminishing range of options as younger, cheaper people flooded the market.

Perhaps it was just as well, reflected Drew, as his thoughts came back in a circle. No one could work for an entire career scavenging for truth and keep his integrity. Drew recalled the French journalist who had told him with a Gallic wink that reporters spent the first half of their careers finding out what they didn't know and the second half hiding what they knew only too well.

Truth was important to Drew, though. In some ways, it was his religion.

He had been very pious as a child, even zealous. His mother, despite her English and German extraction, was Roman Catholic and steadfastly adhered to her faith. She had insisted that Henry Dumesnil convert to the church before she consented to marry him. The young accountant was in love and cared little for the arid religion of his Huguenot forebears, so he readily agreed.

Drew, and later his brother, attended the Catholic school,

dutifully conforming to the strictures of a paranoid church implanting bastions of Roman faith in a Protestant and secular America.

Drew took readily to the religious tutelage. Intelligent and impressionable, he shared his mother's devotion and his father's driving sense of rectitude. He accepted the special status of American Catholics in a hostile world and their mission to bring heretics and nonbelievers to the one, true church.

For that's what they were taught, and it was easy to believe inside the sheltered environment of school, church, and home. Catholics in the middle America of that era occupied an intellectual ghetto as isolating as any walls.

Drew became an altar boy. The solemnity and the ritual of the Mass appealed to his imagination. His responsibility to carry the heavy Latin missal from one side of the altar to the other, to bring the cruets of wine and water to the priest, to ring the bell as the priest elevated the host and chalice that had become the body and blood of Christ the Savior—all this charged him with a sacred fervor.

He followed the ceremony carefully, reading the English version in his missal as the priest intoned the Latin text. Jesus was the Way, the Truth, and the Life. "The truth shall make you free," the Savior told his apostles.

One summer Drew went to Mass every day. He also went to confession every week. The church was refreshingly cool after the hot buzz of a Saturday afternoon in summer. The confessional surrounded him with a comforting intimacy, which itself enticed the truth from him regarding his minor faults and grievances, including his tiny lies.

When he reached eighth grade—the highest level St. Jerome's parish in Springfield, Iowa, could afford—Drew became chief altar boy, an appointment that enhanced his already palpable sense of responsibility for the sacred trust given to him.

The high point of the liturgical year, and the most challenging for altar boys, was the series of special ceremonies marking Holy Week, the commemoration of Christ's passion and crucifixion that culminates in the celebration of his resurrection on Easter Sunday.

From the hours of practice and the careful attention given to all the complex details of the lengthy ceremonies, one moment always clung to Drew afterward. In the Good Friday ritual, the pastor and his assistant sang the Passion According to St. John, alternating parts during the dialogues to "play" various roles.

In what seemed to Drew at the time the most solemn stillness of the afternoon, the elderly pastor raised his thin voice to chant Pilate's querulous question when confronted with Jesus' claim to represent the truth: *Veritas quid est?* Truth, what is that?

The cynicism of Pilate's question represented for Drew the rejection of all that was holy, even though it was necessary in order that Christ could fulfill his destiny and save mankind.

Drew never forgave Pilate or forgot his question. To seek the truth was right and holy; to sneer at it as Pilate did was to invite divine wrath.

Had he been free to make his own decisions, Drew would have gone directly to the seminary from eighth grade to study for the priesthood. But his parents wanted him to stay home through high school. In the secular world of Springfield High School, his childish piety yielded to the more immediate emotional concerns of adolescence.

Although timid, Drew possessed a quick wit and a quiet charm that made him popular. A series of ever more intense infatuations pushed thoughts of the priesthood farther back in his mind. One winter evening in his senior year in particular marked a turning point in his relationship with women and eradicated any desire for celibacy.

But Drew practiced his religion steadily, if more and more perfunctorily, through college.

It was in France that he lost his faith. It was not a dramatic event. Somehow, in that most Catholic of countries—where nearly everyone is baptized into the church but fewer than half the adults practice their religion—going to church became superfluous. Drew slipped into a comfortable agnosticism, shedding his religion like so many other notions from his past that now seemed to him callow and naïve.

He realized later, though, that the strong moral sense instilled by his upbringing remained with him. And life for him had to have a deeper meaning than material success. It was not a crusading spirit, or a sense of mission, but a simple need to see more in life than creature comforts.

In the soul-searching that followed his rupture with Chris-

44

tine—three years ago, now—Drew came to see that his professional integrity had become the driving force in his life. All the religious fervor of childhood and the drive of adolescence became focused for him on the single objective of remaining true to his profession. That was his sacred trust.

III

At 5:01, Drew settled into the sleek leather seat in the back of the navy blue Rolls Royce. Samantha, the slim, finely chiseled Scottish girl who chauffeured Sangrat's Rolls—among what other duties, Drew could not help but wonder—chatted demurely about the rain as the car glided effortlessly through the rush-hour traffic, across Mayfair to Sangrat's office on Park Lane.

Sangrat rose to greet Drew when Samantha ushered him into the sitting room on the first floor of the renovated row house. Oily was the word in Drew's mind as he shook hands with the roundish, balding Lebanese, whose brown eyes glistened shrewdly.

"Thank you for coming," Sangrat said, with his unctuous smile. "Exciting times," he said, offering Drew his own cigars, knowing they would be refused. The secretary brought tea. "Or would you prefer whiskey?" Sangrat offered. Drew, uncertain of how late he would be up tonight, opted for the tea.

"I'm told Kuwait is buying a lot of gold," Drew said, seizing the initiative.

Sangrat finished his ritual with the huge Havana cigar before responding. "That's just what I was going to talk to you about," he said, once he had taken the first few puffs. "My friends are a bit perturbed."

Drew had only a vague notion of just which Kuwaiti investors Sangrat considered his friends. It didn't matter much, though.

"Some people seemed to know about the gold mines before the news came out," Sangrat said. His friends must be very perturbed, thought Drew. First the peremptory summons, and now Sangrat coming to the point without the usual preliminaries.

45

"Some people in Kuwait?" Drew asked, suppressing again his queasiness. What had MacLean done?

"Some in Kuwait, some in other places." Sangrat focused on the journalist. "My friends reacted very quickly, but these others, they made a killing."

No matter how much money they made, they always wanted more. It was their sport. Kuwait had more millionaires per capita than any other country in the world. The small, desolate emirate on the Persian Gulf was the second-largest Arab oil producer. Kuwaitis boasted that their merchant tradition made them more sophisticated than the simpleminded nomad warriors of Saudi Arabia and other neighboring Gulf states. But their merchants had been more smugglers than tradesmen, and their sophistication had not prevented a stock market collapse in 1982 that paralyzed the economy for half a decade. Through the eyes of many Kuwaitis Drew had met, financial markets seemed like a real-life Monopoly game that they played with middling skill.

"Are they still buying?" Drew pursued his own question first. He wasn't going to tell Sangrat about MacLean; he wasn't sure just what he *was* going to tell him.

"That's the other thing," the Lebanese said. "My friends are buying, the price is going up, but"—he relit his cigar—"somebody's selling."

"Maybe those other Kuwaitis are taking their profits," Drew suggested.

"Perhaps they are, but that doesn't account for the amount of gold coming onto the market."

"Maybe the Asians," Drew said. Japan, the Philippines, Korea, and Hong Kong had absorbed a lot of gold in recent years. Indians had always had a great affection for hoarding gold.

"They like to have gold, to keep it. They're not investors," Sangrat said. For the Lebanese, it was clear that "investing" meant speculating.

"Where do you think it's coming from?" As long as he asked questions, Drew didn't have to give any answers.

"I don't know. My friends are beginning to wonder." Sangrat again fixed on Drew. "What have you heard?"

"Not much. The Kuwaitis are seen as buyers, but no one's located the sellers yet." Drew shrugged. "The Russians?"

Sangrat tapped the ash on his cigar. "That's what we presume, but I don't know." He paused. "Can you find out what

Marcus is doing?" Sangrat knew that Drew had spent some time in Switzerland.

Of course, Drew realized. That's the weak link. Philip Marcus was a product of the market. Scarcely human, he was the quintessential trader. Already worth hundreds of millions of dollars, he kept playing the markets, amassing money with no respect for laws or propriety, for human morals or dignity. From his base in Zug, Switzerland, the first-generation American bought and sold oil and gold, grain and money, in every market in the world. He sold Nigerian oil to South Africa and American computers to the Soviet Union. There were very few countries he could go to without being arrested.

"He's very secretive, of course." Drew's thoughts turned to Hannes Kraml, his Austrian friend who had recently gone to Zug to work for Marcus.

Drew recalled the day when Hannes told him about this decision. They had come out dripping after forty rugged minutes on the squash court; Drew actually had one of his rare days of victory over the athletic Austrian.

In the sauna, that bath of warmth to make the punishment of the courts worthwhile, Hannes mentioned with a false casualness that he might be moving to Zurich.

"No kidding," Drew responded. "One of the Big Three?" The journalist knew Hannes had held talks off and on with at least two of the three massive banks who dominated the Swiss financial system and were among the strongest banks in the world. Drew also knew that, much as Hannes liked city life, he yearned for his mountains.

"Actually, the job would be in Zug," Hannes ventured timidly.

Drew looked at his companion curiously. "I remember very distinctly late one night how you loudly proclaimed you would never work for that crook."

The Austrian, whose bland features lent him a deceptively slow look, smiled shyly. "I'd probably had too much to drink."

"It's not me who's passing any judgments, old friend," Drew said. "It's you who's got to know."

"I've been asking around. The operation itself seems pretty much on the level," Hannes explained. "And he does pay really well."

"And the mountains are very close, and he's really no worse

than most other people only he got caught, and . . . and . . . and."
Drew smiled. "You don't have to rationalize for my benefit. My
only regret is that I'll have to find another squash partner who'll
let me win sometimes, and another drinking buddy who knows
that pubs are for drinking beer, and somebody else who likes
driving like a maniac down country roads—I'll probably have to
replace you with three people."

Hannes studied the hot coals of the oven.

"Seriously, give it a try," Drew added, "if it seems all right
to you. Keep your eyes open, and if things start to get a little
funny, just bolt. You know you'll never have trouble landing a
job." Traders of Hannes's caliber were rare.

"I could ski every weekend in season," Hannes said.

"When do you leave?" Drew realized that the Austrian had
long since made up his mind.

"End of next week." Hannes broke into a grin.

"Two more squash games and at least one long pub crawl.
Deal?" That had been three months ago.

Drew saw Sangrat waiting patiently for him to finish his
reverie. "It would take me some time," the journalist responded.

"I think we'd all know a lot more if we knew just how Marcus
fit in," Sangrat said.

Drew had no idea how long it would take him to get through
to Kraml, or whether the trader would talk. "I can't promise
anything," he said to his host.

"Of course not," the Lebanese said after a pause. "But I think
we can help each other to find out what's going on."

When Drew returned to his office, the tension and lack of
sleep from the past twenty-four hours caught up with him all at
once. He felt a sudden emptiness, a profound discouragement
that made him sad, almost as if he alone had the responsibility
for the momentous events going on around him. Gold. South
Africa. The dollar. Kuwait.

What always bothered him about this roller-coaster ride of
crisis and euphoria in the financial markets was how vulnerable
it made the political situation. After all, the world had survived
financial calamities in the past, in spite of the individual suffering they inflicted. But the conditions resulting from a financial
collapse too often gave rise to worse consequences. The Great
Depression had meant a stock market decline and high unem-

ployment in the United States. In Germany, it had meant a banking disaster, hyperinflation, Hitler, and revenge.

Financial crisis increased the volatility of international relations. At times, he wondered what would have happened in 1982, just after Mexico suspended its debt payments and ushered in the crisis they were still suffering from, if King Fahd had been assassinated in Saudi Arabia or if the Soviet Union had invaded Iran from Afghanistan.

Drew started doodling on his desk pad.

1520: *MacLean excuses himself to go to the dentist.*
1538: *gold fixing.*
1545: *Van der Merwe's call.*
1618: *WCN flash.*
1654: *Pretoria's announcement.*
1815: *press conference at New York Fed.*

Gold. Buyers in Kuwait, elsewhere, after fixing. News leads to sharp price rise, profit-taking. Strong demand but steady supply.

It didn't smell right. Panic buying should not be matched by selling. MacLean. Odd duck. Why did he leave Canada? (So why did you leave the States, wise guy?) Where was MacLean now? With whom does he have contacts? Drew underlined the word "contacts" that he had written on the pad. He put a question mark behind it. Marcus. If he's selling, he might have the key to where the gold is coming from. Maybe he's been stockpiling gold for this kind of opportunity. No. Marcus wasn't a stockpiler, he was a trader. Who else could stockpile gold? Russia? He underlined again.

He looked at his doodling. Underlined words with arrows and question marks. It did not make sense.

He looked at the word "contacts."

"Tom," Drew called to the slotman from the door of his office, "who was that Swiss banker MacLean used to hang around with?"

Tom hit some keys and looked up. "Fürgel, I think. No, Fürglin, over at Ticino Bank."

Drew called Preston. "Morgan, what do you know about Fürglin?"

Silence, as Preston's internal computer digested the signif-

49

icance of the question. "Smooth operator. You think he's the one?"

"Could be. Gives me a lead, anyway."

"Stay on the line a moment," the banker said.

If MacLean had decided to profit from the sabotage, a banker like Fürglin would have been in a position to exploit the advantage of having the news ahead of the market.

Preston came back on the line. "Well, he's supposed to have a link to some Kuwaitis, so that part fits. He also runs some fishy money through the Caribbean, but I've no idea who's behind it."

Where had MacLean gone? Drew found himself asking. Off to South America? The questions surprised him. Little more than twenty-four hours ago, his life had been much more innocent.

"You know, company like that can get pretty rough. I hope your man knew what he was doing," Preston said.

"I'll admit I'd feel better if I could track him down," Drew told him. "Thanks, Morgan. Let me know if you can dig up anything more about Fürglin, will you?"

Four

I

Maclean paid no attention to his surroundings as he crossed the Pont du Mont Blanc. The crystal-clear November day lent a blue sheen to the lake stretching out on his left. Geneva gleamed on both sides of the river, and snowy peaks beckoned in the distance.

MacLean distrusted the Continent. It was too pretty to be sincere. The neatly trimmed gardens and parks, the wedding-cake buildings sandblasted to their pristine glory, the sense of comfort and well-being oozing from the shops and finely kept houses—it made him uneasy.

He mounted the cobblestone alleyway bearing the street name of the address Fürglin had given him over the phone. He found the right number, and the brass plaque with the three initials designating the bank Fürglin was sending him to. He pressed the buzzer, and a uniformed concierge immediately opened the door and admitted him. Shabby as MacLean's coat was, the concierge relieved him of it and seated him in the parlor

51

before inquiring his business. As instructed, MacLean said simply that Mr. Fürglin had sent him.

The concierge nodded noncommittally and left MacLean alone. The Canadian glanced at the publications spread out on the coffee table. They seemed to be three-month-old analyses of the Swiss bond market. MacLean didn't feel like reading anyway. He might never read again, he thought; he had had enough in twenty-six unhappy years as a journalist. He sure as hell wouldn't be in any hurry to read newspapers. He smiled grimly.

The sunlight filtered through the chiffon curtains in the parlor, but the overhead chandelier reduced it to a pale rectangle on the beige carpet. The heavy damask drapes and imitation Louis XVI furniture lent further weight to the room.

MacLean looked at his watch, but only five minutes had passed. He wasn't really worried. His price, $2.5 million, wasn't much compared to what Fürglin and his associates had probably earned through his complicity. There was no reason for a double-cross.

The door opened and a tall, elderly man walked in, carrying an attaché case. The man had graying temples, was pleasingly portly, and had the gentle eyes and face of somebody's grandfather. Somehow, MacLean had formed a different image of the famous Swiss gnomes.

"So you're MacLean," the banker said. His voice was as gentle as his appearance promised. He didn't give his name, however, and didn't offer to shake hands.

He set the attaché case on the coffee table, on top of the bond market analyses. He flipped the latches and opened up the case. MacLean had been reassured by the sight of the case. When it was opened, he was stunned. It seemed incredible, the packets of green bills with blue wrappers around the middle. It was too much of a cliché, a hackneyed scene from a B movie.

"Here you are then," said the banker, with a businesslike manner suggesting that he passed out several such attaché cases each day. "It's two and a half million dollars, as specified." He spoke English with just the barest trace of an accent.

The thousand-dollar bills were in packets of fifty each. MacLean didn't feel like counting them. Whether or not it was exactly $2.5 million, it was more money than he had ever imagined possessing. He felt a sudden urge to flee.

The banker seemed to divine that he wouldn't be counting the money. He closed the case, locked it with the key attached to the grip, and handed the key to MacLean. "All yours," he said with his gentle smile. He stood up and opened the door, waiting for MacLean to go out before him. The journalist, still in a daze, rose slowly to his feet and picked up the case. The banker again did not offer his hand, but smiled kindly at him as he walked out the door. "Goodbye," he said after MacLean, who followed the concierge to the front door.

Blinking in the daylight, MacLean stood on the cobblestone street in front of the bank scarcely a quarter of an hour after he had gone inside. He felt like bursting into hysterical laughter. Efficient bastard, that Fürglin. He quickly swallowed his emotion, resisting an urge to clutch the attaché case to his chest and run all the way back to his hotel. The street was deserted except for an old woman in a wool coat who was negotiating the steep path with the aid of a wooden cane.

With as natural a step as he could muster, MacLean started back to the hotel. This time, the neatness of the city didn't bother him. He conjured up the Brazilian beaches, complete with swaying palm trees and half-nude beauties. MacLean didn't swim and had an aversion to the sun, but he had always liked the relaxed, sinful air of the beach resorts he had visited in Spain. Brazil would be even more exotic—and safe.

Not that he was worried. He had the money now. He wasn't even sure if what he had done was illegal. There was no law against knowing something before somebody else. There was no such thing as insider trading in a global gold market. Of course, he wasn't going to pay any taxes on the money, but he wasn't sure Inland Revenue even had a claim on it. At any rate, the Swiss certainly did not seem fussy about attaché cases full of money being carried across their border, nor were the Brazilians, he presumed.

The whole thing had been astonishingly easy. These capitalists weren't really as smart as they thought they were if a nobody like him could plunder them so easily.

He was so wrapped up in his feeling of satisfaction that he only noticed the car stopping at the curb in front of him when the back door opened.

II

The Gulf Stream office building looked just like the parking garage it was. Like most other office buildings in this part of Kuwait, it was built with tiers of parking space around a core of offices and shops. The building had been done in the transition phase after the first oil shock, when new wealth started pouring into the country but before they really knew what to do with it. Newer office buildings looked more like their counterparts in Europe and North America, glistening towers testifying to the primacy of mind over matter. But Dhow Investment Company liked its offices in the older building near the souk, which it kept in spite of its majority ownership in the new office-hotel complex on Airport Road. The hawkers and bazaar booths on the ground level of the Gulf Stream building—just one hundred yards from the covered bazaar in the old core of Kuwait city—were somehow comforting to Yosuf al-Masari, the patriarch of the family that controlled Dhow.

Tamal al-Masari adjusted his headdress as he walked into the reception hall from the parking lot. The evening weather was mild, but he suspected the air-conditioning was still running in the building. No matter, he thought; after their latest killing they had less need than ever to think about making economies. Tamal took the elevator to the eighth floor, the privileged space at the top of the building. His two cousins and his uncle were waiting for him.

Yosuf sat cross-legged on the leather chair at the head of a small conference table. His feet were bare and he fingered his worry beads as the younger men sat down around the table. Tamal was glad he had stopped on the way from the airport to change from his Western clothes. It made everyone more comfortable to be dressed alike.

"We are very rich," Tamal announced to the group. An ironic smile flitted across his cousin Abdul's face. After all, the $70 million they had had before their coup, while small compared to the fortunes of some other families in town, could hardly qualify them as poor. Tamal grinned back at his cousin.

The al-Masaris had accumulated a respectable fortune in the flush years following the oil shock of 1973–74. They had parlayed their Toyota franchise into sizable real estate holdings, including a hotel in Kuwait and luxury apartment buildings in

London and Paris. They had lost money in the collapse of the *souk al-manakh*, the parallel stock market in Kuwait, but not as much as some others.

They could not hope to equal the wealth of the emir's family and their cronies, but they made a respectable showing. When Tamal took charge of the family business, after returning from the States with his Cornell MBA, the al-Masaris started showing a new aggressiveness in their business dealings. Tamal bought his way onto the board of a commercial bank and began playing the markets, demonstrating a creditable skill in moving quickly in and out of world markets with a net gain that was often quite large.

Tamal wanted to overtake the al-Sayeds, their rivals not only in the auto business—al-Sayed had the Ford franchise—but bitter enemies from an obscure feud that went back ten generations. The competition extended well beyond Kuwait into the major financial centers of the world. The al-Sayeds relied largely on their man in London, David Sangrat, whereas Tamal, comfortable in the West, managed al-Masari activities abroad himself. But Tamal did maintain close contact with Philip Marcus through his trading operations.

"The al-Sayeds wonder what hit them," he added. At this, the old man smiled faintly through his white beard. "They are chasing their worthless Christian pimp in London to find out what happened," Tamal continued, with a broad grin.

"How much?" croaked the old man.

"Nearly six hundred million dollars," said Tamal, not prolonging the suspense. With their friends and the credit lines Tamal had had in waiting for just this purpose, he had been able to put $200 million into the market. The ploy had succeeded beyond his hopes, and he insisted that Fürglin realize his profits immediately. The Swiss had done his work well, selling into the panic-stricken market before it gridlocked. He had kept his nerve.

"We tripled our money in two hours and got out with most of it," recounted Tamal. He felt proud of himself too, because it was the organization he had set in place that enabled Fürglin to exploit the opportunity when it came. Tamal had been in Paris closing a property deal when Fürglin launched his operation, and the Kuwaiti's secretary had reached him only twenty minutes later.

"Al-Sayed is still buying gold?" asked Abdul. He didn't have

55

his cousin's experience, but he knew al-Sayed was a shrewd operator.

"Yes, yes, he's following the herd, but he got in too late. We have done much better," Tamal declared.

He did not go into Fürglin's worries about the peculiar behavior of Philip Marcus. Fürglin had gone to Marcus to unwind their position, because the expatriate American normally would handle such large blocks without asking any questions, and found himself talking directly to Marcus instead of the chief dealer for gold. That was unusual enough, but then there was a noticeable hesitation on Marcus's part to take Fürglin's gold in spite of the panic demand.

It had set Tamal to thinking. Maybe Marcus knew something that made him balk at going long in gold. But if South Africa's production was crippled, what could that be? Tamal wondered whether he should short gold in the futures market, just in case the price took a sudden nose dive for whatever reason. No need to bother the old man or his cousins with his speculations, though.

A boy shuffled in with thin green coffee, which he served to the four men. He collected the small cups and brought the traditional sweet tea, again serving a round, while Tamal sketched his plans about where to put their winnings once the markets reopened.

III

Hannes Kraml relished the surge of the engine as he pulled around the Volkswagen, his BMW 735i overtaking the smaller car effortlessly. The lake on his left sparkled already as the sun on the horizon promised a gloriously clear day. Kraml loved his morning drive to the office—the lake, the fresh mountain air, the BMW. He was thirty-two, he was rich and getting richer every day, and he was back in his mountains. No quite Austria, but Alps anyway, just like the ones he had grown up with. After his apprenticeships in Frankfurt, New York, and London, it was nice to be home, even though the Swiss dialect took some getting used to. His wife was happy too. A Swiss girl he had met in London, she had been beautiful enough and devoted enough to his interests to make him forego the pleasures of bachelorhood, or at least abate his enjoyment of them. Now they had their villa at St. Adrian and skiing was just a half hour away.

His quick ride to Zug reminded Kraml every morning how blessed he was. Transacting millions of dollars' worth of business every day was a pressure, but a pressure Kraml had gotten used to over the past ten years. He had traded everything in that decade: currency, gold, deposits, notes, bonds, stocks, futures, trade bills. He had an instinctive feel for the relationships in the market—how a cut in the prime rate in New York affected stock prices in Frankfurt, or how the price of oil in Rotterdam affected the price of gold in London. More important, he knew what the numbers meant, how to find market opportunities, and how to exploit them. Like a champion rugby player in a scrimmage, he saw openings and got through them.

To further enhance his marketability, Kraml had made a point of gaining expertise in computer programming. He had worked on some state-of-the-art trading programs in London to make sure he stayed at the head of a volatile profession.

Coming up to Zug, he steered the BMW automatically toward his office. It had not been an easy decision to join Philip Marcus. After all, the trader had run afoul of judicial authorities in the United States and had a seedy reputation as a result. But his operation seemed first-rate and professional. Marcus had maintained his business contacts in good standing, had an inside track on many deals, and had not lost his touch in making huge amounts of money in the markets. The opportunity afforded by Marcus's operation to play the market was unparalleled; certainly the timid U.S. investment bank Kraml had worked for in London could not match it. And the pay and benefits were outrageously high even compared with Kraml's extravagant London salary.

It had been a difficult decision, but so far Kraml was not disappointed. He *was* dealing from time to time with people of questionable reputation, but that had been true in London as well. It was hard to know when too many of the people were questionable, but Kraml didn't think things had reached that point.

He eased the car into his parking place in the underground garage. He was earlier than usual this morning, after a late night the evening before. But then, the markets didn't gridlock every day. The first night of the crisis he had not gone home at all, but last night Marcus had insisted. For having such a sinister reputation, the guy was remarkably considerate with his subordinates.

Marcus was there when Kraml stepped out of the elevator. He was gliding down the corridor—he walked with a slight crouch that made him seem to glide—pulling at a big cigar in spite of the early hour. He smiled when he saw Kraml. "Hannes, come into my office," he said, moving away. A decade in Europe had not rid him of his Brooklyn accent.

Kraml had not seen much of Marcus since his arrival in Zug. The American spent long hours in his headquarters on the top two floors of the modest five-story building, but he usually stayed in his office. He could be seen sometimes gliding in his peculiar way past the trading room, but Kraml had never seen him actually come into the operational hub.

The Austrian knew that Marcus inspired as much fear as he did respect. The other traders were polite enough, but Marcus's taciturnity seemed contagious, and Kraml missed the camaraderie that generally characterized a trading operation.

Kraml went into Marcus's office, a corner room with windows along two sides. He had been there only once before, on the day of his arrival two months ago. Once again, the sterility of the room struck him. There was nothing on the walls save a map of the world, no plants, no decoration of any sort. Marcus himself had removed his jacket and sat behind a large walnut desk in a starched white shirt. His thinning hair, slicked back with oil, gave him a sleek appearance.

"You've dealt gold," he said. It was a statement of fact; Marcus knew these details about his traders, and he had landed a big fish with Kraml. "Help the gold boys out today, OK?" Marcus ended the brief audience by picking up the phone for a Hong Kong call he had just put in.

Kraml had been working on oil finance, but it made sense to switch him to gold just now. He went into the dealing room, a vast hall with five circular desks of computer screens and a bank of teleprinters on the far wall. The night shift was finishing up some late Asian trades, but already several European shift people like himself were at their terminals. He walked across to the precious metals desk, noticing to his surprise that Blacky himself was holding down the chief trader's position. Blackford Teller III had been Marcus's sidekick long before the two of them left New York to branch out on their own. A WASP with Mayflower heritage, Blacky was an unlikely partner for the poor Jewish boy from Brooklyn, but the years had made them practically alter egos. Blacky was paunchy, balding, and chomping a cigar that might have cost a nickel.

Blacky barely glanced up as Kraml took his place. The young Austrian quickly saw that special times made for special organization at the desk. Normally, the traders fixed the price for a transaction within limits set by the chief trader. This was not the case today. Instead, they had been instructed to deal only at the price Blacky flashed onto their internal monitors. Even while he talked incessantly into his receiver, Blacky changed the price every thirty to sixty seconds. Trading was heavy.

Kraml reached his trading high very quickly. Juggling the half-dozen phone receivers snaking out from his terminal, two or three of them dangling over his shoulders he made the lightning calculations in his head while the three screens in front of him flashed a steady stream of information and prices.

When London came on, the pace quickened. Kraml's instincts, so in tune with the market, made him realize that something peculiar was happening with the gold trading. He had the feeling that Blacky was not responding to the market but controlling it. The price was rising steadily, but apparently at the pace and with the volume that Blacky wanted. He sat there, imperturbably chomping on his cigar, constantly on the phone, working his console to feed prices to his dealers.

Where was he getting all the gold? Kraml wondered. The trader knew that he at least was not talking to any sellers; Bahrain and Kuwait were flooding the market with buy orders.

The morning went by quickly, never hectic but always busy. Things finally let up a bit as the market waited for the morning fixing in London. Blacky talked to the London man about their strategy in the price-setting session and quickly ducked out when Marcus appeared at the door, leaving Frey, the usual chief trader, in charge.

Kraml decided to break for a quick coffee. Rounding the corner to the canteen, he passed Marcus and Blacky flanking a

59

third man, gray-faced, who was wearing a heavy coat and broad-brimmed hat. Not too many visitors came to Zug, but Kraml didn't think much about it until he heard the voice of the stranger. Kraml could not make out the words, although he could tell the language was English. What struck the Austrian was the accent— the unmistakable nasal monotone of a Russian. Like most of his compatriots, Kraml felt an antipathy to the Russians for their long postwar occupation of Austria.

Kraml resisted the urge to turn around and watch the trio. After all, Marcus always had some deal brewing; Kraml just hoped he would not have too much to do with the Russians.

Back at the desk, Frey called out to him, "Personal call." Kraml punched the lighted button.

"Hello, Drew, how goes it?" he said when the journalist identified himself. The two of them had gotten to be fairly close in London, but Kraml felt ambivalent about taking this call. He was still uneasy in his new situation; he felt self-conscious and was worried about giving something away.

"Market's steady enough. Busy, not hectic," he said in response to Drew's questions.

"Sellers? Somebody's selling, I guess," he said. "We seem to be getting some supply, yeah, but I'm not on the buying side." Drew was getting insistent. "No, I don't really know where it's coming from, probably a bit from all over." He didn't really know, but the buying was coming from all over so he didn't think the selling was from all over. It was hard for him to dissemble with Drew; they had closed many a pub in London.

Kraml suddenly thought of the Russian in the corridor. He bit his tongue not to blurt out the news to Drew. But the journalist's next question threw him off balance.

"Well, yes, I suppose it's possible the Russians are selling," he responded, probably too quickly. "But I haven't seen anything myself. . . . Marcus does have some connections with the Russians, I think, yes," he conceded, under a barrage of questions from the journalist.

"Look, Drew, I'll keep my ears open, and let you know what I find out. It's a promise, OK? But it's really busy now, and I have to get back to work." He rang off quickly.

Was Blacky getting all that gold from the Russians? As Kraml puzzled over the problem, Marcus's sidekick returned. The trader turned to catch a last glimpse of the gray-faced man standing at the dealing-room door for a moment before he moved away. Kraml was certain the man was Russian. But how much gold could the Russians have?

IV

Even at this time of year, Miami seemed steamy from the humidity. Halden didn't visit Florida's biggest city often, and the vaporous air always surprised him. The palm trees looked limp under the overcast sky; the heavy warmth was oppressive rather than refreshing after New York's cold and damp.

The limousine sent by Southern Bank passed several construction sites on the road in from the airport. Would the building never stop? The central banker grunted; Miami's prosperity seemed to wax and wane in inverse proportion to Latin America's financial problems. Even without the statistics to prove it, Halden could not help sharing the view that much of the money missing in the big debtor countries had found its way across the Gulf.

The driver pulled into the U-shaped drive off Ocean Boulevard, and Halden got his first view of Southern Bank's massive new skyscraper. He shivered slightly in spite of the humid warmth as he stepped out of the Cadillac. The gold-tinted glass of the fifty-six-story building shone against the leaden sky. The bank now dominated Miami's skyline. The slight feeling of terror he always felt at the thought of interstate banking welled up as he tilted his head back to take in the building's size. He was afraid of the power one bank could accumulate if it was free to stretch its tentacles across the entire country. On his last visit to Miami, the headquarters of what had become the third largest bank in the country had still been a construction site too.

Carol, who had taken an earlier plane to prepare the meeting, came out to meet Halden at the car.

Inside the huge atrium of the front entrance, Halden met a delegation from the bank headed by Hugh Vane, the chairman. Between the grinning Vane's white teeth and white hair, his skin had the odious brown of a suntan that never faded. Halden had never reconciled his notions of hard work with the Sun Belt lifestyle. At least no one in the Southern Bank group was wearing white shoes.

The executive elevator rocketed them up to the conference rooms at the top floor. Halden felt palpable relief as José Martínez broke off from the group of men at the top to greet him with his big, warm smile. This time Halden's own smile was genuine. The two men shook hands and clasped each other's arms with real pleasure. Since Wagner's ouster, they had learned to rely on each other in the endless round of conferences to resolve the debt issue.

The Mexican, who had held on as his country's finance minister through the difficult series of reverses over the past few years, took Halden by the arm to greet the finance ministers of Brazil, Argentina, Venezuela, and Peru. The American knew them all but rarely saw them as a group.

"Thank you for coming, Mr. Halden," said Carlos Angouros, the Brazilian, who had called him the previous night. His voice betrayed a genuine relief. Halden did not tower over the others as Wagner had, but his muscular physique instilled immediate confidence when he walked into a room. The central banker had earned a high regard among the debtor countries for an intellectual toughness that fully matched his physical appearance.

The markets had reopened as planned this morning. Gold had moved steadily upward, although Tuesday's panic had abated. Shutting down the markets had worked like a cold shower to calm the incipient hysteria. The gold stampede already showed some signs of petering out, but markets remained jittery.

One sign of the uncertainty was the desperate lack of liquidity for the Latin American debtor countries. That was why Angouros had called Halden for this impromptu meeting in Miami. "Let's get started," said the Brazilian, leading the group of ministers and central bankers into the conference room. Vane and his courtiers smiled as they backed into the elevator. They were glad to offer their premises for the meeting, but that was to be the extent of their involvement.

"It's the interbank lines again," Angouros said immediately, referring to the short-term funds banks lend each other. "And this time it wasn't only us who got hit." His colleagues quickly buzzed affirmation.

"We really must do something, Mark," Martínez said when the hubbub subsided.

Halden hunched up in his chair, which offered a view of the Atlantic horizon. Yesterday and the day before, he had put up $2.5 billion in emergency loans to tide over the Banco do Brasil and certain other Latin American banks after the big international banks had withdrawn all their interbank lines. One of the great fictions maintained in the wake of the debt crisis that Mexico had set off in 1982 was that these interbank lines were temporary and short-term. The fact was that the funds, amounting to hundreds of millions of dollars, had to be maintained at certain levels to keep up the illusion of sovereign solvency. If the New York Fed had not been there yesterday to tide over the Banco do Brasil, the reality of bankruptcy might have overtaken the bank, and Brazil as well. Can a country go bankrupt? Even Halden wondered.

The interbank lines were not included in the multibillion-dollar debt reschedulings agreed to by the banks and the debtor countries. Nonetheless, there was a clear understanding that they had to be maintained—clear at least until panic clouded the minds of the creditor banks.

"What do you suggest?" Halden said. He had spent more than an hour the previous evening on the phone to bank chairmen, twisting their arms to reopen the lines to the Latin American banks. His efforts had reduced the Fed bailout from $1.5 billion on Tuesday to $1 billion by Wednesday night.

"Would it be possible for the Fed to install an automatic safety net for situations like this?" Martínez asked. It was an idea he and Halden had discussed over many a late-night drink. Halden knew it would come to this sooner or later, anyway. Whether the bailout was automatic or ad hoc, it always came down to the Fed putting up the money. The Fed, the great, powerful, magical Fed—Halden sighed in frustration at the blind confidence placed in his imperfect institution. Even the Fed could not simply print money without paying the consequences. Angouros was listing the advantages of this new plan, parroting without knowing it the arguments Halden and Martínez had long since made.

The gold crisis threatened to light the fuse of the debt powder keg. As Halden listened, a profound sense of futility came over him. The alarming suddenness of the gold mine sabotage threatened to topple the hodgepodge of arrangements and agreements cobbled together in the past few years to avoid the worst consequences of the overwhelming Third World debt. The shock of the sabotage shook that fragile structure with more force than it could bear.

Halden had been a football player at Princeton, a middle linebacker. His was the duty to follow the offensive play, to back up the front line and plug the holes to keep the ballcarrier from crossing the line of scrimmage. It had been a good preparation for his Fed duties, as it turned out.

But his feeling of impotence grew. What if the safety net were put in place? That would not remove the debt. It would remain there, like a sleeping dragon, waiting for the next financial crisis to wake it up and unleash it on a vulnerable world. The only answer would be to slay the dragon. But how?

In the meantime, he would go along with the aid sought by the anxious politicians around the table. It was no solution, but as much of a solution as anything else for right now. Fed chairman Roberts could not say anything against it. Halden sat back, though. He would let the Latin Americans convince him for a while—his Delta flight to London didn't leave until 4 P.M.

Five

I

Drew sat fidgeting in his office. The conversation with Kraml had left him confused, but he hesitated to make too many phone calls. The market was brooding, and no question was innocent.

He jumped up and walked through the office, calling to Tom that he would return shortly. Coming out to Fleet Street, he made two rights, into a narrow lane. Without pausing, he walked one hundred yards briskly and stepped into the Cock and Bull, his regular pub.

It was nearly 3 P.M., and most of the lunch crowd had already drifted away. Drew ordered a pint of bitter. The barman, Ralph, had a friendly smile on his face, but Drew put on a preoccupied look to discourage conversation. He was not in the mood for idle chatter.

The journalist retreated with his pint to the corner of the padded bench lining one side of the pub.

The Russians. What could they be up to? Kraml had sounded edgy on the subject. What connection did Marcus have with the

Russians? Presumably, Marcus had connections with just about everyone who traded commodities, which made Kraml's remark even more curious. The trader had been affirming the connection, as though he himself had just received confirmation. Something seemed to be going on in Zug.

Whether Zug was the missing link or not, there was simply too much gold in the market. Kraml had been uncharacteristically evasive about gold selling. Drew needed to see the Austrian in person, to have a talk more private than international phone lines permitted.

Even if the Russians had been stockpiling gold, which ran counter to all analyses of the gold market, could they be selling enough to compensate for the sudden loss of the South African production?

Drew mulled over these questions. Could South Africa, or some South African firm like Anglo American, be unloading stockpiles of gold? But Preston would have told him if Anglo was thought to have that amount of gold.

The panic had sharply increased demand for gold, and the price had shot up correspondingly. Now the price was stable. Was there a limit, after all, to gold demand, panic or no panic? Or was there a large supply source that was meeting demand at this higher price level?

The amount of trading going on, in fact, was only slightly short of the normal volume in bullion. It was almost as if, aside from the higher price, the mine sabotage had not taken place.

But it *had* taken place. Drew drained his glass. It had taken place the day before yesterday, and the news had shut down world financial markets in unprecedented fashion.

Drew stared at the blurs through the glazed windows of the pub. The mine sabotage had taken place. Van der Merwe had managed to get a telex out about it. The South African government had announced it.

Still, it gnawed at him. He had never seen the telex. MacLean, who might have seen it, had disappeared. Drew could not reach Van der Merwe. The Russians, or somebody, had a lot of gold to sell. His old friend Kraml, as cool under pressure as anyone, was not so cool today.

When he got back to the office, Drew found a short item from the French Press Association on his desk. He looked through the window to Tom, who just nodded solemnly at him.

Drew studied the story.

APPARENT MURDER VICTIM FOUND IN HAUTE-SAVOIE ANNECY, Nov. 17 (FPA) — Departmental police found an unidentified male corpse hidden in an abandoned automobile near here today. The man had apparently been murdered, police said.

The body was stripped of all clothing or identification, but appeared to be that of a balding, middle-aged man. Severe battering of the face and head delayed positive identification.

The automobile, an Opel Kadett, had no plates and the engine number was filed off. Police said these details suggested a professional assassination. There are indications that the crime may have taken place in Switzerland. Swiss police and Interpol are cooperating in the investigation.

Drew looked again at Tom. The slotman arched an eyebrow and shrugged his shoulders. Drew read the story again. He called MacLean's number. No answer.

His phone buzzed.

"Hello, hero. We still on for five o'clock?" It took Drew a few seconds to realize it was Katy Trevera on the phone, not Sangrat, or Preston, or Corrello, or God knows who from the South African embassy. Katy was advertising director for *Money Manager*, and the two of them had a comfortable understanding. Free and easy; no plans, no disappointments. Just a couple of friends who enjoyed each other's company.

"Everything's set for five; Chel will be there," Katy said.

Drew flipped open his agenda and saw that he had indeed penciled in a date with Katy. For weeks she had been after him to come see the exhibit of Chel Hang, a Chinese painter friend of hers. Although he wasn't a great student of art, Drew had realized, after years of traipsing through Europe's best museums and long conversations with artists he had known, that his appreciation of art was as refined as that of most other people. He even bought a piece now and again. He especially liked a situation like this one, where he met the artist through friends. It made painting more personal, somehow.

"Katy, I hate to stand you two up, but you know what's going on in the market. I'm not sure when I'll get away."

"That's OK. Everybody keeps telling me what a hero you are for breaking the sabotage story. I'll let you off the hook this time." There was a subtle change in her voice. "How about a late supper?"

Drew knew that tone, the implied suggestion. Why not? he

67

thought suddenly, with a feeling of relief. After all, the world didn't come to an end just because of a financial crisis.

"That sounds like a good idea," he said.

"Why don't you just come to my place when you're finished. I'll fix a salad."

"See you tonight, then." Drew felt better already. His eyes came back to the FPA news item. He called Corrello.

"Rich, something just came over the FPA wire." He read the dispatch to a silent Atlanta executive.

"You think it might be MacLean?" No beating around the bush.

"I have a bad feeling about it," Drew answered. Those finely honed instincts.

"Don't jump to any conclusions. Just hold tight till I've talked to Madison. I'll call you tomorrow."

Drew sat with a tight feeling in his stomach. Preston had said Fürglin's crowd was rough. But what could MacLean have done to deserve death? Was his cut too big?

With a conscious effort, Drew put the matter out of his mind and went out to the slot to spell Tom.

II

Drew watched Katy through half-opened eyes. She slipped out of bed and tiptoed to the dresser, took a cigarette out of the pack, and lit it. The drawn curtains kept the room dim, but the brief flame highlighted her face. She turned and walked quickly down the hallway to the bathroom. Her hair came down to the middle of her back. There were two dimples at the base of her back; her bottom was round, her hips narrow, her legs long and shapely.

She disappeared into the bathroom. Drew turned over on his back, feeling that pleasant ache from lovemaking. The tension of the past week had made him more passionate than usual with Katy. He realized how much pressure he had been under from the release sex had provided.

Katy came back down the hall. She knew about Drew's addiction to his morning coffee and always kept real coffee on hand to brew for him when he spent the night.

"Coffee's on," Katy said. "It's after nine," she called back, on her way down the hall. Drew reached for the phone on the bedside table. It had been nearly midnight when he left work the night before.

He dialed the office. "Ah, Drew, tried to call you a little while ago but got no answer," Richard, his night editor, said.

"I went out early for a run in the park," Drew lied. He detested jogging, but his flat was near Hyde Park, so the excuse was plausible. "What's up?"

"The Old Lady called," Richard said.

Drew had been half expecting a call from the Bank of England, the Old Lady of Threadneedle Street. "Let me guess. They want me to drop around for a cup of tea."

"I don't know what they're serving, but they said it was urgent and they want you there at eleven. Charley himself wants to see you."

"Eleven it is. Call and confirm for me, will you?" Charley was Charles McQuade Guinness, deputy governor of the bank. Of course, they had to know where that news came from. Had they tumbled to MacLean's scam?

He turned around, and Katy put a mug of freshly brewed coffee in his hands.

"Charley Guinness wants to see me," he explained. The deputy governor was probably the most respected man in the City. Effectively the chief executive of the central bank, his role had grown in importance with a succession of weak political appointments to the governorship.

Katy looked at him ambiguously. "You better run," she said.

Drew ignored her tease. "Yeah, I'd better," he said. Cab to Knightsbridge and home, quick shower and shave, cab to the City. He would just make it.

She was still undressed as he pulled on his topcoat. "Give me a call," she said lightly.

Drew kissed her quickly and was out the door. He felt better than he had in a week.

III

Drew still felt good as he mounted the short staircase into the Bank of England's reception hall.

He hardly noticed the porters in their top hats and mauve

69

tailcoats, although the historic costume had startled him on his first visit a decade ago. The Bank was a financial version of Buckingham Palace, complete with its own colorful guards.

The Bank of England was in many ways the premier central bank in the world. London's key role in international finance during capitalism's golden age made England's bank of issue the model for most other central banks. Although some dramatic banking failures had tarnished the Old Lady's image in recent years, it still functioned as the moral backbone of the major central banks.

Drew went to the desk and announced himself. It was just after eleven. He had put on his blue pinstripe for the Bank audience.

A porter, more soberly dressed than those at the entry, led him through the hallway around the court and up what appeared to be the back stairs. They came to a reception area where another porter relieved him of his coat.

No waiting, Drew marveled, as the oak door at the end of the reception area opened. If only it was this easy all the time! He thought of the accumulated hours he had spent waiting in antechambers like this one.

Guinness himself came out to meet him. They knew each other from press briefings, and Drew had interviewed him once some time ago.

"Good of you to come at such short notice," Guinness said, guiding the journalist back to his office.

Drew was surprised to see other people when he came into the room. He recognized Mark Halden immediately, although he had hardly expected to see him in this setting. Halden's companion was even more remarkable. Drew could not remember ever having seen a woman inside the Bank of England, let alone one as beautiful as this tall brunette.

"Hello, Drew," Halden said, extending his hand. "Been a while since we've met. Paris, wasn't it?"

Now it clicked. The meeting was with Halden; Guinness was there for protocol.

"Years ago," Drew responded. "We both had different jobs then." He smiled.

"This is Carol Connors, one of our top economists." Carol shook his hand firmly, with a friendly, open smile. Despite his confusion at the sudden turn of events, Drew was momentarily distracted by the encounter. Carol's brown eyes were alight with intelligence, but perhaps something more—that slight expansion of the pupils that marks a kindling of interest.

Guinness ordered tea as Drew took his place and concentrated on the two men. He imagined how many bank chief executives had sat in his place, waiting for the tea to be served in Guinness's office, wondering what had prompted the Bank's summons.

Once the tea was poured and Halden had reminisced with Drew about Paris, the Fed president said, "I'm sure you've figured out why we called you."

"South Africa," answered the journalist.

"I've spoken to Tom Madison and another fellow—"

"Richard Corrello," Carol prompted. Drew nodded. Protocol again, clearing the conversation with his two superiors at SBC.

"That was it. They said it was your call. The news came from your stringer, they said. But that's all they knew."

Drew picked up on cue. He recognized the need for the responsible authorities to explore the circumstances leading up to such a market crisis, so he sketched the chronology of Tuesday afternoon, starting with Van der Merwe's phone call. He did not mention the telex or MacLean.

The two central bankers listened attentively. Guinness was a tall man, whose big ears stuck out prominently. Carol took notes, looking up only occasionally to meet Drew's eyes.

"My traders tell me there was considerable movement in the market just *before* your flash," Halden said when Drew had finished.

Drew paused. He took a deep breath and told the three of them about MacLean. He narrated just the facts: Van der Merwe asking about his telex, MacLean's hasty departure for the dentist and subsequent disappearance. They were suggestive enough. Then he added what he had heard about the gold trading from Preston Morgan and David Sangrat, without giving the names of these two sources.

"Looks like we need to find this MacLean," Halden said to Guinness.

"Have you talked to the police?" Guinness asked Drew, who shook his head. "It'll be easier for me to get the machinery moving. Somebody from the Yard will call you."

"There is one other thing I should mention," Drew said, and

told them about the unidentified murder victim in Annecy. The information was greeted with silence, except for the scratching of a pencil as Guinness made a note.

Carol resumed the conversation. "You've had no contact with Van der Merwe since then?" she asked Drew.

"Our contact with him was always spotty anyway, and communications seem completely shut down since the sabotage."

Halden was thoughtful. "Amazing, how thin the thread is," he remarked. He looked at Drew. "The markets are up and running again. But you know as well as I do just how delicate things are." He paused. "Off the record, I had an emergency meeting yesterday with the Latin American finance ministers. The Fed's putting up a ten-billion-dollar safety net for their interbank deposits."

Drew kept quiet but whistled in his mind. What a tip, straight from the horse's mouth. Too bad it was off the record.

"Can you do me a favor, Drew?" Halden leaned forward. "Let me know first if you hear anything else from Van der Merwe." Drew shifted in his seat. "I know it's unusual," Halden went on, "but I asked Madison, and he had no objection. It's up to you."

It was a touchy point. Deep down, Drew believed that the public good was best served by an independent press. But it seemed a small enough favor, and Halden made sense—the markets were very fragile and it would be irresponsible to bring them crashing down just for a two-minute beat. Halden was the one who was really on the line to keep that from happening. But who was to judge? What would Van der Merwe have to say to Drew when he called, and what would Halden's response be? Maybe it's all right this time and not another? Suppose someday the President himself comes to a journalist and says the security of the country depends on suppressing a piece of news. Maybe he's right—but maybe he wants to bomb a Southeast Asian country illegally.

Halden waited; he understood what was going through Drew's mind. Guinness waited because it was Halden's show.

"All I can say is that I'll keep your request in mind," Drew said finally, looking Halden in the eye.

Halden returned the gaze and smiled. "That's all I can ask. I appreciate it." He pulled a slip of paper out of his coat pocket and handed it across the table. "My direct line at the office, my number at home, and"—he smiled again—"my home away from home, the Princeton Club. Any time, day or night."

Drew realized the meeting was over. They all stood.

"There's one other favor I'd like to ask," Halden said. "Could you spare some time for Miss Connors to compare notes on developments in the gold market? She's going to stay in London for a few days to monitor the situation for us."

Drew actually felt the increase in his pulse rate. Before he thought twice, he turned to Carol, "There's no time like the present. I've got to check in at the office, but if you're free we could meet for lunch in about an hour."

Carol smiled and looked at Halden.

"That's fine," Halden said. "Charley and I are having lunch with the governor at his club."

As he gave Carol the address of Erno's Bistro, near Covent Garden, Drew ignored the bemused expressions on the faces of the two older men.

IV

Drew decided to save time by getting out of the cab at James Street and walking across Covent Garden to the restaurant. Despite the late-fall chill, crowds of young people gathered on the cobblestones to watch the performers—here a juggler bravely wearing brightly colored tights, there a mime effectively imitating a mechanical man.

The wrought iron and brick of the old market architecture retained its charm, although Drew felt the gimmicky boutiques filling the renovated halls were tourist traps.

Still, he preferred the gentrified Covent Garden by far to the soulless structures that had been erected in Paris on the site of Les Halles, the legendary stomach of Paris immortalized in the novels of the twenties.

Carol was waiting for him at a small table in the corner. He had been quite lucky to get a table on such short notice. As usual, the trendy restaurant was full.

Drew was confused as he sat down across from this lovely

woman he had just met. Not even her severe navy blue suit could detract from her charm. The single miniature rose on the table lent a dash of fiery red to the tableau and made their tryst almost romantic.

Things were happening too fast. Drew still had a warm emotional buzz from his night with Katy. Then the sudden call to the Bank and the unexpected confrontation with Guinness and Halden. And now . . . and now this. He wasn't sure what "this" was, but he felt a pleasant tingling as he greeted Carol—Miss Connors—that he had not felt since he met Christine.

"It's very kind of you to go to all this trouble," Carol began apologetically.

"As it turns out, those men were going to let you fend for yourself when they went off to their club."

"Still, it's above the call of duty, and I appreciate it," Carol said, with her warm, open smile.

"Don't worry, I hope to learn as much as I tell," Drew said.

The two plunged into a discussion of the past week's events. Carol remained circumspect but nonetheless filled in some blanks for Drew, especially regarding the maneuvering that had resulted in the markets' shutdown.

"Mr. Halden was quite surprised to hear just how the South Africa story got onto the wire," Carol remarked, when the discussion turned to the sabotage.

"Yes, he seemed to think the whole thing was kind of chancy," Drew responded. "But it's not really quite as fragile as it seems."

Carol waited for him to explain.

"All news organizations have their structures in place to gather the news and to vet it—to make sure the facts are correct before they actually reach the public. Those structures themselves are built up over many years and have to survive the test of time. That very survival is part of the safeguard built into the system. It's like with banks—the older the organization is, the more credible it becomes. WCN is fairly young, but the U.S. service has been around for a long time, and we have the benefit of their experience."

Drew paused. Carol continued to regard him with interest.

"Then there's the people involved. A lot of people seem to think anybody can write a news story, but it's not as simple as it looks. Reporting is a skill you learn as an apprentice, usually working under a master—a good city editor, for instance. Over the years, you develop a feeling for the news, a sense of what seems right and what seems wrong. Even though I'm relatively young, thirty-eight, I've had fourteen years' experience in financial journalism."

"Still, the system puts a lot of responsibility on individual judgment," Carol interjected.

"It does. But again, day in and day out, year in and year out, that judgment is refined, put to the test. And there's a very high ethical standard—"

Drew stopped abruptly and reddened, recalling his confession about MacLean scarcely an hour ago. He saw a funny gleam in Carol's eyes.

"You're thinking about MacLean, aren't you?" he asked.

"As a matter of fact, no, I wasn't thinking about him." She paused, as if to mark a change of subject. "You're devoted to your profession, aren't you?"

"I am. But I don't think I'm so special in that. I think it's a safe bet that you're devoted to yours." Drew studied her for a reaction. "After all, to have your responsibility, at your age . . . ?" He trailed off, asking the question.

"Thirty-four. I've worked hard." She looked at him with one eyebrow raised. "But maybe I'm only ambitious, and not devoted to anything but getting ahead." She laughed suddenly. "We're a very serious pair, aren't we? Tell me what it's like to live in London."

Drew spun off his stories about being an American in London, concentrating on Carol's reactions, responding to them. He realized that something was happening that was out of the ordinary for both of them.

"I've got to retrieve Halden," Carol said finally, after she had quizzed Drew about the theater in London. "Perhaps we can pick up our discussion of the gold market later; Halden's going back to New York this afternoon."

She had said it casually, but the invitation was unmistakable. Drew felt giddy. He put Carol in a cab to the Bank, with a promise to call her, and walked the half hour back to Fleet Street to regain his composure. The tingle was still there by the time he reached the office.

Six

I

Marcus put down the receiver and relit his cigar. He spent most of his time on the phone. The constant conversation, cigars, and generous doses of whiskey over the years had made his voice mellifluous. His telephone voice was gentle, almost seductive, save for the rasp deep in his throat.

He swiveled to the window and looked out at an overcast sky casting a dull gleam over the plain squat buildings of Zug. But Marcus paid little attention to the view. He thought of Abrassimov and their discussion of the previous day. He thought of his meeting this afternoon in Berne.

Marcus paused several times like this each day. Although many of his decisions were instinctive, reacting to pressure, he needed to reorient himself periodically.

He was alone; he had to rely on himself. He had always made his decisions alone. At age twenty, he decided college was a waste of time. He went to his father and declared his intention to drop out. Before his father could remonstrate with him and launch into the immigrant's plea that he wanted everything better for his son, Marcus said he wanted to work in the family packaging business.

That assuaged the old man, who reconciled himself very quickly to his son's decision when Marcus doubled sales in a rapid series of major contracts and the acquisition of an upstate factory.

But the packaging business was too small for the young man. Again alone, he decided to seek greater fortunes on Wall Street and joined Davidoff & Co., a medium-sized firm trading in securities and commodities. Johannes Martin, a tough immigrant trader, was pushing the firm out of a comfortable somnolence to become a leader in world markets.

Marcus was just the man Martin needed. The young man's instinctive skill in trading quickly made him a success in the arcane world of commodities. He mastered the pricing intricacies and peculiarities of each market. More than that, he pursued his deals with a preternatural energy.

Marcus realized early on that it was not money that drove him. He wanted to be rich, very rich, but not just to have money. Nor was it power he sought. What was power, after all? No, Marcus sought freedom, freedom to act, to move markets, control them even. That for him was the objective of wealth and power— this freedom.

He had that freedom now, and it belonged to him alone. Martin, his mentor at Davidoff, had tried to restrain him, to curb some of his activities. Marcus decided to break with him and leave Davidoff, which had become the biggest commodities trader in the world largely through Marcus's efforts.

The press described the rupture as a result of disputes regarding Marcus's bonus. As if he cared whether the bonus was $2 million or $3 million. No, it was the freedom Marcus sought.

So he went to Switzerland, with its banking secrecy, to the canton of Zug, with its low taxes—what were taxes, anyway, but an infringement of freedom—and he traded freely around the globe. He quickly built up Marcus Trading to be as big and important as Davidoff. The Internal Revenue Service in the United States found his transactions too free; they shut down his operations in the States for alleged tax evasion. Marcus resented the claim, but he resented the restraint on his freedom of operation even more. He paid $100 million to settle the corporate tax claims, and his offices reopened. He refused to settle the personal tax claims and renounced his American citizenship. The IRS still maintained warrants for his arrest in every country that considered tax evasion a crime. Switzerland was not one of them.

In all this, Marcus had acted alone. True, Blackford Teller had stayed with him, leaving Davidoff to go with Marcus to Switzerland. But Blacky was like a dog, loyal in an unreflective way. The decisions, the actions, were Marcus's alone.

He needed to act now. He had seen Abrassimov; he would see du Plessis today. He knew what they wanted him to do, and he would do it. He would do it because he was the only one who could.

But he would do it his way.

"Come in here a minute," he told Blacky on the internal line. "Bring Frey."

The two men came into Marcus's barren office, Blacky tucking his shirt in as they entered. Frey, a Swiss, was impeccably pressed and manicured, lanky and thin next to Blacky.

"We're going to short gold futures," Marcus told them.

Neither responded. Blacky knew what Marcus had in mind; Frey could guess.

"The market will be confused," Frey said finally.

"It sure as hell will be."

Marcus shook with his funny, silent laughter. Although Marcus's traders would spread the contracts through a variety of middlemen, the market would soon see that someone was shorting gold futures—someone expected the price of gold to go down and was speculating on that eventuality in the futures markets. In time, the shorting would probably be traced back to Marcus.

"But they won't know what to do. They'll stay confused," Marcus added. "We're not going to enlighten them." At this, Blacky grinned lopsidedly.

Marcus could see Frey working it out in his head, but he was not ready to confide completely in the Swiss. It was enough that he and Blacky knew what was at stake.

"OK, boys, go to it," Marcus said, and swiveled back to face the window.

II

Kraml felt the fatigue. He had handled half a billion dollars' worth of gold deals during the day. Only now, with Europe coming to a close, did the activity slacken. Most of the activity in the United States was done on the markets in New York and Chicago. Marcus had his own teams there.

"Just keep on a holding pattern," Kraml overheard Blacky say into the phone.

The American, who looked just the same now as he had at the beginning of the day, hung up the receiver and looked up into Kraml's gaze. Visibly suppressing his annoyance, he opted instead for bonhomie.

"Hectic, huh?" he said, with a slight attenuation of the frown normally fixed on his face. It was a grimace that was the closest he ever came to a smile. Blacky was a very unattractive person. It wasn't only his bland appearance or slovenliness; a fundamental unpleasantness seemed to emanate from him, like body odor.

"Well, it's to be expected, after all the news," Kraml said. "But who is doing the selling?"

Blacky just grunted as he picked up a flashing phone. "Talk to Carlton. He knows what to do," he said curtly to his caller.

Without another word, Blacky got up and shuffled out of the trading room, signaling to the chief dealer to handle whatever transactions came in.

"Friendly cuss," Kraml said to the dealer, trying to keep his face sympathetic. His colleague, a dour Swiss, said nothing.

Kraml felt much less content than he had at the oil desk. Although Marcus's whole operation lacked the ambiance Kraml cherished in a team, at least there had been no mystery at the oil desk. The market was reasonably transparant. It was important for Kraml to be in the picture, to know the overall movements of the market. Otherwise it was like working in a closet.

Like today, he reflected. Blacky was deliberately drawing a curtain across the market. It was little comfort to Kraml that this veil left most other operators in the dark as well. The young Austrian had always enjoyed the complete confidence of his employers, and with good reason. He had always played it straight— not exceeding his limits, not fiddling on the side, not trying to cover up mistakes, not following his own head unless he cleared it with his supervisor. He had a good standing in the market.

But the two days trading gold had made him feel like a college graduate on his first probation. They told him nothing. Even now, as the day's tension washed out, there was no feeling of relaxation. Kraml missed the human warmth. He decided he didn't like Blacky or trust him.

Just then the American shuffled back into the room, carrying a Styrofoam cup of tomato soup.The canned soup, which Blacky imported by the case from the States, was a trademark of his.

"Kraml"—Blacky's voice was always soft, almost a purr—"he wants to see you." He, even for Blacky, meant Marcus.

A momentary chill passed over the young trader. But he dismissed any worries. His book was in order; he'd done everything he was told.

Marcus was on the phone when Kraml came into the office. The trader regarded the world map as he stood there, noticing this time that the time zones indicated on the map were circled in red. Kraml wondered why, because Marcus was famous for calling anyone he wanted, whenever he wanted, regardless of what time it was for the person he called—or what time it was for himself, for that matter.

Marcus hung up and pressed a button for his calls to be held. "Hannes," he began. His low, mild voice made it sound like a hiss. "We run a confidential operation here. You're a good trader, you've already shown that. If you stay with us, if you keep up the good work, we'll treat you well, we'll keep you happy."

He paused to relight his cigar.

"But Hannes," he said, looking at the Austrian for the first time, "no questions. We'll tell you what you need to know." For some reason, he smiled wolfishly at this and dismissed Kraml by turning back to his phones.

There was a buzzing in Kraml's ear as he returned to the trading room. Marcus's hoarse whisper had raised the dealer's blood pressure in a way five simultaneous multimillion dollar transactions never could. He realized he was afraid, afraid of a bully. It was a feeling he hadn't had since his first year in the *Gymnasium* in Linz, when upperclassmen had systematically razzed newcomers like himself.

Working for Marcus was different after all. Kraml had dealt with criticism, accepted the occasional reprimand. But the menace underlying Marcus's remarks was new. There had been no hint of this in the two interviews prior to his being hired. Kraml had met Frey in London, and later came to Zug to meet briefly with Marcus and Blacky. The conversation had been banal. Not like this.

Visibly subdued, Kraml returned in a trance to his place on the desk. Blacky ignored him, as did the chief dealer. It was a different world from the cozy, clublike environment of the City. He felt he was in a jungle, a dark place filled with unknown dangers.

Walking back from lunch that afternoon, Kraml saw Marcus's Cadillac pulling out of the garage as he came in. It was an almost endearing eccentricity of Marcus that he maintained the prestige car of his native country in a part of the world dominated by Mercedes, BMW, and Porsche.

Kraml noted that the ungainly limousine turned left, which meant south—Berne or Geneva rather than Zurich. No farther than the border, in any case—valid extradition orders awaited Marcus in all countries bordering Switzerland.

Acting on a hunch, Kraml phoned a friend of his in Berne when Blacky went on his first tomato soup run of the day. Franz Schmidt, who had started with Kraml in the bank in Vienna, was now economic attaché with the Austrian embassy in Switzerland. Kraml had phoned him when he arrived in Zug, and they were planning a skiing weekend together.

"Couple more weeks and we can go," Schmidt said when Kraml reached him.

Kraml expressed genuine eagerness. "Have a feeling my man is in your neck of the woods today," he went on.

"Then he'll be adding to the excitement," Schmidt said. "Big South African delegation blew in last night. Du Plessis himself. It's the talk of the town."

Kraml thought quickly. It fit. Du Plessis surely needed to explain South Africa's position to the Swiss. It was even logical that Marcus, who had assiduously cultivated the Swiss establishment for the past few years, would be invited to such a meeting.

"Any news on the Russian front?" the Austrian trader asked.

Schmidt paused. "Gold market's funny." It was a statement.

"But very busy. Have to go now. *Servus!*" Kraml said, switching over to another line as Blacky shuffled back.

Trading did get heavy. Kraml watched the wires closely, but no one had picked up on the South African delegation. All the financial reporters were in Zurich or Geneva; the South Africans were in Berne.

It was logical enough. But still, Kraml was too attuned to

81

the market. Something was not quite right. Blacky continued today as he had on the previous day, feeding the market slowly, steadily, keeping the gold price on a leash. Yesterday, a Russian came to Zug. Today, Marcus almost certainly was meeting with South Africans in Berne.

Before retrieving his car in the underground garage, Kraml went to a phone booth outside and called Drew in London.

"Sorry I couldn't talk earlier," he told the journalist. "You know, this Russian connection: there was a Russian here yesterday visiting Marcus." Before Drew could respond, Kraml added, "And I have good reason to believe Marcus has gone to Berne today to meet with the South Africans."

Kraml listened as Drew went through the same checklist of possibilities as he had been turning over in his mind, until the journalist ended up at the same dead end. If Marcus was selling Russian gold, what was he doing talking to the South Africans? And even if he was channeling Soviet production into the market, where was the rest of the gold coming from?

"Drew, there must be something we don't know about." It was one of Kraml's endearing traits that he could draw an obvious conclusion and state it unhesitatingly.

There was silence on the line except for the gentle click every eight seconds signaling another message unit.

"It looks like I have to come over to the Continent next week," Drew said. "Why don't I come see you?"

The crystal dial in the pay phone began flashing, telling Kraml to put more money in. He was out of change. "Yes, we need to talk." The two agreed on Monday evening, and Hannes went around the corner to his office building. It was nearly dark and the streetlights came on as he turned into the garage entrance.

III

Fürglin peered out the window as the Crossair turboprop bounced its way through the valley currents to the Lugano airport. The two legs of the lake opened up between the mountains in a suggestively erotic fashion that appealed to the Swiss banker. The tiny plane landed on the airstrip and taxied up to the low-slung frame building that served as airport terminal for the capital of the Ticino canton.

As Fürglin queued up for a taxi outside, a Rolls Royce Silver Shadow swung around the corner from the service road and glided up to the parking lot. The uniformed chauffeur hopped out and opened the back door on his side to retrieve a valise. On the other side, a thickset gray-haired man with all the elegance wealth can give stepped out and briskly traversed the twenty meters to the terminal entrance. Two men in pilot's uniform greeted him. One took the valise from the chauffeur, and without any delays or goodbyes the three men retreated into the building while the driver returned to the Rolls.

Fürglin watched this tableau with a small smile of satisfaction. He was home. He had seen the Learjet on the tarmac and mentally ticked off now just who the passenger might be. Thyssen-Bornemisza, perhaps, the steel heir who kept one of many homes in Lugano. The fact that Fürglin did not readily recognize the man from photos meant he was probably very wealthy.

The Swiss settled into the back seat of the Mercedes taxi, wondering if he would buy a Rolls once he was ensconced in Brazil. Better not—he laughed to himself—too showy. But there were lots of ways to be discreet and very, very comfortable.

Fürglin dismissed the images that came to mind. He had only fifteen minutes before the taxi would deposit him at the Piazza Manzoni and the headquarters of Banco Ticino. He had prepared Antonelli, the sleepy chairman of the board, for the notion of his abrupt vacation, but he rehearsed his story again. The constant pressure, the stress of trading in the hotbed London environment, capped by the market shutdown last week had taken their toll, he would tell the chairman, who only rarely ventured away from his lakeside tranquillity. Fürglin had engineered a tidy profit for Banco Ticino as well in the gold rush, although not, of course, as tidy as his own. Antonelli couldn't deny him his two months of furlough, hidden away in his country home, far away from telephones.

Of course, Fürglin wasn't planning to sit and relax, waiting for Interpol to catch up with him, but he had to tell Antonelli something.

Fürglin had made a brief, cryptic call to Carajec, his Yugoslav friend, to make his real plans. A short conversation with Gabelli in New York had completed his arrangements. Fürglin was Swiss;

he left nothing to chance.

The lake was choppy. Off-season tourists dressed in wind-breakers and scarves clung to the railings on the top level of the sightseeing boats. The piazza fountains were still going despite the temperature, as the city tried to preserve the resort atmosphere that drew so many Swiss and Germans from the colder north. But Fürglin noticed as he got out of the taxi that very few café patrons braved the chill to sit on the tables surrounding the Piazza della Riforma.

Fürglin went into the discreet side entrance with the elevator going directly up to the offices of the board members. His meeting with "Dottore" Antonelli was even briefer and more perfunctory than he had planned. The pompous old bastard had appropriated the cherished *dottore* title on the basis of an honorary degree that Lausanne had awarded him in recognition of certain generous contributions from Banco Ticino, but it had not made him any smarter. He belonged to the old generation of Swiss bankers, who waited for wealthy customers from less fortunate countries to bring their money to him. Their gratitude for this privilege expressed itself in a willingness to accept rates that obviated any strenuous efforts on the bank's part to make a profit.

Fürglin was a member of the new generation, which knew that Swiss bankers were going to have to work harder. International competition had reached the point that many banks were aggressively moving into the market for funds management that the Swiss had monopolized for so long. And Swiss banking secrecy was no longer what it used to be. As Swiss banks expanded their own business abroad, foreign governments had more leverage to pry open the lid of secrecy on numbered accounts. The United States had been particularly keen on getting documents to crack some huge cases of insider trading. Countries like Haiti and the Philippines successfully blocked funds of their deposed dictators. All in all, Switzerland was not the safe haven it used to be, and that meant Swiss bankers had to double their efforts to drum up business.

The problem was, Fürglin didn't want to work so hard all his life. If being comfortable in this day and age meant trading these restful mountains for Brazil's beaches, he at least was willing to make the sacrifice.

He would miss the skiing, though. Fürglin gazed at the massive white peaks from the window of the suite at the Splendide

Royale that the bank kept for its visiting executives from abroad. *Tant pis.* He sighed.

He called Carajec. "All set?"

"Don't worry. I'll be there." Carajec also spoke English as a precaution, although their brief conversation was cryptic enough.

Fürglin relaxed. He knew he could count on Carajec. The big Yugloslav knew how to be serious about serious things, and Fürglin had let him know this was serious.

Carajec owed him a lot. Fürglin had backed him when the young immigrant on the make had wanted to launch his charter service. The ambitious young man wanted to try the charter business from Campione, the Italian enclave across the lake from Lugano, and he had impressed Fürglin enough so that the newly minted loan officer gave him the seed money he needed.

Carajec had prospered, although Fürglin felt fairly certain that not all his income came from tourists. But he was a good customer for the bank, a friend to his first backer, and an amateur speedboat champion. Tonight, banker Fürglin was going to take a little spin on the lake with his customer friend in Carajec's world-class speedboat.

Fürglin would have liked to go to the bar, but he didn't want to run into anyone he knew. He'd already told the hotel he wouldn't be staying, but was leaving this evening for his country house. With about three hours to kill, Fürglin stretched out on the sofa and, like a man without a care in the world, promptly went to sleep.

At 9 P.M., he was at the Debarcadero Paradiso, dressed in a summer-weight suit and a trenchcoat, carrying only a leather flight bag. Carajec's boat came gliding out of the darkness, its powerful engines reduced to a gentle purr. The waves slapped the fiberglass hull as Fürglin stepped onto the boat without a word. Carajec pulled away from the dock and headed south for the bridge.

"You like the drama," Carajec finally said, once they were under way, speaking Italian now but keeping his voice low.

Fürglin cut off the conversation. "There will be a lot less drama if we keep this quiet."

He did feel slightly ridiculous, even though he was nervous. He'd been out with Carajec often, and many times had gotten off at Gabelli's villa, not even thinking about its being an unofficial crossing of the Swiss-Italian border. Tonight's quiet exit from

85

Switzerland was just a precaution, perhaps an unneccessary one. But what did a little caution cost? He'd seen too many bankers go to jail to feel like taking chances now.

He knew it was hard for Carajec, an ebullient personality, to keep quiet. But Fürglin adamantly remained silent, forestalling any conversation. The banker had also instructed Carajec to furnish himself with an alibi, "as a precaution." If anyone asked, four drivers would swear that the Yugoslav had spent the evening with them, discussing a first-class boat and bus tour to Lago Maggiore that was scheduled for the next day. Carajec had enough marginal activities of his own not to question the banker's instructions.

In spite of all the caution, Fürglin was enjoying himself. He had come to the lake region later in life, when he began his bank training, and still experienced the outsider's wonder at boats, which transform an obstacle into a pleasant highway.

The trip was over quickly, without any incident and without any further conversation. Fürglin just nodded at Carajec as he stepped onto the cement landing dock in darkness. The villa was dark and shuttered, but Fürglin discerned two dim shapes near the door, a man rhythmically stroking a dog.

The man at the door whispered something to the dog and then went inside without turning on a light, leaving the door open for Fürglin to follow. Fürglin nodded again at the man when he lit a candle inside; Antonio knew him well. The stocky gray-headed retainer shuffled ahead of Fürglin, carrying the candle to light the stairs to the guest room on the garden side of the villa.

A plate of cold cuts and an ice bucket with a bottle of wine were on the table in the room. Gabelli was a generous soul, thought Fürglin, grateful for the small favor. But then, Gabelli owed him about a million small favors by now.

Fürglin had nothing to say to Antonio, who left quietly. The banker had planned this down to the last detail. At 7 A.M., Antonio would take him to Linnate airport at Milan, for the flight to Rome and the connection to Kuwait. Fürglin had not come to the villa, and his friend Gabelli was an ocean away in New York.

Attacking the mortadella, Fürglin felt pleased with himself. His precautions may have been superfluous, but he had too much at stake now to risk any mishap. The food and the wine increased his sense of well-being, which enveloped him still as he crawled into the four-poster bed and once again fell quickly to sleep. Being a fugitive wasn't so bad.

Seven

I

The doorman swept open the cab door with a flourish that would have honored the Prince of Wales. The gentle self-mockery of his smile perfectly suited the incipient euphoria Carol and Drew felt as they entered the glittery elegance of the Dorchester.

Drew ordered champagne cocktails for them in the bar, decorated in a lighthearted modern chic despite the old-fashioned glamour of the hotel. They clinked their glasses together in a giddy toast and sat facing each other in a sudden silence.

It was a comfortable quiet. The two of them had established an easy rapport. They had gone to see the revival of *Travesties*, followed by a light supper of salmon and white wine at Leicester Square and now the nightcap at Carol's hotel.

There were only a few people in the bar. The muted lilt of whispered French drifted over from another young couple two tables away. The black and pastel decor gleamed here and there from spotlights punctuating the dim room. The candle on each table created a small circle of intimacy.

Carol broke the silence. "We haven't talked too much about gold, Mr. Reporter."

"No, Miss Central Banker, we haven't," Drew responded. "Do you think Halden will forgive us?"

"Did you find out anything this afternoon?"

Drew looked at her for a moment. The candlelight reflected a limpid clarity in her brown eyes.

"The more I know, the more confused I get," he said finally. He told her about his inconclusive conversation with Kraml.

"Don't feel alone. There was a very discreet meeting at the Bank this afternoon. Guinness called in the fixing banks to discuss the situation. He let me sit in on it." Carol sipped her cocktail. "They have the same question: Who is supplying the gold to the market?"

"Do they have the same answer?"

"The same collection of maybes."

Carol was quiet for a while.

"The key seems to be the South Africans," she resumed suddenly. She looked at Drew. "Do you think they could be selling gold?"

Drew bit off his instinctive negation. The loss of 80 percent of South African production was the cause of the crisis, after all. The mystery about who could have so much gold and would be willing to sell it was predicated on that situation. It seemed obvious that South Africa could not be the source of the gold. And yet, Carol's question was the logical conclusion of the information they had.

"I don't see how," he said.

"Do you think your friend could find out more about what Marcus is really doing?"

"I'm going to see him next week. I'll ask him."

"And this reporter of yours—Van der Merwe?—can you reach him?"

Drew toyed with his glass a moment. "I think I may go to South Africa," he said.

And odd look came into Carol's eyes. She said nothing.

"I'm going to Geneva. Scotland Yard called—Guinness works fast—and they think I should have a look at this murder victim in Annecy."

"How terrible!" Carol's exclamation was spontaneous.

Drew had been shocked himself when the detective sergeant rang up in the afternoon. Idle speculation about mob-style murders was one thing; that Scotland Yard took his suspicion seriously enough to make the trip to Annecy thrust the journalist into a new dimension.

The call from Kraml had unsettled him in a different way. MacLean and his possible fate were worrying, but Kraml's suspicions had a different order of importance. They lent further weight to Drew's instinct that Marcus was instrumental in whatever was happening in the gold market.

Now Carol felt the South Africans were the key. The South Africans were in Berne, presumably meeting with Marcus.

Drew had made one other phone call before leaving for the theater to meet Carol. He reached Christian de Narcy, who always stayed late in his office, and arranged to meet the French banker Monday for lunch in Paris. Drew was sure that de Narcy, heir to generations of financial wisdom, could help him sort out the bewildering tangle of events.

Drew noticed Carol watching him, patiently, somehow tenderly. An unasked question yawned between them. "I'll be here through next Friday," Carol said. Drew nodded. They looked at each other with a quiet confidence. "Right now, I'm going to plead jet lag and thank you for a wonderful evening," she said.

At the elevator, they kissed, briefly.

"Good night, Drew," Carol said, stepping into the elevator. "Be careful."

The admonition stayed with him on the cab ride home. He didn't feel alone, carrying her concern with him. Somehow, those two words, spoken simply and sincerely, were as intimate as anything they could have said in parting.

II

Drew blinked when they came into the room. The harsh fluorescent light reflected brightly off the whitewashed walls. The unpleasant odor of formaldehyde affronted his nose.

It was his first trip to a morgue. There were indeed square

cabinet doors lining one wall. But the white-coated assistant took Drew and the plainclothesman to a table at the far end of the room. Drew, who had taken his coat off in the reception hall, noticed the chill in the air.

A white cloth over the table clearly outlined a body. Drew felt detached, as though he were sitting comfortably at home watching some detective series on television. The laboratory assistant pulled down the cover.

Drew nearly retched as he was plunged into the overpowering reality of death. He fought the impulse to turn his head away. Despite the work of the coroner's staff to clean up and restore the body, the face was scarcely recognizable as such, while the head was unnaturally oblong, with purple lumps that made it resemble an eggplant.

There was no question of recognizing MacLean from the face, but the very thought that this mutilated corpse might be that of a man Drew had worked with for three years was nauseating.

Having forced himself to look at the head, he found it difficult to divert his gaze from its riveting ugliness. The assistant had completely uncovered the body. Drew swallowed hard and willed himself to objectivize the corpse in front of him. He looked at the shape of the shoulders, the torso, the legs. He imagined the body standing up, dressed in MacLean's clothes.

"He seems right for the height," the journalist whispered to the policeman in French. It seemed inappropriate to speak in a normal voice. "The shoulders are bony and flat the way MacLean's seemed to be."

The slight bend in the legs corresponded to MacLean's bowlegged stature as well, but Drew was not sure whether that was due to the body's position on the table.

He returned to study the head. Some wisps of hair remained on the back of the battered skull. They acted upon Drew like icons, to reveal the identity of the victim. He suddenly had no doubt that the corpse was MacLean's.

"Excuse me," he said, leaving the room quickly and crossing the hall into the toilet, which had been pointed out to him as if by happenstance when they were going in. There he retched painfully; he had avoided eating anything for fear of just this reaction, but the nausea continued to rack him.

As frightening as the physical reaction was the numbing

coldness in his brain. The recognition of his former colleague froze all emotion and thought in one blast of incomprehension. Drew could not fathom murder and brutality. It did not belong to his sheltered world of words and paper and business suits. For him, violence and even death were the fictions of movies and books.

The palpable evidence of physical violence brought home to him in a new way the moral disruption it reflected. For Drew, the brutal punishment meted out to MacLean seemed appropriate to the violation of his integrity as a journalist.

MacLean had been party to a scam, Drew felt sure. He had taken the telex from Van der Merwe and passed on the information to an accomplice, probably Fürglin, who was allied to investors in Kuwait and elsewhere. With a half hour head start they had been able to buy massively in the bullion and futures markets before the news broke and sent prices skyrocketing. MacLean had violated his sacred trust as a journalist and now lay mutilated and dead on a morgue table.

Drew became dimly aware of his feeling. His reason immediately tried to excuse MacLean, to rationalize the Canadian's behavior, to reject his own condemnation of MacLean. But the feeling of justice was too strong. He knew that whoever did this to MacLean was not motivated by a respect for truth, but in Drew's mind the violation of truth had ineluctably carried Mac-Lean to his fate.

A sharp rap on the toilet door interrupted Drew's internal conflict.

"Ça va?" the policeman called.

Drew emerged ashen-faced. "I'm pretty sure it's him. The hair is just the right mixture of gray and color," he managed to say.

The perpetrators had made some effort to render the corpse unidentifiable but, through the pressure of time or indifference, had not removed the victim's teeth. Scotland Yard had located MacLean's dentist and was sending his dental records to Annecy. When they arrived, the records would almost certainly permit positive identification.

In the meantime, Drew's companion took him to the police station, where he signed a brief statement identifying the body on a preliminary basis.

III

Fürglin throttled the choke and went flying over the dune, landing on two of the three wheels. The balloon-tired Honda tricycle righted itself, recovered traction, and hurtled along the packed sand to the next dune.

The Swiss banker was delighted with his "toy," one of a garageful that Tamal al-Masari kept at his weekend house on the Gulf for the amusement of his children, his guests, and, on occasion, himself.

Fürglin thought it was good to visit his Kuwaiti partner. Al-Masari had loaned Fürglin his stake for the gold play, but of course it was Fürglin's cunning and patience that made the play possible. The Swiss banker had multiplied the wealth of al-Masari's family. The meeting reminded everyone of that. It also muddied Fürglin's tracks in case anyone was trying to find him.

The weather was nippy, but not nearly as cold as in Europe. The sky was gray, and the Gulf equally dull. Solitary tankers dotted the water's surface. Fewer than before, Fürglin reflected.

The banker rounded another dune and nearly ran into Mahout, al-Masari's oldest son, who swerved his tricycle, balancing it precariously as he avoided a collision. Fürglin guffawed with delight, righted his own vehicle, and bent forward, accelerating on the straightaway before him. The speedometer climbed to 60 kilometers per hour, which seemed thrillingly fast on the ungainly motorcycle. Fürglin extended his left leg, decelerated, and banked in the direction of the clubhouse.

The bungalow was identical to several others spaced out in a row along the shore. Inside he found al-Masari playing cards at a felt-covered table in a corner of the lounge. The Kuwaiti waved to his friend, and disengaged himself from the other players.

"Had enough?" he said to Fürglin. Face still flushed with the wind and the excitement, the Swiss only nodded.

"How about a whiskey?" asked al-Masari, reaching into a cupboard and pulling out a bottle of Chivas Regal from one of several cartons. Fürglin nodded again, marveling as he had on a previous trip at how well stocked the club bar was in spite of Kuwait's ban on alcohol. Al-Masari had explained to him that each member brought home a case when returning from abroad, declaring to customs that it was for his own personal use.

"It's chilly, I suppose," the Kuwaiti said to his guest as they settled into the leather sofas opposite the game table.

"Oh, ça va, ça va," Fürglin said. "I like those tricycles."

"You must come in the summer sometime to try our motor-powered surfboards."

Fürglin nodded, thinking to himself that it would take more than a surfboard to lure him away from the Copacabana. "It's funny," he said. "You people have all the money in the world, and you have to haul back cartons of whiskey to have a drink."

"We are adapting slowly to the twentieth century," his host responded nonchalantly.

A miniature gong sounded across the room. Immediately, the men at the card table rose. Some were dressed in burnooses. One wore a designer sweatsuit from France, and another sported a flannel Western shirt and blue jeans. All were under forty. It was Kuwait's young financial set, as down home as they got.

Two big platterfuls of rice were already sitting on the table as the men took their places. Fürglin was given the place of honor at the head of the table. Two boys brought plates steaming with grilled mutton chops, which they deposited on the table. The group politely waited for Fürglin to serve himself. The Swiss ignored the serving utensils placed by each platter. He knew from his last trip that these, like the tableware at each place, were just for show. With a gusto he truly felt, he reached out his right hand and grabbed a juicy chop from the platter. A burst of Arabic greeted this display of cultural savoir-faire, and hands — right hands, always—depleted the mounds of meat on the other platters.

Fürglin did not have as much luck with the rice. He could not quite master the trick of twirling the grains into bite-sized ovals, as his hosts did. "Don't worry, it takes practice," al-Masari murmured next to him.

After the meal, the Kuwaiti walked with his guest along the "beach," a desolate stretch of sand marked with black and gray lines of muck from the polluted waters of the Gulf.

"There's something going on," al-Masari said, finally coming to the point.

The Swiss nodded. He'd gotten the drift of al-Masari's concern in the brief snatches of conversation they had managed between meetings at the airport the previous evening, his home in Kuwait City, and the weekend bungalow.

"You're right," Fürglin said aloud. "There is too much gold on the market."

"Marcus seems to be the funnel, but who's supplying?" al-Masari continued.

Fürglin had trouble focusing his mind. He had $20 million banked in the Bahamas and a discreet refuge waiting for him in Brazil. The money was more than his moderate greed had ever hoped for. It dazed him. It took him some time to realize that al-Masari, who already had a multiple of this fabulous sum, was anguished by how to get more.

"Maybe the South Africans were hoarding part of their production just in case something like this happened," offered the banker.

"Perhaps," agreed the Arab, plainly not satisfied. "But everybody had the impression before that South Africa was selling and bartering everything it had just to get essential imports."

"Maybe the sabotage wasn't quite as bad as they made out," said Fürglin.

Al-Masari grunted, then stopped abruptly. He looked quickly at his companion.

"What's the matter?" said Fürglin, watching the nearly invisible progress of a tanker on the horizon.

The Kuwaiti paused a moment. "That might be the case," he said finally. He changed the subject. "It was a drastic measure you took with that journalist."

"Oh, I don't think two and half million dollars was too much, given the situation." Fürglin turned to his companion with a smile, which disappeared when he saw the look of horror on al-Masari's face.

"He has been murdered," al-Masari said, recovering.

"Murdered?" Fürglin's surprise was genuine. The bank had told him that MacLean came right on schedule to pick up his money. "How? Why?"

"He was found in Annecy, across the French border," al-Masari explained, scrutinizing the Swiss carefully. "It's all right, my friend. It need not concern us."

Fürglin didn't pursue the subject but walked silently at al-Masari's side, solemnly reflective. The Kuwaiti made no attempt to hide his suspicion, but Fürglin could think of no way to allay it.

94

Very quickly, Fürglin's concern turned from MacLean to himself. He could not figure out who would have put out a contract on MacLean or why, but those same people might have designs on him.

"Perhaps it would be well to short gold in the futures market," the Kuwaiti said, returning to his top priority.

"You think the supply really is greater than the market knows about?" Fürglin said. "But why be greedy? Why not just sit on your profits? Why take a needless risk?"

"You don't understand our world, my friend," responded al-Masari, looking out toward the Gulf. The slender figure was dressed in a well-used sweatsuit and shabby tennis shoes. The sole sign of wealth was the leather jacket he had thrown over his shoulders, an exquisitely worked piece from Italy. "It's not just the money." He did not say what else it was, and Fürglin did not feel like inquiring.

"Well, it's the money for me," the Swiss said, smiling smugly. Money and the pleasures it could buy: the beach, the girls, the freedom.

"You may find yourself bored in Brazil," al-Masari suggested.

Fürglin turned sharply toward the Kuwaiti. The news about MacLean had made him nervous. How innocent was this remark of al-Masari's? How had the Kuwaiti known about MacLean's death anyway?

The Swiss said nothing. He was dependent on the Kuwaiti's good will until he arrived in Rio and confirmed that his money had been safely transferred to his Nassau account. Al-Masari was smiling enigmatically. Fürglin walked on in silence.

Eight

I

José Martínez opened the safe in his office with quick, sure movements. The Mexican finance minister's face was drawn, his eyes bloodshot. But his starched white shirt was fresh, he had shaved, and his hair was combed in the neat, waxed style that was his trademark.

José Martínez had not slept that night. His wife and children were already in bed when he returned home from his meeting with the president. He sat in his study, sipping bourbon, all night long. He brooded, and thought, and made up his mind about what he was going to do.

He had arrived early this morning at the Hacienda, his ministry, his home away from home. It was Sunday, but the guard was not surprised to see the minister. Martínez worked often during the weekends.

It was quiet. Martínez had not called upon a secretary or assistant as he usually did when he came in on Sunday. Today he needed to be alone.

Martínez relished the tranquillity. He imagined how different it was right this moment at Zócalo Square, where the president would be coming to the balcony to address the crowd. The television news had announced the previous evening that the president would be making an important speech today. The party left nothing to chance; busloads of enthusiastic fans would guarantee the president a fervent audience, even if the speech were not so important.

But it was indeed important. Martínez had been made privy to its contents last night, during his hour-long session with the president.

Martínez's temple throbbed with the memory of that meeting. How he hated that man, the president of Mexico. Sitting there with Jésus Moncloa at his side, the two of them gloating over Martínez's defeat.

What a defeat they had prepared for him! The president was going to announce a repudiation of all foreign debt, effective in two weeks. It was a repudiation as well of Martínez's policy of conciliation with foreign banks and governments, of his efforts to reach a compromise that respected all legal and diplomatic commitments his country had made.

Repudiation was like a declaration of war. But the president shrewdly delayed the impact, turning his threat into an ultimatum. The banks, and the governments that backed them, had two weeks to concede terms that would nullify the repudiation. It was a gamble, a desperate act by a president too convinced of his own power to consider the consequences of his actions.

A deluded president, egged on by an ambitious Rasputin. Moncloa was a Socialist, but Martínez had always been able to convince the president that Mexico's obligations to the United States should prevent anyone espousing Socialist principles from coming to power.

Until now. Now, Moncloa had prevailed. He had convinced the president to brandish repudiation in the face of the Yankee dictator.

Of course, Martínez could not continue as finance minister. Repudiation went against solemn personal pledges Martínez had made, not only to Halden and other U.S. officials but to his colleagues in the other debtor countries who looked to him for leadership in the endless agony of negotiating and debt resched-

97

uling. His resignation was expected and accepted on the spot.

Martínez took the papers from the safe. He sorted through them quickly, removing several dossiers and replacing the others in the safe. There were certain facts that must disappear with him.

He went into the small room between his office and his secretary's reception room and quickly fed the dossiers into the paper shredder. Then he carried the receptacle full of confetti out into the hall, to the incinerator shaft, and dumped the contents into it.

Martínez came back into his office. Several documents were neatly laid out on his desk. On the top, a brief letter to his wife. He had written nothing for his sons. There were many things he was aching to tell them, but they were too young to understand.

José Martínez was forty-two years old and his life was over. His single ambition for the past twenty-five years was the presidency. Last night he had learned he would never be president. Nor would he ever again hold government office in Mexico.

He had invested too much in his ambition to accept the humiliation. It would be easy for him to retreat to the United States. A Harvard professorship, a seat on the Council of Foreign Relations, a voice in the deliberations of the U.S. administration regarding its southern neighbors.

But he would be tainted with failure, clearly distinguishable to all those he came in contact with. No comfortable academic title could compensate for the princely wealth and status he was about to lose after hoping for so long to augment it.

Martínez turned on the radio behind his desk. The strident tones of the president, with his harsh northern accent, blared forth. "Dictatorship," "Yankee," "imperialism," "repudiation"—the words thundered.

With an angry movement, he switched it off. He reached into his briefcase and pulled out a glistening, well-oiled Colt .45.

Halden would know what he meant, and that might be revenge enough. Martínez had a boundless confidence in the American central banker. Halden would appreciate the hopelessness of Martínez's situation—and of his own.

The room was completely quiet now. With quick, sure movements, Martínez put the pistol in his mouth and pulled the trigger.

II

The countryside remained placid as the French bullet train sped through the rolling Burgundy plain at 180 miles per hour toward Paris the next morning.

The view reassured Drew, who was still shaky after his look at MacLean's corpse. The dental records had arrived and confirmed Drew's tentative identification. The journalist had spent the remainder of Sunday with the police, telling them what he knew.

The identification of the corpse had removed any doubt about MacLean's participation in a scheme to beat the markets, though it raised a whole host of other questions. A warrant was out for Fürglin's arrest, but the Swiss banker had already fled London. Interpol was after him, starting in Lugano, where his bank was based.

Drew checked his bags at the Gare de Lyon. He needed to hurry to keep his lunch appointment. Emerging from the station, he joined the taxi queue; within two minutes, he was seated in a Peugeot 505, speeding to the Pré Catelan restaurant.

It was one of those breathtaking late autumn days in Paris. The sky was a deep bright blue and the midday light etched the white stone buildings in arresting detail. The sheer grandeur of the Place de la Concorde impressed Drew once again, as it always did despite his innumerable taxi trips across the wide carrefour.

As the taxi came to the end of the Champs-Élysées and began negotiating its way around the Arc de Triomphe, Drew tried to arrange his thoughts for his meeting with Christian.

The banker had been his usual diffident self when Drew called him. While Drew waited on the line, he shifted his other appointments around to invite the journalist to lunch at the Pré Catelan restaurant in the Bois de Boulogne.

Christian de Narcy was probably Drew's best source, and a friend as well. Just slightly older than the American, the Frenchman represented the youngest generation of a family whose banking tradition went back two and a half centuries. Older than the more illustrious Rothschilds, the de Narcys had managed to preserve their discreet influence in European finance through countless wars and revolutions. The family had deliberately kept its banking operation small, with the result that they escaped the wholesale nationalization of French banks under the Socialist government in 1981.

De Narcy, in fact, had been the one who taught Drew that a bank's true strength does not lie in the size of its assets. The published statements of the de Narcy bank gave hardly any indication of its true influence. Christian was a merchant banker in the truest sense of the word, using his wits as his main capital. The bank's principal assets were off the balance sheet, hidden in decades of unrealized capital gains. As the family heir, Christian was one of the twenty wealthiest people in France.

The taxi turned into the park at Porte Maillot, speeding down the tree-lined avenues crisscrossing the woods at Paris's western end. It finally stopped in the gravel drive of the manor house that was now one of the city's most highly rated and expensive restaurants.

As Drew stepped out, de Narcy's chauffeur-driven Renault came up behind the taxi. The banker buttoned his double-breasted brown suit as he came up to Drew.

"Welcome back," he said warmly in English.

The Pré Catelan showed its best side in the summer, when the bucolic ambiance of the woods together with the fine food and wine relaxed the most determined businessmen. The chill November air chased them inside today, but the late fall colors remained enchanting through the terrace window.

Drew felt better already. De Narcy radiated that easy self-confidence that comes with birth into wealth and position. It elicited the appropriate measure of deference from the normally haughty maître d'hôtel.

Lunch at the Pré Catelan was a tradition for the two men. Drew occasionally hosted the banker at a more moderately priced restaurant in the city when time was too short for the trip to the Bois, but de Narcy liked to bring them out here whenever possible to enjoy some of the particularly refined pleasures that life in France is all about.

"You have already been to Annecy then?" de Narcy asked.

"It was pretty grisly," Drew said, folding open the oversized menu, "but it was MacLean. My instinct unfortunately was right."

"Well, it won't be the first or last time something like that has happened," the banker remarked, perusing the wine menu.

Drew wasn't sure whether he was referring to MacLean's abuse of inside information or his murder. "Have they caught the Swiss fellow yet?"

"No, he's skipped the country, but Interpol is on the case."

"They'll have trouble catching him," de Narcy stated matter-of-factly. "It's odd that whoever was involved with your MacLean went so far as to have him killed."

Drew just shook his head. None of it made any sense to him.

"Will you have any trouble from it, home office or anything?" the Frenchman asked.

"We're trying to keep it out of the papers," the journalist responded, smiling at the irony.

"In the end, it's a small sideshow," de Narcy continued. "Unfortunate for you, but beside the point really." He paused again. "What do you think is really going on?"

The sudden pointedness of the question was unsettling. Drew knew from experience that de Narcy did not ask rhetorical questions; he genuinely wanted his journalist friend's opinion.

"I'm not quite sure," Drew began cautiously. "The one thing that still puzzles me is the gold selling."

De Narcy nodded in a brief, sharp movement, as if acknowledging another correct answer from a star pupil. "Just so. It has many people puzzled. But the price remains high."

"It has to," Drew said. "With four fifths of South Africa's production out, the price has to stay up."

De Narcy went through the ritual of extracting a cigarette from his case and fitting it into a holder. It was his only affectation, although Drew sometimes wondered whether the banker wouldn't sport a monocle in later life.

"Are you sure the report is accurate?" he asked.

A chill rippled through the journalist. He bit off his first response and thought a moment. The telex, the phone call, the announcement, the market. He had never seen the telex, but MacLean's corpse seemed massive evidence that it had arrived. Nor had he had any luck in reestablishing contact with Van der Merwe, but there was no question it had been the stringer on the phone.

Drew measured his response. "I'd say we have about as much certainty about it as we do about most things we report." The words hung in the air. De Narcy just looked at him as he puffed on his cigarette, holding it between his thumb and forefinger.

There had been no independent verification, Drew reflected. The South Africans had rejected any attempts for security reasons. Likewise, they had released no photographs.

"The market's response seems to verify it," Drew ventured.

"The market," de Narcy said, "will jump off whatever cliff it's confronted with." Drew was well acquainted with the banker's strong opinions about the speculative chaos that passed for financial markets. "And besides, this gold selling *has* made the market confused and jittery." The banker paused again. "Is it possible that the South Africans are holding out on the market?"

De Narcy's unexpected question gave Drew a sudden insight. Kraml's call had bothered him, and now he knew why. It made no sense for Marcus to be dealing with both the Russians and the South Africans—*unless for the same reason.* But if the Russians and South Africans were selling gold together, what about the mine sabotage?

What about the mine sabotage? The question rebounded in Drew's mind. The sabotage. What if the South Africans were exaggerating the impact of the sabotage? What if—Drew reeled with the thought—they had invented the story and were continuing to put their full production on the market? They would be reaping enormous profits with the price of gold tripled.

He rejected the idea. It was not thinkable that the news mechanism could break down to that point. But it had broken down with MacLean. Was it possible that it had broken down elsewhere too?

"I need to talk to my stringer," Drew said, giving voice to a sudden decision. De Narcy had patiently let the journalist work through the possibilities.

"Have you heard anything about Marcus?" de Narcy asked. That name again.

"I'm trying to find out," Drew said. "What do you know?"

The banker shrugged. "We avoid dealing with him," he said. He paused. "If Pretoria *is* holding out"—de Narcy kept it in the world of conjecture—"you're right: the market will catch up with it sooner or later. But with things the way they are, a lot of damage could be done in the meantime."

"Things the way they are" was de Narcy's tactful way of referring to the collapse of the postwar monetary system a few years earlier. The Third World debt crisis had brought down the last semblance of order in international monetary relations. Only the vast liquidity in the world markets and the nimble imaginations of the bankers had kept the world from recognizing that fact. It was the insight Drew had gotten through his conversations with de Narcy and one or two other clear-sighted financiers.

"The market is extremely tight because of the gold news. Mexico is likely to declare a default, Brazil can't sustain the run on its interbank lines, our own recovery depends on trade that depends on finance that is not available as long as the gold situation is unresolved." The banker ticked off the potential damage to the world financial system. As usual, he had thought his position through. "The sooner we know, the better," de Narcy concluded.

The banker, Drew was well aware, had a high respect for the role of information as a constructive force.

Drew reacted to the succession of elegant dishes with automatic appreciation. De Narcy's suggestions had even pushed yesterday's grim encounter out of his mind. His tentative resolve to go to South Africa as soon as possible hardened into a firm decision. He *would* convince Corrello and Madison, he *would* get the visa, he *would* find Van der Merwe, he *would* find out what in the hell was going on.

III

Drew asked de Narcy's driver to drop him at the Galerie Vivienne, near the Banque de France, where he found a quiet jewelry store he remembered for its original yet affordable earrings and necklaces.

He studied the window for some time before entering the shop, getting ready for his usual difficulty in coping with the insistent attention of French sales clerks. He finally spent an unsatisfactory quarter of an hour sorting through trays and trays of simple jewelry. Nothing seemed quite right for Carol.

Stepping back out into the gallery, its tile floor always elegant under the filtered glow of the skylights, Drew noticed a man with his back to him, studying the display in the *papeterie* opposite.

He had noticed the man before, because of his hat. Not many men wear hats, and certainly not many in their early thirties, as this man appeared to be. He seemed to have little else to do except browse in the Galerie Vivienne.

Drew went out the side entry of the gallery to walk up to the Place des Victoires, a favorite sight of his in Paris. It was one of the few traffic circles without a metro station or bus stop. The figure of the mounted Sun King in the center presided over a maze of entries and exits, streets spinning irregularly away from the Place, in contrast to the regular wheel-spoke planning of Étoile or Nation.

Drew glanced over his shoulder as he left the gallery; the man with the hat came around the corner, following in Drew's footsteps.

Drew turned left up the rue de Banque toward the Place. As he reached the circle, he turned left again, looking down the street to see if the coincidence was going to be prolonged. The man with the hat had also turned up the street.

So intent was Drew on the man behind him that he paid no attention to a white Renault R5 turbo making its second turn around the tiny circle. Only when Drew stepped into the next street to cross did the R5 spurt ahead. The sound of the motor and the squeal of tires on the cobbled pavement made Drew turn his head in time to see the squat car bearing down on him. He jumped back just as the car sped past him, swerving quickly out of sight. Drew noticed only the 75 of a Paris license plate.

He swung around quickly, aware of how fast his heart was pumping. There was no man with a hat anymore. Because the Place des Victoires was not along a major artery, there was very little traffic. There were a few pedestrians, but they were mostly on the other side of the Place, near the clothes shops there.

No one was paying any attention to Drew. Screeching tires and endangered pedestrians were commonplace in Paris.

Drew himself wondered whether it wasn't just another incident typical of Paris's lunatic driving customs. People were killed every day crossing the street, by accident.

He leaned against a parked car while his knees steadied. But his heart kept pounding, as fear gave way to anger. He pictured himself underneath a white cloth on a morgue table. The affront to his moral sense from the murder of a colleague became much more personal. His repugnance turned to hatred for those who threatened him.

It was a new feeling for Drew. In his society, relationships were rarely naked enough to inspire strong feelings. Long-established social structures diffused harsh emotions, especially negative ones.

Drew rarely raised his voice in anger and had never been in a fistfight or a brawl. He had taught himself to curb his anger, to suppress the urge to smash things when he did get mad.

But now he felt released from all those bonds. There was no doubt in his mind at that moment that someone had tried to kill him.

The white Renault did not reappear, nor did the man with the hat. When a taxi came into the circle, Drew hailed it on impulse and told the driver to take him to the Gare de Lyon.

On his way to the airport, after he had retrieved his luggage at the train station, Drew tried to sort through the tumult in his mind. If someone was following him, if, God help him, somebody *had* tried to run him down, they were evidently professionals.

But who could it be, and why were they after him? MacLean's murderers? He wasn't looking for the killers; Scotland Yard and Interpol were. He was a managing editor trying to fill a hole. He was a journalist trying to get to the bottom of a story.

What had happened? He had seen a man with a hat, and a car had nearly run him down while he was crossing a street. He had in fact not been looking when he started across. Why would anyone want to kill him? How could he report a suspicion that someone was trying to murder him if he had no idea why or who? Drew had enough experience of French police to know their response to such a vaguely founded suspicion.

It occurred to Drew that perhaps he should heed the warning, if that was what the near-murder was. Let the police do their work hunting MacLean's killers. He was out of it. There was not even any conclusive evidence that the scam he suspected had taken place.

As for the rest, the uncertainty in the markets, the anomalous gold dealing, the murky South African situation—these were certainly not his responsibilities. He was just a journalist, trying to report what's going on.

What *is* going on? he wondered. Attempted murder was for

105

investigative reporters tracking mob influence or police corruption, not for managing editors of commodities news services.

It all seemed so melodramatic. After all, it would be terribly risky if he disappeared. Or would it? Risky to whom? Whoever had staged this attempt on his life was running much greater risks than killing an obscure financial journalist.

One thing had become much clearer: there was definitely something to know about this report of mine sabotage. The attack against him verified his suspicions that more than the market scam was at stake.

Nor did the anger leave him. It supported his already strong convictions about getting at the truth. For the first time in his life, he felt ready to defy any danger to get a story.

IV

Richard Corrello looked through the tinted glass to the bright sky outside. A slight haze hung over the city of Atlanta, but there was green farmland surrounding it. His office on the thirteenth floor offered the view of a distant horizon.

Corrello didn't usually spend much time gazing out the window, regardless of the view and the splendid Georgia weather. But Drew's call had disturbed him. He knew he had to go to Madison immediately, and he was dreading the encounter.

Drew had called him from the airport in Paris, just before eleven o'clock.

"It was MacLean. I could identify him tentatively, and the dental records confirm it." Drew's voice was as clear as an interoffice call.

"Shit," Corrello said.

"There's more, Rich," Drew continued. "I've had a very disturbing lunch with an old banking source of mine here. He raised the question of whether the sabotage report was accurate."

Corrello was quiet. He suppressed his defensive reaction because the question was too realistic. After all, United Press had reported the end of World War I three days before the fact. Reporters made mistakes.

"We weren't the only ones who reported it," Corrello said coldly.

"We were the only ones who *had* a separate source," Drew said. "Notice the past tense—the separate source seems to have vanished."

Corrello listened as Drew told him why he wanted to go to South Africa.

"I'll have to clear it with Madison."

"I'll call you tomorrow from London. They're boarding my flight."

Corrello was in charge of news in an organization that lived off the news. But it was the money men who ran the show. Madison, trained as a certified public accountant, was chairman and chief executive officer.

It fell to Corrello to maintain and defend the group's journalistic strandards. He picked up his phone and pressed one of the buttons along the bottom. "Rita, it's me. Is he free?" No frills, no useless chatter. Madison's secretary knew the voice of everyone who had access to that line. She knew as well that it must be urgent simply because Corrello wanted to talk to Madison right now.

"In ten minutes," she said.

"What's up?" Madison snapped when Corrello entered the office. Madison could be quite charming when he saw the need to be. Seeing less and less need, he was charming less often these days.

"Drew called," Corrello said.

"Is he still gallivanting around in France." It wasn't a question. For being one of the shrewdest managers in the country, Madison still had the old-fashioned notion that any American traveling in Europe was on vacation.

"It was our man who was murdered," Corrello said.

"Drew's man, you mean."

"In point of fact, he was already on board when Drew took over," Corrello said. Whatever Madison's faults, he did not demand a yes-man. Corrello never hesitated to contradict him. "There's more."

"You've got to be kidding. What more?"

"One of Drew's bankers is asking whether we have verification on the story."

At this, Madison looked up from the papers he had been shuffling. He gave Corrello the stare that had chilled boardrooms across the country.

"Do I really have to listen to this?" he said evenly.

"Drew wants to go to South Africa."

"Drew can go straight to hell," Madison snapped, standing up. He started around the desk, thought better of it, returned to his seat, and sat down.

"Look, Rich, isn't this a bit out of our line? I mean, aren't we supposed to be taking pork belly prices in Chicago and delivering them to the meat packers in Kansas City?" He paused and continued in a more natural voice. "Of course the story is accurate. Every newspaper in the country reported it. The goddamned South African government confirmed it. And just because some queerbait European banker thinks he knows something, I've got a managing editor who wants to go traipsing off halfway across the world."

"Drew's worried about the stringer who reported the news," Corrello said. He knew the best way to get through to Madison was just to keep on a straight tack to his objective.

Madison snorted. "Is he dead too?"

"We've never been able to reestablish contact with him."

"I wish to hell we never had in the first place," Madison said with feeling. "So we had a scoop. If the story's fake, we'll lose more business than we gained." He thought for a minute. "If this thing blows up in our faces, I'll have Drew's ass."

Madison did not have to say to Corrello who else's ass was on the line.

"If Drew did go to South Africa, he could get some verification of the sabotage and find that stringer," Corrello suggested, after what he deemed an appropriate pause to let Madison know he had gotten the message.

"What are Dow Jones and Reuters doing? Don't they have stringers in South Africa?"

"They're much more prominent; their people were kicked out first," Corrello said. He didn't add that the other two agencies had been paying staffers in South Africa, not relying on a stringer for one of the most important commodities markets in the southern hemisphere.

"What if Drew finds this stringer? Then what?" Madison asked. He was weakening.

"Well, I suppose he'll find out his source. Confirm the accuracy of the report." Corrello smiled. "Knowing Drew, he'll dig up a scoop or two of his own while he's there."

Madison frowned. Corrello understood his dilemma. The last thing in the world Madison wanted was further complications from another scoop. On the other hand, the agency's sales manager couldn't stop talking about how the sabotage beat had lifted subscriber sales.

"What kind of scoop?"

"If he gets a visa at all—and he thinks, the situation being what it is, he might—he'd be one of the few journalists allowed in since the state of siege was declared," Corrello said. A former reporter, he was on Drew's side, uneasy himself about the gold selling in the market.

"What are we going to do about this corpse?"

Corrello was used to Madison's shifts. "Nothing just yet. The British papers will tumble to it first, because Scotland Yard was involved. We'll wait and see if the American papers pick it up. Anyway, it'll seem a small footnote."

"Let's keep it that way," Madison declared. "Tell Drew to go on to South Africa but not to do another goddam thing on the story without clearing it with us."

Nine

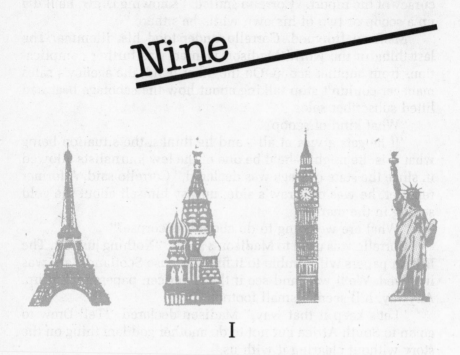

I

Drew's Swissair flight arrived punctually; within fifteen minutes he was comfortably installed in Kraml's BMW. It had been only two hours since he telephoned Corrello from Roissy airport in Paris.

"Nothing like Swiss efficiency," Drew said to the trader, as the two of them sped along the Autobahn through the flat farmland surrounding Kloten, the Swiss village that gave its name to Zurich's airport.

Kraml grunted. "The Swiss are boring," he said with an Austrian's automatic disdain for efficiency. But the young dealer was clearly nervous. Drew had noticed this the moment they met when he emerged from the gate.

Kraml ignored the exits for Zurich. Drew was to spend the night at Kraml's home south of Zug.

"You've put on weight, Hannes," Drew said, to make conversation.

"Family life," said Hannes, making a joke.

"How is your wife?" Drew continued the formalities.

110

"She likes it here. She's Swiss, you know."

The banalities only seemed to increase the tension. The two men continued in silence.

"I'm worried," Kraml finally said. "I think Marcus is working some kind of fiddle, but I can't figure out what it is."

"What's going on?"

"Well, Marcus and Blacky seem to be *controlling* the gold price. They're playing the market, but always in control."

"How do they do it?"

"That's what I can't figure out. Either they have some gold stashed away somewhere or they're pretending they do."

"What's the feeling in the market?"

"Always nervous, very nervous," Kraml paused. "Then today, Marcus got even funnier. He started shorting gold in the futures market."

Officially, Kraml did not even know this, but he had uncovered the transactions during the afternoon.

"There's something else strange," Kraml continued. "He's not the only one. Another Swiss group seems to be shorting gold. No telling who they're trading for."

"What do you think is behind it?"

Kraml shrugged. "I don't know."

"Could Marcus have built up a position in gold?"

"It's too big. Not even Marcus could afford to stockpile that much gold."

"Somebody else?"

"No, no. It's too much." Kraml showed his frustration. "The only ones who could have that much gold are the producers."

Drew thought for a while. "Do you think it's possible that South Africa is the source of the gold?"

"But their mines have been bombed."

"What if they had stockpiled some gold?"

"Impossible. Everyone knows the South Africans were selling every ounce of their production when the attacks took place."

"What about the Russians?"

"They're selling, all right," Kraml said. "And our visitor the other day points to Marcus as their dealer."

"Could they be the source of the gold?"

"Dammit, Drew, you know better than that. Everybody knows both the Soviet Union and South Africa desperately need

111

hard currency, so they were producing to the maximum and selling everything they produced. And then the South African mines got bombed. So there should be a lot less gold on the market, unless some goddam trader has developed a Midas touch." Kraml took the exit for his lake road.

"You know how the markets work," Drew said. "We don't really *know* how much gold the Russians can produce, or how much they're selling. We make guesses. Then we see if the trans-actions in the market are in line with those guesses. It's like physicists with the laws of nature. They make hypotheses and then test them empirically. For a long time, a hypothesis can look like it's right, and then something happens that proves it to be wrong. So you come up with a new hypothesis."

"What's your hypothesis?"

"I'm not sure yet," Drew hesitated. "Granted, it would be very hard to accept that South Africa had stockpiled any pro-duction."

Kraml just grunted.

"But maybe all our estimates about the Russians are wrong. Maybe they've made a new find we don't know about yet. Or maybe the South African sabotage wasn't as bad as we were led to believe," Drew concluded. "There are any number of reason-able hypotheses."

"Yeah, real reasonable, if you know about them." Kraml wasn't satisfied. "I think Marcus *does* know. I think he may be the only one who does."

"And I think you're right about that," Drew said. "Look, can you poke around some more?" He saw the Austrian grow even more tense. "Don't get yourself into trouble, though." For some reason, he had a flash of that corpse in Annecy.

"I'll be careful," Kraml said.

"I'm going to try to go to South Africa and see what I can find out," Drew said. "I haven't talked to our stringer since he sent us the telex about the sabotage." The telex he had never seen, Drew thought guiltily.

Kraml turned into a well-manicured drive, leading to a two-story house. Drew realized suddenly he was looking forward to a relaxed evening and hoped that the presence of Hannes's wife would steer the conversation away from the gold market. The thought of Carol flashed quickly through his mind.

II

"I don't like it," Carol said, as they sat together in the Cock and Bull. "Central bankers have no more to do with murder than journalists do."

Drew had just finished telling Carol about his trip to Annecy, his visit to the morgue, and the Renault in Paris.

"I think we should just report all this to Halden and Guinness and let them pass it on to the proper government authorities," she said.

"Pass on what? MacLean got involved with some thugs who swindled the market. Financial markets are jittery because there's more gold than there's supposed to be, and I was daydreaming when I crossed a street in Paris. What's the CIA going to make of all that?"

Drew was exasperated. He knew Carol was right, but he knew as well that their instinct for what was happening would be difficult to convey to those not familiar with financial markets.

"There's something more," Drew continued. "I feel very much personally involved in all this. It was my colleague—my subordinate—who swindled the market and got himself killed in the process. It was my story—my decision—that closed financial markets around the world."

He paused; Carol waited patiently.

"If the story was wrong, if the South Africans are somehow still supplying gold to the market, do you realize how that would make me feel?"

"It's not your fault, Drew. No more than the debt crisis is the Fed's fault. You were doing your job."

"My job is to report what's going on. I'm trained to sift out truth from lies, but this time I may have made a mistake and passed on a whopper."

"You had every reason to accept the report. Agencies bigger than yours, journalists older than you, accepted the declaration of the South African government."

"But my report made it possible for them to accept it. It tipped the balance in making Pretoria's announcement credible."

Drew punctuated this last statement by pounding his fist onto the table.

"I can't just sit and wait for things to happen," he continued.

"Marcus is playing a key role, so I've got Hannes digging into his operation. And if I can get to Van der Merwe—"

"Has it occurred to you that Van der Merwe might be dead too?"

Drew looked at Carol. The whole conversation seemed ludicrous. Carol's features were alluring in the semidarkness of the pub, and he wished he could devote himself to her. She was right, though, Drew realized for the first time. After everything that had happened, he had to face the possibility that his stringer had met a fate similar to MacLean's.

"Did you know Martínez shot himself?" Carol said.

"The Mexican finance minister?" Drew was genuinely shocked. "The wires said he died of a heart attack in his office."

"They're trying to hush it up. Halden called me on Monday."

"Is the situation in Latin America so critical?"

"The Mexican president is threatening repudiation. The gold crisis has dried up liquidity so much that all the makeshift solutions to the debt crisis don't work anymore."

Drew was silent as he tried to work out all the connections. Carol took his hand.

"There's a meeting in Rio at the end of the week," she said softly. "I'm meeting Halden there."

The next couple of days were very full. Drew rode herd on the nervous markets. The gold situation and the declarations of the Mexican president—as well as the suspicious death of the finance minister—brought the markets to a near standstill, interspersed with bouts of frantic trading.

As Drew anticipated, the South Africans granted him a visa quickly. They could not risk arousing any suspicions regarding their own truthfulness.

Carol meanwhile interviewed executives and traders and the major British clearers and merchant banks. She worked late into the evenings writing her report, calling Halden with a brief summary each day.

Wednesday and Thursday passed quickly. Carol's flight for Rio was at ten o'clock Friday morning; Drew was to leave for Johannesburg on Saturday. They had no time for each other.

Ten

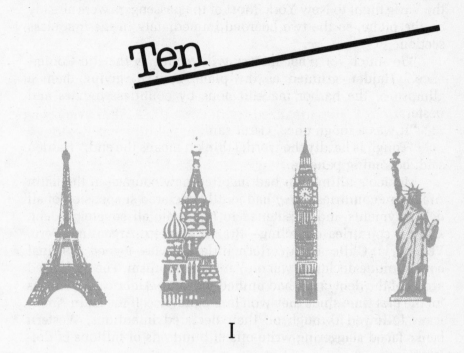

I

The girl was stunning—tall, her tawny skin darkened further by the sun, the silky brown hair flowing down her back, stopping just above her shorts, which two elegantly molded legs kept swinging suggestively back and forth.

"It seems such a waste," Halden said, watching the girl's progress in front of them. "To come all the way down here, spend two days in a hotel, and then just leave."

Carol murmured something that Halden construed as agreement. She had been withdrawn since her arrival from London. Her report on the gold market had been extraordinary, even by the high standards she set. It had all the usual detail and thoroughness, but also an unusual amount of feeling, of involvement in the subject. She looked tired, though.

"Be nice to take some time off—spend a day on the beach, night on the town," Halden continued as they reached the end of the airport concourse and their gate. He had done neither in years.

The Brazilian girl had disappeared as they checked in on the Varig flight to New York. Most of the passengers were already on the plane, so the two boarded immediately in the first class section.

"So much for what history will record as the Rio Conference." Halden grunted as the plane banked, giving them a glimpse of the harbor made famous by countless movies and posters.

"It was a tough one," Carol said.

"Tough is hardly the word; I think it means the end," Halden said, becoming pensive.

Mexico's ultimatum had inspired new courage in the Latin American countries. They had jointly declared suspension of all debt payments and threatened to repudiate all sovereign debt. All the countries attending—Brazil, Mexico, Argentina, Peru, Venezuela, Chile, even forlorn little Bolivia—signed the final communiqué declaring war on Yankee capitalism. The prolonged agony of the debt crisis had unified the Latin American countries for the first time since they won independence. If the Latin Americans followed through on their declared intentions, Western banks faced staggering write-offs of hundreds of billions of dollars.

"The initial impact of the declaration will be in the interbank lines," Carol ventured in the silence.

"I'm not so sure; I hope we can keep bank lines on ice for another week or two," Halden responded, as much to himself as to his companion. Halden's safety net of Fed support in the interbank market had succeeded in calming the turbulence there.

The Fed guarantee of interbank lines had given Halden enough leverage to win one concession at the conference: the Latin Americans would wait two weeks to implement any decision to repudiate the debt. Even though most of the countries had already ceased making any payments on their debt, a formal repudiation would shock the market psychologically. Halden wanted to mitigate the shock by postponing formal default as long as possible.

"Will we go to Washington right away?" Carol asked.

"I'll go. Roberts and Johnson will be waiting for me. You'll have to brief the fellows in New York."

Halden was worried, but he hoped to keep the situation stable for the next week or two. The Fed guarantee, comforting calls to the banks, confident statements to the press would calm the incipient panic. Fortunately, the Latin Americans had issued many ultimatums before; the U.S. Press was likely to view the latest declarations with skepticism. They would expect someone to come up with yet another face-saving agreement so the world's money machine could keep clunking along.

But Halden knew this declaration was different, and he was fairly sure that neither the administration nor Congress was in the mood for further concessions.

Even if American public opinion could be coddled along to avoid a panic and a run on the banks—no small "if" in itself—Halden was more worried about the effect of an international run of confidence on the dollar.

"It could be awful," he said aloud.

Carol pretended not to hear. She continued writing up her notes from the conference.

"Do you think there could be a run on the dollar with the announcement of the payments moratorium?" Halden asked her.

"Isn't the problem still the same—run from the dollar to where?"

"The yen, deutsche mark, Swiss franc, even the pound sterling." Halden listed the other main international currencies.

"Those currencies don't have the depth; the countries would stop exchanging them." Carol repeated the consensus view.

"Gold?" Halden suggested softly. That was the real wild card. What was happening with gold? How much gold was there in the market? That was the big mystery. If the market knew for sure there was enough gold, there might be a massive flight of capital out of the dollar.

"The gold supply is limited," Carol responded. "And now production is supposed to be greatly impaired."

Halden looked at the economist sharply. He had noted the qualification in her statement and looked to see how significant she meant it to be. Carol's face was impassive.

"What you say is logical, but people aren't always logical in a panic situation," he said.

"But the moratorium doesn't change that much, in reality. The market will see through it," Carol said.

"Yes, but the balance is so delicate," the Fed president said. "What would happen if there was a crash?"

Carol faltered momentarily at the unexpected question. "A financial crash can lead to war," she ventured.

"It did in the 1930s," Halden conceded. "But there were a couple of crashes in the nineteenth century that didn't. Besides, the only dangerous war nowadays would be between the Americans and the Russians, and the Russians wouldn't really be affected by a crash too much."

"But the Soviet Union might invade the Middle East or even Western Europe if the financial system collapsed," Carol protested.

Halden continued as though she had not spoken. He did not hear the undertone of anxiety in her voice. "Who would be in the best position—natural resources, energy, industrial base, internal market?" Halden's question this time was rhetorical. "We'd certainly be better off than Japan or Europe."

A crash would wipe out Japan's mortgage on the United States, the billions of dollars of government debt and other dollar assets Japan had acquired with the surplus it earned on its exports to the United States—earned by postponing the prosperity of their own people, by taking advantage of America's open borders and high standard of living.

"In fact, we'd be in a fairly strong position to dictate the terms of a new monetary system, wouldn't we?" Halden pursued his flight of fancy.

Carol smiled uneasily, acknowledging her superior's joke.

"Makes you wonder why we try so hard to avoid a crash, doesn't it?"

Halden lapsed into a long silence during the generous meal served in first class. He only picked at his food. He thought of José Martínez. More than anything else, the Mexican's suicide made Halden think that some radical, cleansing solution was needed.

He saw the outlines of how the United States could take the initiative to wipe out all the distortions of the past few years, how they could regain control of the situation. He could work out the details; Peter Wagner would help him.

But he needed to know what was happening in the gold market. He could not leave anything to chance.

118

"Your conclusion, if I read correctly, was that the gold market will remain unstable in the near future?" Halden asked.

"Until there's some clarity about the supply, yes."

Halden studied her for a moment. "Did you see much of this journalist, Dumesnil?"

"We met a couple of times," Carol said. She smiled. "He's actually quite nice."

"Do you think he can get to the bottom of this gold business?"

"If anybody can, he will."

"Keep in touch with him. Let me know what he's doing."

Carol looked at him noncommittally. "He's very keen on journalistic independence."

"Yes," agreed Halden. "But he's smart. He appreciates our position."

Carol did not respond.

II

Blacky shuffled out of the room with more purpose then usual. Hannes Kraml assumed he was going to confer with Marcus. For once Frey, the chief dealer, was also absent. The market was like a graveyard. It was Monday afternoon, the Rio communiqué had made a slight ripple, but most operators had simply squared positions and were waiting to see what would happen.

Kraml saw his opportunity. He started working his keyboard. His previous furtive attempts to enter the master dealing program had been quickly blocked. Marcus had a sophisticated software that restricted access to only a few of the dealers.

Kraml drew on his systems experience. He had worked together with computer specialists to design two major programs. He had learned a few secrets from the specialists, secret passageways that might not have been sealed up in Marcus's program.

Kraml worked intensely, quickly. He found an opening and worked back until he had the key to entering the program. Apparently Marcus had not anticipated this type of security breach and had taken few precautions against it.

Kraml's console was situated so that he could keep an eye on the door into the dealing room.

119

The trader found his way to the gold master program, the internal record of Marcus's position. He saw accumulated futures contracts confirming that Marcus was massively shorting gold. Perhaps it was just a hedge, Kraml thought, a cheap way of protecting a long position in the spot market, although he would have thought that a decline in the gold price was unlikely in view of the South African situation.

Kraml had to work a little harder to get to the bullion position, but he finally had the picture on his screen. What he saw stunned him. They were just digits shimmering on the cathode-ray tube, but for Kraml the impact was as breathtaking as for Ali Baba stumbling upon the treasure hoard of the forty thieves.

Kraml felt flushed; his breathing was irregular; he wiped his palms on his pants. He systematically studied the position, grasping its dimensions. He knew exactly what he was seeing and what it meant.

No wonder Marcus could control the gold market. The answer to the mystery was here. Kraml became frightened. His knowledge was dangerous.

He flashed quickly over the keyboard to get out of the file. Only then did a quiet shuffle draw his attention to the door. Blacky was poised at the threshold.

A sudden fear gripped Kraml. How long had Blacky been there? The trader had been so mesmerized by the screen that he would not have seen the American if he stood there quietly.

Kraml tried to control his breathing. Blacky paid no attention to him but shuffled around to his chair and sat down heavily.

Relief crept over the Austrian. Surely Blacky had not noticed anything.

The next half hour passed painfully for Kraml. Blacky occasionally responded to the phone, but the market remained quiet.

Finally, Kraml was out in the street at the phone booth. He rang Drew's private number and cursed when the answering machine came on. He left a message for Drew and took his winding road home, deeply preoccupied by his discovery.

III

Marcus sat in darkness, sipping his bourbon. Only the faintest sound of traffic reached him from the streets below.

Marcus liked to sit in his apartment in the evening with the lights out. The penthouse was on the top floor of his office building. The living room where he sat took up nearly half the floor, giving out onto a terrace that faced the mountains in the north.

The room was not empty like his office. In fact, it was filled with antiques and art treasures. The objects were not priceless—Marcus knew the market price for each piece in the room—but very, very valuable.

He appreciated them just as much with the lights off. It was not their aesthetic value he cherished. They were investments, like everything else; he kept them here to impress visitors, usually foreigners, because the Swiss, like him, had little energy left over for beauty.

Marcus relished the absence of interruptions. A telephone sat on the table next to him, but very few people knew the number. Marcus used it for private calls, like the one he had just made to Berne.

He would miss Kraml. It was not a personal sentiment, rather the grief of an accountant for a lost profit center. Kraml was a valuable asset, a natural resource. Talented, experienced, the Austrian could easily have taken Frey's place as chief trader in a couple of years. Frey lacked the intelligence, the quickness to be really great.

Kraml had that spark. It was his undoing; he was too quick, too resourceful. When Blacky reported what he had seen Kraml doing, Marcus drew the inevitable conclusion. The number in Berne had been given to him for just this type of problem.

It was a waste, really, Marcus reflected. The news about the gold would get out soon anyway. That's why he was shorting gold futures. But it was important that the leak not come from him. His clients would not like that, especially if they found out about his profits in the futures market.

He pondered his clients. He wondered if Abrassimov was also banking on the collapse of the gold price. The old Russian had taken a few licks in his time, but experience had made him very clever. The South African, du Plessis, was no match for him.

121

Such unlikely allies. Not that it bothered Marcus. He would work for Satan and the Archangel Michael if there was a profit in it.

What bothered Marcus was the Russian. He understood du Plessis; the man was transparent. But Abrassimov was not the same. Du Plessis could hardly see beyond next week; Abrassimov took a long view. Marcus would watch the Russian closely.

The phone rang. Marcus picked it up without saying anything. He listened silently to the voice on the other end, which gave only a time and place.

Marcus hung up the phone and drained his glass in a final toast to a lost profit center.

Eleven

I

Tony Edwards was not being very cooperative. The managing editor of the *Johannesburg Sun* refused to meet Drew's gaze.

"As I said, we've not heard from him for quite a while," Edwards mumbled in that curiously inarticulate way many accomplished editors have.

Drew had been escorted perfunctorily into the tiny cubbyhole to confront an obviously embarrassed Edwards, who immediately stubbed out his cigarette and reached for his jacket.

"No, don't bother," Drew had said. "I'll take mine off too." The office was half the size of Drew's in London and twice as full of furniture. There was no window, and the late spring temperatures made it stifling.

The *Sun* was Van der Merwe's main string. Although an Afrikaner, he had orginally preferred the English-language daily for its objectivity. But that was before the *Rand Daily Mail* was folded, for "economic" reasons, and all newspapers, regardless of political leaning, lost their independence and followed the government line more or less overtly.

"Van der Merwe was working less and less for us anyway," Edwards resumed. "The political situation, as you know, has become—well, quite delicate."

"But you must know how to reach him," Drew insisted.

"He told us nothing about going away. You've tried his flat; he hasn't been to his office here in nearly two weeks."

Edwards reached for his cigarettes but checked himself. His sandy hair and eyebrows made his face so bland that it would be difficult to recall his appearance the minute he was out of sight.

"I believe somebody mentioned something about an inheritance," Edwards said as he grew uncomfortable with the silence. "It may have been Tony himself—I called him Tony, it was our little joke; he called me Antoine." Edwards smiled shyly. "Come to think of it, he mentioned something about an aunt passing away and some money."

"Some money?"

"Oh, not a fortune, you know. But perhaps that's it. Perhaps he's just gone off for some holiday with his inheritance."

"It's an odd time for a business journalist who's just broken the story of the year to take a vacation."

"Well, that's perhaps part of it." Edwards leaned over and lowered his already quiet voice practically to a whisper. "That story was not very popular in Pretoria."

"So you blackballed Van der Merwe?"

Edwards straightened up. "Of course not. We're operating in a difficult social environment that is practically in a state of civil war, but we are, after all, a free press."

Drew realized that Edwards would not help him. Even if he did know something about Van der Merwe's whereabouts, Drew had no leverage to pry it out of him.

"Where did this aunt live?"

"In the suburbs, I suppose." Edwards seized his cigarettes, withdrew one, and lit it in a fluid motion more graceful than Drew would have expected.

"Do you know her name?"

"I'm afraid not."

"Maybe I should just look in the phone book under Van der Merwe," Drew said, deadpan.

"Oh, you'd have a good deal of trouble with that. You see,

Van der Merwe is the most common"—Edwards paused when he saw Drew's expression—"name in South Africa. But of course you know that."

Drew nodded. "Have you had any verification of the gold mine sabotage?" he asked.

Edwards took a long drag on the cigarette, which steadied his hand and gained him some time to formulate a response.

"It's all quite official, as I understand, although it's really out of my bailiwick." He looked at his watch, apparently surprised to see what time it was. "I'm afraid I'll have to show you out. You understand, deadline and all. And there's really not anything more I can tell you about Van der Merwe. I'm sure he'll be turning up bronzed and relaxed one day soon."

Drew was surprised to see the sun when he came back to Fox Street, after the harsh fluorescent light in the timeless, windowless office. Much of the street was in deep shadow from the mining and bank buildings lining Johannesburg's main business street.

After a moment's hesitation, Drew turned left and headed back to the Carlton. The Sun had been his only other lead, after calls and visits to Van der Merwe's flat had revealed no sign of the stringer.

He couldn't even get into the front door. The neighbors who responded to his buzzing on the interphone claimed not to know anything about the missing journalist.

Drew did not believe the inheritance story, and he certainly didn't think Van der Merwe had picked now to take some time off.

Tinny strains of Musak greeted him in the lobby of the Carlton. Drew brightened when he saw the message handed over to him by the concierge. It said RAMPART, followed by a phone number.

Drew hurried to his room to dial the number. He let it ring a dozen times but there was no answer.

"Damn." Drew sighed wearily, stretching back on the bed. Cyril Rampart, a young Xhosa who was a director at the Heritage Foundation, had been invaluable to Drew on his previous trip to South Africa. The thirty-four-year-old graduate of the London School of Economics had introduced the visiting journalist to black leaders in Soweto and Bophuthatswana. Although Rampart was extremely discreet, Drew had gotten the impression that he was in contact with the ANC.

Drew decided to order supper from room service rather than brave the hotel restaurant again, with its token blacks and ambivalent visitors. Before he could pick up the phone, it rang.

"You called the number I gave you," a familiar voice said. "Be in the hotel bar tomorrow at six." Drew heard a click, and the dial tone returned.

He didn't understand Rampart's sudden need for secrecy, but there were many things that baffled him in this second trip. It was an odd mixture of feigned normalcy and state of siege.

Offices were full and the business crowd during lunch at the Rand Club had been as animated as on his previous visit. Yet no one lingered on the streets, and security in the office buildings was heavy and ostentatious.

It was nearing 7 P.M. Drew wanted very badly to call Carol, but they had agreed he would not try to reach her at the Fed. It was only lunchtime in New York.

Drew had woken her up earlier that day. He had passed by the hotel to call her before his lunch appointment. Her sleepy "Hello," had transported him halfway around the world.

Drew was impatient with their separation, but it was impossible for them to plan a meeting until the situation was clearer. He told her briefly about his problems in Johannesburg.

"I'm worried about you," Carol said. "This thing with MacLean is scary."

"I'm not sure the South Africans had anything to do with MacLean," Drew reassured her, "And they hardly want an American journalist to disappear while visiting the country."

Carol was hardly mollified. "Be careful. When are you going back to London?"

"It depends on the interviews, but as soon as possible."

"Halden was strange on the way back from Rio. I want to talk to you about it. Not now, not on the phone." Drew heard her sigh. "Maybe I'll come to London."

II

Drew drained his beer glass and looked at his watch. Nearly six-thirty. The bar, restful if somber with its dark oak paneling, was more than half full. Drew had nursed his beer, waiting for Cyril to show up, and hesitated to order another.

The day had been uneventful. He had appeared promptly at the Information Ministry office when it opened and was duly handed an envelope. But it contained only a single sheet of paper and the paper noted a single appointment—with Andreis du Plessis, director general of the Finance Ministry, for the next day at nine o'clock. The American had requested interviews in four different ministries. Drew was incensed at the short shrift he was getting but knew it was useless to remonstrate. And du Plessis, after all, was the key official for him to see.

For lack of anything better to do, Drew had visited the stock exchange during its trading session. One of Van der Merwe's brokerage contacts had shepherded the American along but deflected all conversation about the gold mines and claimed to know nothing about Van der Merwe's whereabouts.

The Johannesburg market suffered, of course, from the loss of the mining stocks, which had been suspended from trading. Curiously, though, the country's very isolation had invigorated the stock market, as domestic institutions jockeyed for positions in the major nonmining companies.

Drew signaled the black bartender for another beer. He clung stubbornly to his faith that Cyril would come.

He was halfway through the second drink when a black man dressed in a sober gray business suit got up from a small table tucked away in the far corner. As he passed through the lounge on his way out, he paused briefly next to Drew at the bar.

"Come with me," he said.

The man, who looked to be in his mid-thirties, was a stranger to Drew, but he quickly signed his tab and followed the man out of the bar.

"George Myeti," he said, as they stepped onto the escalator leading down to the bar.

Drew shook his hand, and said, "Cyril sent you." His companion only nodded.

After the parking attendant had retrieved Myeti's car and the two of them were heading toward the southwestern edge of town, Myeti explained that he worked with Cyril at the Heritage Foundation. He said they would meet Drew's friend shortly but volunteered no further information. Drew respected his silence.

Shortly before the entrance to the highway, Myeti pulled into a side street. "I'm going to ask you to get into the back on the floor and to keep down. The police are not stopping cars, but they are watching."

Drew did as he was asked, trusting his instincts that Myeti was who he said he was. He had figured out by now that they were going to Soweto. Whites had always been required to have special passes to visit the black townships, but the rule had been strictly enforced only since the state of siege was imposed.

The Ford Scorpio was big, with sufficient room even for someone Drew's size to fit into the floor space in back. Myeti had spread a blanket there, and Drew installed himself on his back with his legs pulled up. The position was cramped but not painful; Drew kept his mind off it and allayed his anxiety by letting his thoughts dwell on his brief time with Carol.

Myeti drove slowly. Drew remembered that a nine o'clock curfew was in force in all the townships, but they made the fifteen mile trip in slightly less than half an hour and arrived well before eight.

"Stay down," Myeti said, as he stepped out of the car, leaving the motor running. Drew heard the clink of a chain, followed by the creak and scrape of a rusty gate being opened. Myeti drove into a carport shielded by a tangled growth of dark bushes.

Drew remained still until Myeti had closed the gate and locked the padlock on the chain. The black man opened the door for Drew, who extricated himself from the back of the car, slowly straightening and flexing his legs.

Imitating his companion's silence, Drew followed Myeti around to the back of the house. In the fading light of the dusk, the journalist saw a fair-sized garden surrounded by a stone wall. The wall and bungalow, also constructed of stone, resembled a small fortress.

They entered a large room that seemed sparsely furnished. Drew's eyes adjusted slowly to the dim light inside. There were no lamps.

A broad-shouldered black man of medium height, dressed in a khaki shirt and dungarees, emerged from the shadows and greeted Drew warmly. "I'm glad you made it; sorry for all the cloak-and-dagger."

Drew, surprised at the surge of relief he felt, shook hands with Cyril Rampart.

128

"Are you hiding out?" he asked.

"Let's just say I thought it best to take an indefinite leave of absence from the foundation," Cyril said, in a tone serious enough to belie his smile. "Myeti told me you had called there for me. It was fortuitous, because I need very much to talk to you."

For the first time, as his eyes adjusted to the light, Drew saw that there was a fourth man in the room. Cyril beckoned to a dim figure behind him. "I think you two already know about each other."

As the figure came closer, Drew discerned a white man in his early forties, balding and slightly shorter than Cyril. Drew did not recognize him until he spoke. "Hello, Drew," he said, holding out his hand. "Good to meet after all this time. Antoine Van der Merwe."

The voice stopped Drew even before he heard the name. The two of them had spoken regularly over the past three years but had never met face to face.

"Where in the hell have you been?" Drew said, recovering to shake the proffered hand.

Cyril answered for him. "Here and in some other houses in the township."

Myeti hissed a warning. He had stationed himself to one side of the window facing the street. Drew followed the lead of the others and moved into a darker corner of the room. He saw the flash of a searchlight outside the window, although the high stone wall kept the beam from entering the room.

"Police?" he whispered.

"Vigilantes."

Drew heard the crash of breaking glass across the street, followed by a woman's scream and several shouts. There was considerable commotion and a single gunshot. Drew saw a glow from flames that seemed to be coming from the same direction. Just moments later, the glow vanished. Within ten minutes, it was quiet again on the street.

The darkness was nearly complete. There were no streetlights to alleviate the African night. Still no lamps were turned on in the house.

Drew heard someone moving, closing shutters. Finally, Cyril turned on a small lamp, dimmed by a dark cloth. The men sat around the table where the lamp was.

"The situation is very tense," Cyril said, keeping his voice low. "The police and their stooges are looking for ALF agents, the vigilantes are looking for stooges, there is the curfew, and we have very little to eat."

Drew's eyes kept moving back to Van der Merwe. He had been trying so hard to find the stringer, he could hardly believe they were finally sitting next to each other.

"Tell me about the telex," he said, unable to contain his curiosity any longer.

"It was a plant," Van der Merwe said, darting a glance in Drew's direction and then looking at his hands in front of him on the table. "They said I would be paid, but it's not like I had any choice," the Afrikaner continued, looking at Drew again. "I'm sorry."

"What do you mean you're sorry? Was there sabotage or not?"

Van der Merwe looked at Cyril, who spoke. "You may have suspected that I'm working for the ANC, which is true," he said to Drew. "We have been working for a political solution, but this was too slow for some people, who now work for ALF." He paused. "We are told by ALF that they have planned for some time to sabotage the mines, but they claim they have not done so yet. They say the government is lying about the mines."

Drew felt suddenly numb, as the blood drained from his face. His limbs seemed leaden. If there had been no sabotage, if his story had been false, if the market collapse had been a mistake—the implications struck at his soul.

"Are you being told the truth by ALF?" he asked.

Cyril shrugged, a slow, measured motion. "There has been strange behavior around the mines. Convoys are moving in and out constantly, and the perimeter is heavily patrolled. The workers are being held at the mine sites, even now. There are many rumors that the mines are still in operation."

"But why?" Many answers to his questions swirled in his mind.

"You know the price of gold now," Cyril said simply.

Drew's head swam. If the South Africans were still producing and selling their gold, now that the price had tripled. . . .

"Has there been any verification? Has anyone seen the mines?" Drew looked around the table. The three South Africans

130

shook their heads. The American turned to Van der Merwe again. "What are you doing here?"

"I was very suspicious of their intentions. I did not like the setup. They promised money, made me spread the story of an inheritance, invited me to buy a farm on the Cape." The stringer spoke quickly.

"They?"

"They. Who knows who they are, really? Two men; they said it was important for national security. They arranged to send the telex from the Sun office. They stayed with me and then made me call you." Van der Merwe's face was thin and haggard. "You must believe me, I did not want to.'

"What happened then?"

"They said I should go home and pack my things and meet them at the address they gave me. I pretended to be very grateful, very interested in the money. But I did not trust them. It is too violent here; too many people simply disappear. I went instead directly to the ANC, because I thought they could get me out of the country."

Drew looked around the table. The covered lamp made a small circle of light, casting long shadows across the features of his companions.

His finding Van der Merwe had solved his initial quest but set a much more daunting one for him. He had hoped Van der Merwe would verify the sabotage for him, or at least put him on the trail of verification. Instead, Van der Merwe's story impugned the very fact of the sabotage and put the burden on Drew of confirming the falsehood of his own story.

For Drew, his obligation was clear; he had to establish the truth. Already, the sinking feeling he had, in realizing that the sabotage might be a hoax, had yielded to a determination to get the real story.

"Is it possible to see one of the mines?" he asked.

Van der Merwe and Myeti looked at Drew as if he had suggested a flight to the moon. Cyril smiled at his friend. "The army is doing everything in its power to prevent people from doing just that."

Drew looked at Van der Merwe. "Surely you see we have to find out the truth. If the sabotage is a hoax, we have to know, we have to get the news out."

The Afrikaner clasped and unclasped his hands, he looked to Cyril in appeal. "Your friend is probably right that his life is in danger," Cyril responded. "And it would be foolhardy to try to get close to a gold mine now."

Drew had never been in a situation where he felt so desperately helpless. He could not abandon his investigation, but he saw no way to go any further without assistance. He had always relied on himself, but never before had the challenge been so great.

"I must try to see a mine, to find out whether they are still operating," he said. He swallowed hard. "I need help."

Van der Merwe avoided Drew's gaze and looked again to Cyril. The Xhosa did not acknowledge the Afrikaner's appeal but studied his own big hands. His brow furrowed a brief instant before he spoke.

"We'll go with you, Drew." He threw a sharp, angry glance at Van der Merwe, who bit off his protest. "I have an idea of how we can do it."

Drew ignored the apprehension on Van der Merwe's face. He nodded at Cyril in silent gratitude. There was a buzz in his head from a sudden, new surge of feeling: fear. Drew was more afraid than he had ever been before.

132

Twelve

I

Hannes Kraml concentrated on his driving. A mushy sleet covered the road in the dim light of a late dawn.

He did not slow down. He trusted the BMW to hold the slick road.

Steering the car around the road's familiar curves relieved the stress of the past twelve hours. For Hannes, living with the secret he had discovered was nearly unbearable. He had been unable to reach Drew and did not want to confide in his wife.

He was afraid now, speeding toward Zug. But he had to show up for work or risk arousing Marcus's suspicions. Hannes had hardly slept. Damn Drew, he cursed aloud in the car. Where was he?

The Mercedes behind him was tailgating again. Mercedes drivers were the worst, thinking they owned the road.

Hannes downshifted to take a 45-degree turn, timing his acceleration carefully to move deftly out of the narrow bend. He felt a harmony with the powerful car that increased his confidence. Also, he knew the road well enough that he could practically drive it blindfolded, in spite of its winding along a steep ravine on the right.

The Mercedes had dropped back, losing ground on the turn. It tried to catch up, but Hannes was enjoying the sport now, surging ahead in the BMW. The road carried little traffic this early.

Hannes turned up the windshield wipers to top speed. The sky was growing lighter, but the low clouds and sleet reduced visibility.

Bank to the left, more gently back to the right. Hannes let up on the acceleration and downshifted to take the deadman's curve, a short 90-degree turn along the ravine. Several triangle-shaped signs alerted drivers unfamiliar with the road to the upcoming curve. Hannes saw the Mercedes gaining, but he knew it would be braking before the curve, allowing him to pull ahead.

He was well into the curve when he noticed a flash of movement. Some damn fool was on the road! Hannes saw the figure in front of him suddenly, wearing a yellow jacket. Hannes's preoccupation with the Mercedes had slowed his reaction by crucial fractions of a second. He braked and swerved, but the BMW was too far gone in the curve. The car's momentum carried it through the metal railing, over the narrow embankment.

In the moment before impact, Hannes knew fear. It was not so much fear of death; it was rather a fear of the man who wanted him dead. He had seen no features of the yellow-jacketed figure, but now the face of Marcus loomed before him—warning, mocking, vindictive, triumphant.

II

Du Plessis remained behind his desk but stood when Drew came into the office.

"Thank you for taking the time to see me, Mr. du Plessis," Drew said, shaking his hand. "It's nice to have the opportunity to talk with you again."

Drew was wearing his lightweight gray suit with a blue shirt. Du Plessis was unaware of the new steeliness in Drew's eyes.

The director general waited for his visitor to start.

"Obviously, the first question on my mind concerns the mine sabotage," Drew said. He had decided that a direct frontal assault was the only way to pry any information out of du Plessis. "How extensive was the damage to South Africa's gold production?"

The Afrikaner took some time answering, as though deciding how much to tell the journalist. But Drew was convinced that du Plessis had long since made up his mind what to say. He looked at the thin-lipped, severe man across the desk from him. He had interviewed du Plessis during his previous trip to South Africa, and later he had run into him at a BIS meeting in Basel.

Andreis du Plessis had presented the cultured face of apartheid to a financial world not too concerned with civil rights. Articulate, intelligent, respectable by all the criteria that counted in that closed community, he had been a tangible reason for bankers and monetary officials to believe in the future of South Africa.

But bankers, too, finally had to yield to the pressure of public opinion. Du Plessis no longer made public appearances abroad. Rumor had it, though, that he still found a hearing in quiet, discreet meetings with financiers, usually in London or Switzerland.

"You will understand that considerations of national security prevent me from answering your question with any precision," du Plessis responded finally. "We have imposed a complete news blackout on the subject in our own country. You are the first foreign journalist I have met with since the sabotage took place."

Drew waited.

"The damage was extensive, as we indicated in our original announcement." Du Plessis's eyes bored into Drew, recalling to him what had precipitated the original announcement. "We're still assessing the damage. But"—he paused, to heighten the impact of what he was going to say—"it's certain that our gold production has been reduced by more than half for several months."

Drew was taking notes as the official spoke. Without looking up, he said, "Our information is that nearly four fifths of gold production has been taken out."

"I cannot, as I said, be any more precise for reasons of national security," du Plessis said. "I don't know the source of your figure," he added, as though daring Drew to use unverified information.

"What has the impact been on South Africa's economy, on its foreign trade?"

"As an American, you should know that South Africa does not have much foreign trade anymore," du Plessis said, with a theatrical smile that had no mirth in it. "The United States, after all, has successfully pushed for an international boycott against us.

"It's an example of what we have always wanted to avoid here," du Plessis continued. "Because of certain faults in the American democratic structure, it is very easy for a vocal organized minority to impose its will on a whole country."

Drew looked up into the sober face of the Afrikaner official and bit off his response, deciding not to rise to the bait. "It is well known, though, that South Africa still does considerable trade on a barter basis, or through so-called 'neutral' businessmen," he said.

"Fortunately, not all of our friends have abandoned us. And here and there we have found new ones."

"Which friends are you referring to?" Drew asked, intrigued by this new line opened up by the official's response. Israel reportedly had intensified its relationship with South Africa, in spite of U.S. pressure. Latin American countries had found a clandestine barter trade with South Africa helpful in relieving the worst effects of the debt crisis.

Du Plessis just smiled enigmatically.

"Do you mean Israel? Argentina?"

"I'm not going to tell you," du Plessis snapped. "I'm not going to expose our friends to American slander because of their willingness to help us."

Undaunted, Drew went on. "Has the mine sabotage affected foreign trade?"

"We are nearly self-sufficient. We continue to import vital necessities through bilateral agreements with our trading partners." Du Plessis paused. "Don't forget, gold is not our only exportable commodity."

South Africa had been nearly self-sufficient in grain production at one point but had been importing massive amounts before the embargo. Drew had not seen any hungry whites, but

136

Cyril's remark about food shortages in the townships confirmed reports in the Western press.

In addition to gold, South Africa was a major producer of platinum, chromium, and other strategic metals, as well as the world's leading producer of diamonds.

"And the higher world price for gold partially compensates for the lost production," the South African said quietly.

"Do you think the present price is justified?" Drew asked.

Du Plessis shrugged. "The market, in its wisdom, has set the price."

"The market seems confused. Gold seems to be coming into the market in larger quantities than expected, given the lost production here," Drew prompted. But du Plessis only looked at him.

"Do you know where the gold is coming from?"

"Perhaps the higher price has drawn out some stocks," the director general speculated.

"Has South Africa stockpiled gold that it's selling now?"

"Again, national security keeps me from answering you. But I think Western experts who follow this market generally felt we were selling or trading our full production."

"Do you know if the Soviet Union has increased its sales of gold?"

"You must go ask the director general of the Soviet finance ministry that question." Du Plessis smiled his humorless smile. "We have our estimates of Soviet production and sales, of course, but they are only estimates, and they are ours."

"Do you think the Soviets are responsible for the sabotage of your mines?"

"As we reported, the sabotage was the work of the ALF. We have said for many years that the ALF, like the ANC, receives substantial support from the Communist bloc." The South African official grimaced. "For many years, we received the support of the American government, because they accepted this. They realized that our fight is their fight."

"Do you think the Soviet Union played a direct role in the mine sabotage?"

"This is a question better raised with our National Defense Ministry or our Foreign Ministry," du Plessis said. "But I am sure they would not answer you, for reasons that are obvious."

137

"I've requested interviews in those ministries," Drew said. "But they've been turned down."

"You are a financial journalist, are you not? You have the opportunity to ask your financial questions in the Finance Ministry."

"Do you have now, or have you had, any agreement with the Soviet Union to coordinate sales of gold?"

Drew himself was surprised at his question. It came out spontaneously as a way to get himself out of the corner du Plessis was pushing him into.

Du Plessis seemed taken aback. His face, expressionless until that moment, stiffened and his eyes widened involuntarily. He recovered quickly.

"I think the history of our opposition to the Soviet Union dictates that such an arrangement would be out of the question," he said evenly.

"Yet the Soviet Union finally joined the diamond cartel controlled by South Africa."

"That was strictly a business decision. It was not possible for the Soviet Union to sell its diamonds outside the cartel. But the Soviets have been selling their gold quite successfully without any arrangement with us." Du Plessis looked at his watch. Drew realized his time was nearly up.

"Would it be possible for me to visit a gold mine, to see the damage for myself?" he asked, certain of the answer.

"Out of the question. I've explained the situation to you. Now, if you'll—"

"There are rumors of activity at the mines."

"Of course, we have started immediately to repair the damage. It will take months."

"There's been no independent verification of the sabotage. There's too much gold in the market. Some traders are beginning to wonder if there really was a sabotage."

Du Plessis's smile was icy. "Surely, Mr. Dumesnil, no respectable trader would dare question the credibility of your own renowned news service." He rose and extended his hand. "Have a safe trip home," he said, cutting off the journalist's protest.

As he drove back to Johannesburg through the flat, dull countryside outside Pretoria, Drew felt a cold anger growing within him.

Du Plessis was a skilled interview subject. He had effortlessly parried Drew's attempts to pry more information out of him. Like most veteran journalists, though, Drew had developed an alarm system against the falsehood or, what in fact was worse, the half-truth. A hunch, a sixth sense, whatever name it had, Drew's experience in hundreds of interviews—thousands, even—told him that he was far from plumbing the depths of du Plessis's knowledge.

In the end, the South African's performance had not been convincing. The burden of proof, as far as Drew was concerned, was very much on those claiming there had been sabotage.

The more it appeared likely that the sabotage was a hoax, the greater became Drew's resentment of the manipulation. Pretoria had coldly calculated how it could dupe Western journalism and Western financial markets and had then unscrupulously done so.

The anger went deeper, though. Drew had struggled to keep his integrity as a journalist, and in profound ways this crisis was revealing to him just how important this integrity was to his whole sense of identity. The falsehood perpetrated by du Plessis, if it was that, amounted to a violation of Drew's integrity, as violent in its psychological impact as rape.

Drew felt shame as well, shame at his victimization. He was deeply discouraged. But he found the shame and discouragement fueling his anger now. The magnitude of the hoax—if it was a hoax—went far beyond Drew's personal feelings. His sense of duty obliged him to redress the damage done to society by the falsehood. Half formed in Drew's mind, too, was the realization that in uncovering the truth now, he could make amends for his former vulnerability.

As he drove past Johannesburg's northern suburbs, Drew almost reveled in the resolve he felt. The anger from his encounter with du Plessis surmounted his fear at the adventure he was about to embark on with Rampart and Van der Merwe. The need to establish the truth overrode all personal considerations.

III

Abrassimov closed the dossier on his desk, removed his glasses, and lit a cigarette. Du Plessis's call was due in ten minutes.

The vice-chairman was used to his cramped quarters, though spacious by the standards of the crumbling building at 37 Plyushchika Street. Construction of new offices in Kirovskaya had, predictably, been delayed, so the largest bank in the world remained housed in the plain nineteenth-century building, and Abrassimov stayed where he was.

Little matter, though Abrassimov. He did not need to impress anyone. For years, the cream of Western banking had trooped through this tiny office or the shabby conference room down the hall, courting him, bidding for his business—his business being to please take their money.

And he had taken it, negotiating Vnesheconombank into one of the best credits in the Euromarket, getting margins within a fraction of triple-A-rated U.S. companies.

The foreign affairs bank, previously known as Vneshtorgbank, was the Soviet Union's main link to the Western financial world. It negotiated hard-currency loans, invested the funds profitably abroad, and handled all foreign exchange trading. Over the years, Western dealers had learned to respect the "Redman" who had become one of the most important players in international financial markets.

Vnesheconombank was also the selling agent for the Soviet Union's gold production. Western experts estimated annual Soviet output at 350 tons, about half that of South Africa's. Abrassimov smiled to himself. Western experts were wrong. The Soviet Union had not disclosed any statistics on production since 1935, though, so Western experts had some excuse.

Of course, they had not fooled the South Africans. Abrassimov remembered his first face-to-face meeting with du Plessis, eighteen months ago.

"We know that you are selling less gold than commonly thought," the Afrikaner said. "Western estimates say you are selling your full production of three hundred and fifty tons a year. We think it is closer to two hundred thirty tons."

"It's actually closer to two hundred twenty," Abrassimov conceded. "Our traders have become very sophisticated, manipulating futures markets to disguise physical sales, which are made through a variety of new channels, not all of them official. It is very difficult for Western observers to follow. They think we are more desperate than we are."

"We also think your production has increased well above historical estimates," du Plessis continued. He paused.

"We are stockpiling two thirds of production," Abrassimov readily conceded. Obviously, their intelligence in this domain was excellent.

"Which puts your production on par with ours," du Plessis said, a glint coming into his eyes. "At least, with our official production."

"But you, too, have increased production, isn't that right?" Abrassimov said.

"Three years ago we abandoned our policy of mining only a certain percentage of reserves," du Plessis explained. "Instead, we pushed existing capacity to the maximum. We did not inform anyone of this change in policy."

"How high is your current production?"

"A thousand tons a year."

Abrassimov grunted, his opinion of the low quality of Soviet intelligence confirmed again. Their best estimate had been 850 tons.

"The extra production has been very useful in securing essential imports," du Plessis added.

This exchange of information had also been essential to the talks between the two countries, talks about mutual interest.

The light flashing at the base of his telephone interrupted Abrassimov's reverie. He picked up the receiver.

"The journalist is becoming dangerous." Du Plessis did not bother with small talk.

"Dumesnil?"

"He was here, asking about the sabotage. Asking whether we were working together."

Abrassimov was silent.

"You did not succeed in Paris," du Plessis continued.

"It was intended as a warning, you will remember," the Russian responded placidly.

"He did not heed the warning. He has become too dangerous."

Abrassimov sighed. The Afrikaners were exacting. First the Canadian, even though his only mistake was to thwart their timing. Then the Austrian. Now the American.

"You ask much of us," Abrassimov said to the South African.

"What has become of the stringer?" The Russian deliberately reminded du Plessis of Van der Merwe's successful evasion of their plans for him.

"He is no danger. He cannot leave the country; he will cause no harm. But Dumesnil is a threat."

"You're right," Abrassimov said with a note of weariness. "He must be taken care of. I'll take charge of the matter personally."

With no further comment on the journalist, du Plessis expressed his concern about the gold market. "The situation is delicate. The market is confused at the amount of gold that seems to be for sale. And the trading in gold futures is unsettling."

"It is unsettling," Abrassimov murmured. "Do you think Marcus is hedging?"

"I presume so, but there must be others as well."

"Following their natural predatory instincts."

There was a silence. "We can reduce our sales until the market is firm again," the Russian suggested.

"It might be useful." Du Plessis accepted the concession matter of factly. "Perhaps the Rio cconference will support the gold price."

"The Latin Americans do seem more serious this time. But I wonder if Western speculators will be worried enough to move funds out of the dollar into gold." Abrassimov's own traders had reported a ripple in the gold market from the Rio communiqué, but nothing lasting.

"Not even the Fed can hold up the fiction of solvent debtors much longer," du Plessis said.

The Russian shrugged, oblivious to du Plessis's inability to see the gesture. Abrassimov had no illusions about the ruthlessness of the Americans in defending their own interests. "We knew the situation in the markets would be very risky, but so far things have gone well."

There was little else to discuss. The events of the next few days would do much to determine their actions.

Abrassimov sat quietly at his desk after du Plessis's call, hunching up unconsciously against the late afternoon chill.

He wondered if the South African was suspicious. Du Plessis was difficult to read. Abrassimov felt he understood the younger man—he saw the similarity in the devotion each of them had to

142

their countries. But the Russian had little experience of these sober, bland Afrikaners, whose reserve masked a fanaticism more like that of a mullah than the cynical patriotism Abrassimov was used to dealing with.

In the end, Abrassimov realized, du Plessis had no more choice with Vnesheconombank than he did with Marcus. Even if the South African distrusted Soviet intentions, there was nothing he could do about it.

The Afrikaner was right to worry about the market's confusion. So far things were working, but that much gold could not continue to come onto the market. Abrassimov was willing to slow down Soviet sales; the gold could sit in the vaults a little longer. The Russian knew he would be free to sell all the gold he wanted shortly, and at an exorbitant price.

IV

Carol looked up to see Vic Daniels, the Fed's chief trader, standing in front of her.

"Here are the printouts on Comex and Chicago," he said, putting a stack of computer listing paper in front of her. "The Bank of England will transmit bullion statistics overnight."

"Thanks, Vic," Carol said with a smile.

She studied the thin, wiry man standing there. His curly dark hair was salted with gray, his tie loosened. His fingers were stained brown from nicotine, but out of deference to others—and the New York City ordinance—he smoked only in his office. He was in his late thirties, but looked at least ten years older.

"Since when does the Fed's top dealer play delivery boy?" she asked finally.

Daniels smiled ruefully and reached absentmindedly in his shirt pocket for a cigarette before catching himself.

"Needed a change of scenery," he said, smiling still. Carol had developed a thick skin for chauvinist remarks, especially from men like Daniels, for whom such comments were simply a bad habit.

"Thought you'd be too busy for sightseeing," she responded good-humoredly.

Daniels glanced at the door behind him. Carol had a quiet office on the ninth floor. It was narrow, with a window looking out onto Maiden Lane. A metal bookcase filled with books and documents covered one wall. The desk was positioned so that Carol faced the door, with her back to the window.

"I'm a bit concerned about Halden," Daniels said, lowering his voice.

Carol wrinkled her brow, suppressing her own agreement for the moment. "In what way?"

"He's moody, more withdrawn than usual. Of course, he's under a lot of strain, too."

"I think Martínez's suicide hit him hard," Carol said.

"There's other things, though. As you know, he's obsessed by the gold market"—the figures he had brought Carol were for the report on gold trading she submitted at the end of every day—"and he's monitoring the Latin American safety net very closely."

"That's all natural enough, given the situation."

"It's hard to explain—there's something that goes beyond just natural interest. For instance, the other day he asked me what would happen if the Fed all of a sudden stopped supplying the overnight credits for the Latin American banks."

Carol felt a chill pass over her.

"You know he's not a big one for hypothetical questions," Daniels continued. "I was so surprised I just stuttered a bit and finally said, 'Well, the whole fucking market would just go to hell in a breadbasket.' That made him laugh, as if it were all a big joke—but I think the question was serious."

Carol was on the point of repeating her conversation with Halden on the plane back from Rio, but she checked herself. It would only add to Daniels's worry, without contributing to any solution. After all, what could they do about Halden's odd behavior anyway?

"He's only human," Carol said. "This whole thing has him rattled. He's traveling a lot, not sleeping much. Maybe his own worries get the best of him sometimes."

Daniels scratched his head with both hands. "Maybe you're right," he said, with a deep sigh. "I guess we're just used to him being imperturbable."

"Thanks for coming by, Vic," Carol said in gentle dismissal. "I'll plug these figures right into the report."

"Right," the trader said, sounding relieved, as though he had discharged an important mission. "Hang in there," he said as he turned to leave.

Carol swiveled back to her computer screen and quickly entered the futures statistics into the report she had written. She worked automatically while her mind sorted out her conversation with Daniels.

Halden had been withdrawn since their return. Usually he would take a few minutes for conversation, no matter how pressured he was. Lately, though, he had been distracted, even abrupt in his encounters, at least with her—guarded, she realized, afraid he would accidentally confide some secret he preferred to keep.

Halden's question to Daniels about the Latin American safety net bothered Carol. Together with his question to her about a crash, at best only half in jest, it showed a dangerous turn in the central banker's thinking. For most of the professionals in the bank and at the Federal Reserve Board in Washington, Halden was the only top official who really seemed to understand the full implications of the debt crisis. His stalwart resistance to rash action had reassured all of them.

But now he seemed ready to bandy about doomsday scenarios like the most untutored analyst at the National Security Council.

Carol printed out her report and decided to deliver it personally. Perhaps she could get a reading on Halden that would calm her worries.

She walked into Halden's reception room on the tenth floor without knocking. It was nearly six. Halden's secretary, who had put in considerable overtime in the past two weeks, had left early today.

Carol walked to the door of Halden's office and looked in. The room was empty, but Halden's jacket was draped over his chair, so he was somewhere in the building.

Carol crossed the thick carpeting, admiring the view of the Stock Exchange from Halden's window. She put her report down on the desk mat, so that Halden would see it when he returned. There was already a light blue folder, similar to the one containing her report, on the desk. She was intrigued, because light blue in the Fed's obsessive bureaucracy was reserved to her department. Normally, all reports passed through her, but she had no idea what the folder on Halden's desk might contain.

With sudden decisiveness, she picked up the other report

and opened it. She noticed the initials of one of her assistants; Halden had evidently gone to the economist directly for the information. The folder contained a concise listing of known holdings of U.S. debt securities by foreigners.

Carol was puzzled. The information was banal enough. Her department kept running tabs on foreign holdings, and Halden could request that information anytime he wanted it. Why had he gone outside channels for it, then? The report was dated that day—there was no reason for the request not to go through her.

Carol was not a stickler for bureaucracy. Although she was thorough and methodical herself, the Fed's undeviating adherence to its myriad rules often exasperated her. But that very insistence made any divergence so much more remarkable.

She returned the folder to the desk as it had been. It was a small anomaly in Halden's behavior, but it added to her concern about his state of mind.

Her thoughts turned to Drew. She trusted him implicitly and wanted badly to talk to him. He could be more objective about her concerns regarding Halden and the Fed. She was perhaps too close, too involved with the personalities.

It comforted her, anyway, to think of Drew. Their time together, brief as it was, had sparked feelings that were new to her. She wished very much he were not half a world away.

Thirteen

I

It was nearly midnight when Cyril turned off the lamp and they went out the back door. Drew followed behind the black man, with Van der Merwe bringing up the rear.

Cyril had brought them camouflage green fatigues, light and comfortable in the evening cool. They climbed into a Range Rover while Myeti opened the gate for them.

Soweto was dark and quiet. There had been no passing gangs this evening; there was no sign of life in any of the houses. Cyril did not turn on the vehicle's lights but drove guided by the faint starlight.

They avoided the national roads, which often had roadblocks after curfew. Instead, they took to the patchwork of unpaved streets linking the black townships together. The going was slow, but Cyril had taken the route often in the weeks since he had gone into hiding.

They were headed to Orville township, where Cyril had grown up and where he still had cousins. The township was located ten miles from the Kampfontein mining complex, one of the older and smaller mines along the Rand.

There were several paths through the bush between the township and the mine that Cyril and his cousins had frequented when they were children. He reckoned that the older mine, which was near depletion, might be less carefully guarded than some of the bigger, better known ones.

If indeed there was anything to guard. Although Drew's instincts told him du Plessis was lying, and the evidence in the markets did not exclude the possibility that South Africa was still producing, the journalist wanted to be careful about jumping to conclusions.

Cyril eased the four-wheel-drive vehicle over a section where the road had virtually disappeared in the wake of rains earlier in the spring. The three of them were silent, although small grunts escaped Van der Merwe whenever the jeep bounced sharply.

The Afrikaner was not pleased about having to come along, but Drew had insisted, because of the stringer's role in breaking the sabotage story, that he be a witness if they found evidence it was a hoax.

The moon rose eventually, enabling Cyril to move faster over the dirt road. Once he pulled aside and stopped in a clump of trees because he thought he saw headlights glimmering through the bush ahead. They waited fifteen minutes, but when there was no further evidence of another vehicle, they regained the road.

The landscape was desolate. Occasional thickets of trees punctuated the stretch of bush on all sides. Game had long since deserted the region. The roads were not straight but zigzagged to connect the small townships dotting the area. The three men passed through several dark, still settlements, some no better than shantytowns.

Drew had the eerie feeling that they were the only creatures alive in the bush. He had visited a game reserve during his earlier trip, and a highlight of the stay had been the jeep ride at night with its searchlight suddenly revealing a herd of zebra or wildebeest. But tonight there was no sign of life.

Cyril drove the Range Rover into a large thicket, picking his way through it until the vehicle was shielded on all sides. "End of the line," he whispered. They gathered dead branches to cover the jeep, so it would not be visible if a helicopter passed over during the day.

They emerged from the thicket as the moon was settling on the horizon. It was still about an hour until dawn. Their plan was to reach the perimeter before daylight. Cyril pointed out the low silhouette of Orville township behind them as they set out through the bush, following the barest rudiments of a path.

Cyril kept up a fast pace, virtually a trot. Drew was winded quickly but then found a gait that enabled him to keep up. He looked around occasionally to check on Van der Merwe, who was breathing heavily.

Once Cyril allowed them to stop and rest, their backs up against a tree. The night was still. They resumed their trek just as the first glimmers of light appeared to the east.

Drew blanked out his mind and focused only on the bouncing figure of the black man ahead of him. He did not hold back, because he knew they would have all day to recover their strength. They planned to hide near the mine and wait for night to fall again before penetrating the perimeter.

They arrived at last. Cyril gestured to the hill that blocked the rising sun from their view. The bush had been cleared one hundred yards in front of a high chain-link fence. Rolls of barbed wire followed the contour of the fence. More barbed wire stretched tautly between struts on top of the fence, to a height of eight feet.

Cyril darted rapid glances around the perimeter for any signs of a patrol and then motioned to a small, low thicket to their left.

Drew felt a great sense of relief as they crawled deep into the loose bush and remained huddled there. His ears pounded with the effort of the trek; he took a sparing drink from his canteen. Cyril was already stretched out, using his rucksack as a pillow, his eyes closed, his face impassive.

Van der Merwe continued to gulp and swallow. Drew admired the older man's pluck. He was even more out of shape than the American, nor did he share Drew's single-minded obsession for the truth, but he had his own sense of loyalty and integrity that kept him from complaining about their mission.

Drew soon stretched out too. The sun was already bright, making the sky overhead a clear, lustrous blue. The thicket provided an adequate amount of shade. Despite the rising temperature, Drew quickly fell into a peaceful sleep.

II

Drew peered through the twilight toward the perimeter. A gentle breeze in his face indicated they were upwind. A low hiss from Cyril directed Drew's attention to three uniformed men and a sentry dog coming from the west. The setting sun silhouetted the patrol as it moved unhurriedly toward the hiding place of the three intruders.

Drew felt sweaty and uncomfortable. The heat accumulated during the day emanated from the ground. The wind was strong enough to rustle the leaves of the low bushes concealing him, a further protection from the keen senses of the patrol dog.

The soldiers themselves were silent but did not seem particularly alert. Perhaps it was near the end of their shift, or too many uneventful patrols had dulled their expectations. They paid more attention to the fence than to the empty countryside, scanning it in the failing light for any sign of tampering.

Drew heard Van der Merwe's heavy breathing beneath the rustling leaves. He realized that his own breathing was like a gentle grunt as they waited anxiously for the patrol to pass.

By the time the patrol had disappeared over the horizon, the sky had deepened to a dark blue. The fence had vanished against the hulking hills that were outlined by the faint light of the departed sun.

At least the darkness brought some relief from the heat. Cyril maintained a cautious crouch, listening for any sound of the patrol coming back. "Looks like this is it," he said, picking up his light rucksack. He donned a pair of leather gloves and pulled out a heavy wire cutter from a pouch on the side. Drew followed suit.

Listening again, Cyril took a tentative step from the thicket. Insects throbbed in the bush behind them; there were no sounds of men or machinery.

"OK," Cyril hissed, staring toward the perimeter at a gentle trot, keeping his head down.

Drew followed as quietly as he could. The moon had not yet risen, but Drew's eyes had adjusted to the glow of the stars. A stronger light in the east gave the ragged edge of the hill a faint halo.

Van der Merwe followed Drew. The three men arrived at

the barbed wire and began cutting through it, holding the heavy shears with both hands. Drew was quickly drenched in sweat.

They cut a path just wide enough for them to step through sideways. Cyril began cutting through the chain link while Drew arranged the barbed wire behind them to make their passageway as inconspicuous as possible.

By now, Cyril was swearing fiercely in a low, violent whisper. The thick link fence yielded grudgingly as the black man forced his body through the narrow three-foot slit he had cut. Drew helped Van der Merwe through and then followed him. They all collapsed on the hillside to rest.

Cyril returned to the cut fence and tied a white handkerchief at the base, anchoring it and covering it with loose dirt. It was a calculated risk, and scarcely visible unless sought for, but it marked the spot of their entry in case they needed to exit in a hurry.

They started up the low hill in the direction of the Kampfontein mine. Although the government had never listed the mines actually closed down by the terrorist sabotage, most reports suggested that virtually all the Rand production had been affected.

Cyril led the way without hesitation, as both white men concentrated on keeping their footing on the rocky ground. Twisted, dwarfed bushes covered the hillside; there was no evidence of any sort of footpath.

They came over the first ridge. The glow in the east was stronger now, clearly emanating from powerful electric lights, like a city below the horizon.

The intruders stopped periodically to rest and listen for any sign of patrols or other activity. Apparently, the fence and perimeter were considered sufficient protection. Drew wondered during one of these pauses how the ALF could have managed a coordinated bombing of so many mines.

After slightly more than an hour of arduous passage in the dark, Cyril stopped Drew with a gentle pressure on his arm.

"The minehead is just over the next ridge," he said in a hoarse whisper.

"Do you hear what I hear?" Drew whispered back.

"I sure do." Cyril grunted.

The unmistakable sound of diesel motors, purring heavily in the night air, was rounded by a soft cacophony of clattering noises.

"It *sounds* like a mine," Van der Merwe said.

The three men proceeded carefully up the hill, keeping low and crawling often on hands and knees. They neared the top and slid the last few yards on their bellies.

Drew came even with Cyril and cautiously raised his head, using a low thornbush for cover. He nearly reeled backward from the sight, which hit him like a body blow. Floodlights transformed night into day below them, like an enormous football field. The light, blinding after the darkness, revealed hundreds of men, scurrying like so many ants amid an overwhelming confusion of dirt and machinery.

"That's orebody." Cyril jabbed a finger at rail trucks emerging from one opening in the rock wall. "That's a pithead." He pointed to some grinding machinery next to the rail tracks. "And those are miners, those are tracks, those are soldiers, and this fucking operation is a gold mine that has never seen a terrorist bomb."

Cyril spat out the angry words. Drew could feel the big man next to him quivering in rage.

Recovering from the stunning first view, Drew tried to concentrate on the scene in front of him. He realized that the figures scrambling on the surface were only a fraction of the crew that must be working the mine.

Many of the figures, he noticed grimly, were carrying automatic rifles. They wore military fatigues and their faces gleamed white. The truck drivers and equipment operators also were white. Most of the other men milling purposefully around in the massive cavity were black. Soldiers surrounded the operation, carrying their guns with both hands, evidently ready to keep anyone from entering or leaving.

Drew suddenly felt violently ill, as though he would retch. Nausea seized him, and he grew lightheaded. He gripped Van der Merwe's shoulder fiercely, afraid he would fall over.

None of them said anything further. The clatter and whir of shifting rock and the grunt of machinery mesmerized them for several moments.

Damn, damn, damn! Drew's head swam with sudden rage.

The personal, crippling blow that came with the realization he had been duped gave way to seething anger at the perpetrators of the hoax.

"Goddam them to hell," he said, louder than he intended.

Neither Cyril nor Van der Merwe responded. Drew saw du Plessis's mocking smile, mocking him, mocking the world. There had been no sabotage—only lies and murder to perpetuate a perverse regime.

Cyril gestured to the two others to stay where they were. The black man backed slowly down the hill.

Drew lost sight of him and waited and listened anxiously, unsure of what was happening.

A branch snapped behind him and Drew whirled around. In the glow of the floodlights he saw a young South African soldier coming toward him, the stark light giving his intent expression a ghoulish contrast.

Then Drew saw the rifle pointed at him. Time stopped, and the world was reduced to the tiny round hole that threatened to spew fire and lead into him. The journalist saw the eyes of his assailant juxtaposed with the rifle opening, a curious gleam lighting them with the quintessence of human mortality—the intent to kill another man.

Even as he yelled to Van der Merwe and threw himself to the ground, Drew heard a sharp crack, a stifled grunt, and muffled sounds of struggle. He scrambled to his feet and saw two figures wrestling on the ground. Cyril had attacked the soldier from behind. A white arm raised up, holding a flashing blade. Drew lunged and caught the deadly wrist in both his hands. Cyril broke free from the soldier's grip, wrested the knife from him, and, with only a split second's hesitation, plunged it into the young man's breast.

Blood spattered both Drew and Cyril as they rolled free of the dying man. Drew glimpsed the wide eyes of the dead soldier, robbed of their curious gleam.

The journalist turned to see what had become of Van der Merwe. At first he did not see the crumpled figure in the shadow of the ridge. He heard nothing over the clank and roar of the mine as he approached the huddled stringer. When Drew reached to grip Van der Merwe's shoulder, the stringer fell back easily. Drew gasped. The Afrikaner's face was covered with blood, and the place where his right eye should have been looked like raw meat.

Drew felt Cyril's hand on his elbow. "He's dead," the black man said. "They may have heard the shot."

Drew looked helplessly at the corpse, still warm to the touch. Cyril tugged at him again, starting down the hill. Drew turned and followed him.

They ran, tripping on the tangled brush and uneven stone, falling, scraping their clothes against the thorns and jagged rock. Cyril kept his orientation, and they covered the ground back to the fence in less than half an hour.

Breathing hard, they crawled along the base, digging through the dirt, groping for their marker. They found the slit, and Cyril held back the chain link for Drew to scramble through.

They had heard no sound of pursuit, but they never stopped long enough to pay attention. Nor did they hesitate now. Drew held back the fence as best he could while Cyril squeezed past him. They crawled through the barbed wire, paying no heed this time to its appearance.

They dashed across the perimeter area. The hundred yards seemed a continent wide to Drew, who expected a helicopter searchlight and machine-gun fire at any moment. So fierce was the pounding in his head, there could have been a fleet of gunships overhead, waiting for the right moment to fire, and he would have been oblivious to their presence.

The two men did not pause until they reached the protective thicket that had been their refuge before. They stopped, panting laboriously, drenched again in their own sweat. This time, Drew did retch, a soul-wrenching revulsion shaking his whole body. The nausea made him dizzy; he felt disembodied. The violence, the sheer physical stress paralyzed him. The stunning suddenness of Van der Merwe's death revolted him, while the profound shock of the deception he had been part of numbed his brain. He gulped desperately for air. Cyril slapped him sharply on the back, forcing him to breathe.

"Don't go hysterical on me." Cyril slapped him again on the back. "Come on, you're tougher than that."

The words calmed Drew. He looked at Cyril in the dark, who returned his gaze steadily.

"It's hard, the first time, to look death in the face," he said to Drew. "Thanks for saving my life." Drew felt tears streaming down his cheeks, but he had stopped heaving and was able to breathe in deep gulps.

They listened for several moments but still heard no sounds of soldiers or dogs. A luminous half-moon hung low in the sky.

"Let's go," Cyril said. He clapped Drew on the arm and set off in a loping gait back toward the road.

Fourteen

"It's very dangerous," the old man said to Halden, looking evenly at him from the cracked leather armchair in front of the fire. "But I can't argue with your analysis of the situation. It may be your solution is the only alternative you have."

Peter Wagner's face looked troubled by the complexity of the problem and the responsibility the two men were taking on themselves.

The two warmed themselves by the fireplace, holding snifters of brandy to restore warmth to their bodies after their short hike in the crisp Maine autumn.

Wagner was a widower and lived in his Maine cabin alone with his Irish setter, Samson. Despite a distinguished head of white hair, Wagner, a tall and bony man, looked more at home in the flannel shirt and corduroy pants of the Maine backwoods than he had in his navy blue pinstripe testifying before Congress.

One of the duties of the chairman of the Federal Reserve

Board is to account to lawmakers for the Fed's conduct of monetary policy, its view of the economy, its surveillance of the banking system. The explosive growth of banking and finance had elevated the Fed chairmanship into one of the most powerful positions in the country.

Even the President had to defer to the Fed chairman. Once appointed, the chairman enjoyed an independence enforced by law. Of course the politics of reappointment had encouraged many a Fed chairman to heed the wishes of the chief executive, but Wagner had leveraged his statutory autonomy by never needing to use it.

Halden admired Wagner without reserve. Wagner had brought Halden from his obscure post as president of the Federal Reserve Bank in Kansas City, one of twelve regional banks that together constituted the central bank of the United States, and had made him his confidant, his protégé. When Halden took his turn in the rotation to sit on the Open Market Committee, the panel composed of the seven governors of the Federal Reserve Board and five Federal Reserve Bank presidents, the two invariably steered the board to adopt the policy measures they had already decided upon. Shortly after the debt crisis broke in 1982, Wagner had encouraged the ineffectual president of the New York Fed to step down and installed Halden in the key position, which Wagner himself had filled before ascending to the chairmanship.

"You see what I was telling you all those years," the old man resumed. "How difficult it is to take on the responsibility for these decisions. You're the only one who really understands them, the only one who foresees the consequences."

Halden willingly played the attentive pupil. This was what he had come for, after all, the reassurance that he was doing the right thing, that he *had* to do it.

The past week of intensive preparation had made him more confident. He had consulted his experts, gathered information to refine his plan. He had been careful to discuss only isolated facets of it, to short-circuit normal chains of command, to keep anyone from getting an idea of what he was doing.

His plan was too big, too dangerous to share with anyone but Wagner. Halden had come to believe in the past few weeks that the world monetary system was past saving. The crash in the wake of the gold mine sabotage had definitively destabilized the delicate balance of an increasingly makeshift arrangement. The only constructive action at this moment was to prepare the transition to a new type of monetary order, purged of all the problems and anomalies that had accumulated in the old. That meant choosing the time—through a preemptive strike against the old system.

The old man came back to Halden's proposal. "It's funny to spend so long repairing something, fixing it up to keep on running, only to push it off the cliff in the end. Are you sure the damage can be contained?"

"I've used the computers, everything I could think of to play out the various scenarios." Halden paused. "Peter, I feel the system will collapse very soon anyway, and it is much better if we initiate it in a reasonably controlled environment."

The older man was reflective. "You're undoubtedly right about the collapse, Mark. You know I've been expecting it for many years. The system has been surprisingly resilient, but it's resting on too many hollow structures. It has to collapse."

He looked into the fire for several moments.

"Tomorrow morning we can go over the details together," Wagner said, looking up again at Halden. He paused. "It's something neither Roberts nor Johnson could grasp, let alone the cowboys in the White House." He sighed audibly. "Will you warn anyone?"

"No. I would have talked to Martínez, but there's no one else I trust."

"You think gold can be the catalyst for your action?" Wagner asked.

"It's the wild card of the monetary system. There's something very funny going on. The sabotage should have reduced supply much more than seems to be the case. The market's nervous as a result, and I feel something is going to break soon." Halden did not explain to Wagner that he expected a certain American journalist to be the source of that break.

Samson stirred in his corner. Then the dog sat up and began a scratching routine. "Time for his food," Wagner said. "And I'd better scare up our steaks."

Fifteen

I

Drew replayed the message.

"Here is Hannes," the voice on his answering machine said. "I have found something astounding, crazy. I must talk to you as soon as possible. Call me only at home. *Servus!*"

Drew tried Kraml's home number again, but again got no answer. The trader had not said what day he was calling, but it seemed to be sometime early in the week.

It was Sunday morning. Drew had just come from the airport after his long flight from Johannesburg.

The message bothered him. There was a strain, an urgency in Kraml's voice that went beyond his normal high-strung tendencies. There were several later beeps on the tape, signaling calls without messages, that Drew feared were later attempts by the Austrian to reach him.

Drew unpacked, showered, tried Kraml's number again. The phone rang several times, but finally a woman answered with the name Kraml as though it took great effort.

"Hello, it's Drew Dumesnil in London," he said in English. "I've been out of town but I have a message from Hannes to call him at home."

There was a silence on the other end, so long that Drew was ready to repeat his greeting in German, although he knew that Brigitte, Kraml's wife, spoke fluent English.

"Hannes is dead," the woman said finally, hesitating to find the English words. "He has been killed on the highway."

Drew was numb. He switched to German, trying to console the young widow while finding out just what had happened. Kraml's car had gone off the road on a curve along the highway to Zug on Tuesday morning. The trader had been crushed; the car was going at a high speed and there was a deep ravine. The curve was marked DANGER and had caused several fatal accidents before.

Brigitte Kraml was obviously having trouble coping with the loss and seemed to be under sedation. But Drew pressed her for details of Hannes's behavior the night before the accident. He had been nervous and irritable, she said, and had not slept well. He had called London often, she added.

Drew finally let her go, promising to attend the funeral the next day. Kraml was to be cremated, but Mr. Marcus had insisted on a memorial ceremony, the woman explained. The trader's employer had been deeply touched by the tragedy and had been most generous and sympathetic. Marcus was paying the funeral costs and said he would pay Kraml's salary to the widow for a year, although Hannes carried considerable insurance and her own family was quite well-to-do.

Drew sat ashen-faced next to the phone. MacLean dead. Van der Merwe dead. Now Kraml. The trader's death may have been the unfortunate accident it appeared to be. Just like Drew's own death might have seemed if the Renault had hit him crossing that Paris street!

MacLean had been involved in a scheme to beat the market. What had Kraml done? Was Marcus in on the scheme, and Kraml had found evidence of it? So what? Marcus used inside information to beat the markets every day. Kraml would not find that worth a panic call to a journalist.

No, it had to be related to the Russians and the South Africans. What had Kraml found out? Why had he been killed?

Drew didn't know what to do about his discovery in South

Africa. He felt he needed some evidence to corroborate what he had seen, but he wasn't sure how to get it. He had hoped Kraml was going to get something from Marcus. The suspicious death of the trader proved to Drew that there was something to find out from Marcus, but the journalist needed more tangible evidence to break the story.

II

Drew's cab delivered him to the funeral home the next morning, just as the ceremony was beginning. He slipped quietly into the back row as a cleric of some sort solemnly read a psalm. Drew saw Kraml's wife in the front row, flanked by an older man and woman he presumed were her parents.

In the second row was a thin man with hunched shoulders, whom Drew recognized from photographs as Philip Marcus. Next to him was a short, flabby man Drew took to be Blackford Teller, Marcus's alter ego.

Drew studied Marcus as the clergyman droned on. Marcus seemed confident, in control. Drew could not imagine him as a fugitive. And yet, that was just what he was to the U.S. government. With all his millions, Marcus could scarcely set foot outside Switzerland without risking arrest. He could live very well in Switzerland, of course, and did by all accounts. At least, he had acquired the trappings of the good life: the villa outside Zug, the chalet in the mountains, the cars.

But, in fact, Marcus had no time for his good life. He lived exclusively for his business, and his business was making more and more money.

Drew recalled the banker character in Zola's *L'Argent*. He had to rise at five each morning to receive long lines of brokers and agents with their offers; he was reduced to living on milk alone because of stomach problems; he supported a large family without ever having the time for them. Like the French writer, Drew wondered at the motivation of these billionaires. Small wonder they did not feel bound by the social and moral strictures of normal people. The modest motivations and contentments of normal people were foreign to them.

But the journalist caught himself. Who, after all, was normal?

What was normal about his own unthinking devotion to his work, his twelve-hour days, his single-minded pursuit of whatever journalistic task was set him? Like Marcus, he too had power of a sort, to compensate him for this devotion. He was just now getting a sense of how much power. But the power was not really his; he did not really control it. Neither did Marcus, for all his millions.

A reedy electric organ punctured Drew's reverie. He stood with everyone else. A number of young men there appeared to be Kraml's colleagues.

The organ piece marked the end of the ceremony. Drew maneuvered forward to speak to Kraml's wife.

"I have something for you," the woman said after he had expressed his condolences.

She was bearing up much better than she had on the phone. Pretty in the striking Swiss way, her pragmatism was asserting itself as Kraml's death became a fact of life.

"I'm sorry I didn't think of it yesterday. I was in bad shape, you know." She drew an envelope out of her bag. "Hannes spent most of Monday night writing this down for you; I suppose he wanted to mail it, I don't know. But here it is, anyway."

Drew slipped the envelope into his coat pocket as Aunt somebody came up to the widow. The journalist turned and nearly walked into Philip Marcus.

"Mr. Marcus, Drew Dumesnil." They were too close to attempt to shake hands. Marcus looked at the journalist blankly. "I work for World Commodities News, and I'd like to talk to you about the gold situation." Drew didn't hesitate. It was as close as he would ever get to Marcus, and the worst that could happen is that he would walk away.

Marcus looked straight at him, and Drew had an inkling of how the rabbit felt when fixed in the stare of a snake.

"Not here," Marcus said.

Drew waited while Marcus murmured his sympathies to the widow, promising his assistance whenever she needed it. Then Marcus turned abruptly and moved quickly through the entrance of the church. Uncertain, Drew followed him outside. Marcus's limousine was waiting at the curb. The journalist barely caught Marcus's quick gesture to get into the back.

"It's a seven-minute ride to the office," Marcus said, as the Cadillac pulled away.

"Are you selling gold for the Russians?" Drew asked.

Marcus flashed a quick, wolfish smile. "No comment," he said.

"The South Africans?"

Marcus leaned back. "I'm a trader. I trade for my own account, I trade for clients. I have many clients." He paused to light a cigar.

"There was no sabotage; the South African gold is coming onto the market." Drew's remark was not a question.

Marcus's eyes hardened. "I'm a trader. I don't make policy or produce gold or bomb gold mines. I trade commodities." He paused. "I don't report the news, true or false. I read the papers, I do what my clients tell me."

"You knew there was no sabotage; you're selling the South African gold," Drew persisted. "You're part of the fraud."

Marcus shrugged. "Even if what you said were true, you may as well blame the metal itself for the evil it causes. I've got as much moral responsibility as a gold bar."

"It's not that easy."

"Who said it was easy?" Marcus hissed with sudden vehemence. "I've spent my life stripping away all the hypocrisy that moralists wrap around us. I've sacrificed more than most people ever think of having to get free of that." He settled back into the seat. "The world is the way it is, and I'm just part of it."

"Did you kill Kraml?"

Marcus gently tapped off the ash of his cigar. "I liked Kraml." He looked Drew in the eye. "I miss him a lot. He had a lot of talent. But he apparently got careless on a dangerous road. Or are you going to blame me for the weather too?"

The limousine drew gently to a halt. The door on Drew's side was opened.

"You know less than you think, Dumesnil, and you can't prove even that."

"We're not in a courtroom," Drew said, standing outside the car.

A slight glaze came over Marcus's eyes. "You would do well to keep that in mind." The chauffeur shut the door. Drew watched the limousine disappear down the garage entrance. He turned and walked away briskly, following the signs to the train station, where he took a taxi for Kloten.

As the white Mercedes cab sped along the highway to the

airport, Drew opened Kraml's envelope. There were three pages of the trader's minute, neat handwriting, in a laborious English. As Drew started to read, a chill rippled through him.

Drew—

I've tried calling but you are not there. I'm writing this down so you will be sure to know what I have found out.

I succeeded in picking a way through the program—you remember the computer work I did for Highland Bank—and getting through the security barriers. It was not too easy, but it was not too hard either. I don't think they expected a trader to know much about software.

First I saw the futures position. Marcus is nearly $2 billion short—he seems certain that the price of gold will fall.

It took me longer to locate the physical trading position. When I found it, I thought I had made a mistake, it was simply not to be believed. I have reproduced the figures from memory.

Midas is South Africa, I am sure. The coded information on the bullion corresponds exactly to the South African bars. The figures show that they are channeling enough gold into the market each month to represent more than their full production. The figures anticipate delivery for the coming months.

Croesus must refer to the Soviet Union. Again, the bullion specifications prove it. Also, the amounts are so big—bigger than what the Soviets usually sell—that it must be a major producer.

If Marcus has both of these producers, with code names, they must be in collusion. You see how important this is. You were right to question the South African sabotage. It is very significant that the Soviet Union and South Africa are working together. They can control the gold market.

Drew grew cold as the meaning of Kraml's message became clear. Not only had the South Africans perpetrated a massive hoax on the markets, they had enlisted the Russians as allies! His heart sank at the end of the letter.

I'm not sure whether they will be able to see that I have been in the program. I had no time to be careful. I confess I am frightened. It is very serious and they are dangerous.

The third page contained three columns of figures. Kraml had reproduced the tables he had seen so briefly on the computer screen. His trader's head for figures had enabled him to retain

164

the details of Marcus's entire gold position. One column was headed Midas, the second Croesus, and the third PMTC, for Marcus himself. Entries for each week corresponded to thousands of ounces credited in each column. Each figure was followed by a baffling string of letters and numbers that Drew realized were the telling bullion descriptions.

Kraml had delivered him his documentary proof! Drew felt a sting in his eyes and a tightness in his chest. He had sent Kraml to his death. He had known it was dangerous but had still asked his friend to do it.

Drew saw Marcus's mocking smile in front of him. Marcus and du Plessis: for Drew, they were the incarnation of evil, falsehood, and death. His rage strengthened his resolve.

III

Drew noticed the man as soon as he came onto the platform. Not that the middle-aged commuter, with a navy blue overcoat and an umbrella slung over his arm, was particularly noticeable. It had been a bright, sunny morning as Drew walked up to the Knightsbridge tube station, but it was quite normal for Londoners to carry umbrellas even on sunny days. The weather could change quickly.

Still, Drew noticed this man. The journalist had been nervous since reading Kraml's letter the previous day, as though it were a voice from the grave summoning him to the other side. He had been looking over his shoulder, sitting in corners in public places, and, indeed, crossing streets carefully.

London and all the everyday bustle he was accustomed to had calmed him somewhat. He was taking the tube to the office as he normally did, but he regretted his thoughtlessness already. He should have just hailed a cab for once, to avoid the unnecessary exposure.

Drew felt hunted. Kraml's discovery and subsequent death had removed any margin of doubt about the stakes involved in his own investigation of the mine sabotage. He had been awake most of the night, and only a long phone call to Carol had provided him any solace.

Drew had his leather overnight bag slung over his shoulder.

He was leaving that afternoon for Atlanta to discuss the gold hoax with Corrello and Madison at Sun Belt Communications. He and Carol had decided he should talk to Halden as well.

The man with the umbrella paced nonchalantly along the platform. It was after the rush hour, and the trains seemed to take a long time to arrive.

Drew moved along the platform to keep a distance between himself and the middle-aged man. Perhaps he was succumbing to paranoia, he thought, but he sensed menace in the man's approach, in his carrying an umbrella.

The man kept coming in Drew's direction, which only steeled his resolve to keep away from him. The rush of wind and screeching wheels told him the train was nearing the station.

Drew was so preoccupied watching the middle-aged man that he did not notice the younger man wearing a trenchcoat and hat who hovered behind him, scarcely a yard away.

The crowd, considerably larger after the wait, moved expectantly to the edge of the platform as the train came into the station. The man with the umbrella headed in Drew's direction, more purposefully now. The train stopped.

Suddenly, in the commotion of people boarding and leaving the train, the man in the trenchcoat and hat shoved past Drew, coming between him and the man with the umbrella. The newcomer reminded Drew of the man in Paris who had followed him. It could have been the same man, but Drew had too little time to notice.

The newcomer grappled with the middle-aged man on the platform as people pushed past them toward the exit. Neither made a sound until the man with the umbrella groaned and slumped to his knees. There were gasps as he fell against the passersby.

Drew was already at the exit, looking back over his shoulder. The man in the trenchcoat and hat had disappeared. A small group of people clustered around the prostrate figure of the middle-aged man.

Drew let himself be swept along by the crowd to the escalator, taking the steps two at a time on the left side of the moving staircase, which the disciplined British keep free for those in a hurry.

Drew certainly was in a hurry. He did not understand the

166

sudden intervention of the man with the hat. He did not want to know why the man with the umbrella had slumped down, nor did he want to encounter the man with the hat to ask him.

Drew came up opposite Harrod's and hailed a cab going in the wrong direction. He jumped in breathlessly and gave the driver the address in Fleet Street.

He wondered if he should call the police. But why? To tell them that a man with an umbrella seemed to be walking in his direction until a man with a hat bumped into him?

At the office, Drew watched the Press Association wire for any report of an incident in the underground. Three quarters of an hour later the item came over the ticker. BIZARRE MURDER IN KNIGHTSBRIDGE TUBE STATION. Drew still had trouble believing it. Middle-aged man, identified by the police as Bulgarian, dead on the platform from a fast-acting poison apparently administered by an umbrella found near him. The assailant was believed to be a man who had been struggling with the victim on the platform. The killer had escaped in the crowd.

A second take came from the archives on a previous series of umbrella murders. The tabloids would have a field day proclaiming a new wave of terror.

Drew was baffled. Perhaps the man with the umbrella had been targeting the man with the hat the whole time. Were the trenchcoat and hat some sort of uniform for secret agents? It seemed too pat. But was it a coincidence that a man identical to the one who followed him in Paris was on the same tube platform in London?

Was Kraml's death an accident? There was no doubt in Drew's mind that it was not. But he could not go to the police about the subway incident without telling them what was in Kraml's letter. And he could not do that until he talked to SBC.

Drew had not told Corrello anything over the phone. When he called Monday afternoon, he just said he had some urgent new information regarding the sabotage that he could not take the responsibility for alone.

"You know Madison's not real pleased with this whole South African business," Corrello had warned Drew. "You're skating on mighty thin ice, so you'd better be careful."

"Being careful is the whole reason I have to talk to you," Drew said.

"OK, come in tomorrow, and I'll be sure Madison has some time for you."

Drew knew what needed to be done, but this time he wanted as much backup as possible. If Madison operated according to journalistic ethics, he would approve the exposure of the hoax, since it meant correcting what they now knew was WCN's mistake.

The journalist did not have many illusions, though, about the reception that awaited him. He would go through the motions nonetheless; he would do what he had to do correctly.

Sixteen

I

Madison glowered at them from behind his desk. Drew sat with Corrello, the two men looking like recalcitrant students sent to the principal for a lecture. It had never occurred to Madison to talk with employees in the comfortable sitting area in the opposite corner.

"What in the hell do you mean, the gold mine sabotage was a hoax?" he growled, suppressing his rage with evident effort. "How can it be a hoax? The government announced it, we reported it, every agency and newspaper in the world reported it. The market did a deep knee bend. The goddam stock market was shut down. No hoax can make that happen!"

Corrello remained pale during this outburst. He had been meeting with Drew for the past hour and was only beginning to grasp the enormity of what Drew had discovered.

Drew, too, seemed intimidated by Madison's anger.

"I've seen a mine in operation!" Drew raised his voice.

"They never said *all* the mines were hit," Madison snapped.

169

"Look at these figures," Drew said, passing a copy of Kraml's letter across the desk.

Madison took the papers in his hands but threw them angrily down.

"It was a hoax, arranged by the South African government, perhaps in collusion with the Soviet Union." Drew pressed on. "There has never been any independent verification of the sabotage; troops have sealed off all approaches to the mines."

"I'm listening to some sort of fairy tale, South Africa and the Soviet Union," Madison muttered.

"Our stringer was forced into filing a false story to lend added credibility to the government announcement when it came," Drew said. He had not talked to anyone, not even Carol, about Van der Merwe's death; he did not feel it would serve any useful purpose with Corrello and Madison.

"But the goddam markets don't fall for any old bullshit you put out!"

"They have to react, Tom," Corrello interjected. "They can't go around checking everything. They count on us to keep bullshit off the wires." He had had a sick feeling in the pit of his stomach ever since Drew had expounded his theory to the SBC executive. Corrello had seen how it could be done; he was afraid it *had* been done.

Madison picked up Kraml's letter. "What are these figures?" he asked.

"Kraml went into the master trading program to learn Marcus's position and found a physical gold position in millions of ounces—amounting to tons—worth billions of dollars.

"They were coded Midas and Croesus, but Kraml knows the gold market inside out. From the type of bullion—the quality of fineness, and so on—he knew where the gold came from. He even recognized the amounts as roughly corresponding to the monthly production figures for South Africa and the Soviet Union. And that was what really stunned him—because the figures were projected into the next six months!"

Madison was following closely. "But granting this Midas or Croesus was South Africa, couldn't the figures refer to stockpiles of gold?"

"Conventional wisdom is that South Africa has always needed to sell all the gold it produced, so it certainly could not

170

have stockpiled to that extent. The figures seem to indicate that South Africa continues to produce at its normal rate—even higher."

"Conventional wisdom!" Madison erupted again. "We're sitting here talking about an absurd international plot by two major countries to swindle the world gold market, and you talk about conventional wisdom!"

Madison had been bouncing restlessly on the edge of his seat. He finally stood up and came around the desk to stand in front of Drew. The movement was so quick Drew could only meet his gaze looking up into his angry eyes.

"Dumesnil, goddammit, I warned you about this story. I told you it was your fucking responsibility, and I told you you goddam better be right."

Drew had no response to that. "Two men have died, maybe three," he said finally. He had not talked to Corrello about the apparent attempts on his own life in Paris or London, nor about the circumstances surrounding his visit to Kampfontein.

The chairman and chief executive officer of Sun Belt Communications went back to his seat.

"Kraml was killed in a single-car accident on a road he'd driven every day for months just after he cracked the computer program, before I had a chance even to talk with him," Drew said. "It was not an accident. He was afraid, once he saw what was happening. That's why he took the precaution of writing it down."

"Yeah, we're lucky as hell he was so cautious." Madison remained furious.

"I've been over the letter with Drew," Corrello said. "I don't know the market that well, but it explained the significance of the figures very precisely."

"This guy gets one glance at a computer screen and he has all the figures in his head?"

"It was his business." Corrello's own temper was rising. "That's why his salary was higher than mine."

"The idea seemed to be that by faking the sabotage of the South African mines they could drive up the price of gold," Drew continued. "The reduction of supply would do that, and so would the general unsettling of the market."

"What did that Canadian have to do with all this?" Madison

171

snapped. His mind did not work in a logical manner, and he was accustomed to asking questions as they occurred to him.

"I'm not sure whether MacLean's swindle was part of the whole plan or whether it was just a coincidence," Drew said. "I don't think MacLean was in on the hoax, though, or he would have made sure the story got on the wire."

Madison snorted when Drew mentioned "coincidence."

"So who's bumping these guys off? The fucking KGB? Jesus, you guys've been reading too many goddam thrillers."

"I identified MacLean's body; I went to Kraml's funeral."

Corrello spoke again. "Tom, we've got to decide what to do about this."

Madison was silent. He continued to glower at his two subordinates as if damning them to hell would remove the problem.

"I don't see that we have to do any goddam little thing," he said at last.

Drew and Corrello sat frozen. They were too stunned to even make a protest.

That made Madison smile. "You assholes," he said. He paused to savor his victory. "Fucking asshole journalists. You guys think you have the responsibility of the whole goddam world on your shoulders. Truth, beauty, freedom, huh? Well, screw that.

"I don't know if there was any hoax or plot or Communist subversion. Your precious little figures seem to be damn flimsy evidence." He tore the copy of Kraml's letter into several pieces and thrust them savagely into the wastebasket. "Let alone your goddam hallucinations."

He glared at Drew.

"But I do know this—the fucking *New York Times* can go win itself another Pulitzer by uncovering this maybe-hoax. What *we're* going to do at SBC is increase our quarterly earnings, quarter after quarter after quarter. And I don't see how owning up to the biggest goddam boner in the history of business journalism is going to help us do that!"

Something snapped inside Drew; he felt his tension wash away in an immense flood of relief. He had known from the first numbing realization of the hoax that it would be his responsibility in the end—his alone. Madison's tirade cleared the way for him; he knew there was no approval Madison could give him for what he wanted to do.

"But Tom, if the New York Times does find a hoax, we'd be sitting there looking pretty stupid, wouldn't we?" Corrello tried to maintain a reasonable tone.

"We'd be in damned good company: AP, Reuters, the Times itself bought the story. Not to mention 'the markets,' " he mimicked savagely. "Besides, I think the whole idea that this is a hoax is a pile of cow manure." The worst of his fury spent, Madison seemed keen on repairing his language.

"Let me make myself clear, Dumesnil—Corrello, you're a witness—I absolutely forbid you to pursue this South African thing one step further. I don't want to see anything on our wires about South Africa or gold that isn't picked up from another agency. I'm going to make a careful review of your status with SBC anyway, but if you fuck me over on this, I'll destroy you. Do you understand what I'm saying?"

"Yes, I understand you," Drew said quietly. He had grown cold, impervious to the menace in Madison's voice. Now was not the time for impassioned eloquence in defense of journalistic principles. He needed to stay where he was a little while longer.

II

Drew came through the exit gate and looked around anxiously. Carol stood to one side, spotting him at the same instant. They looked at each other, hesitating a brief moment before rushing into each other's arms.

Carol picked up Drew's briefcase so that he had a hand free for her to take and lead him to the parking lot of the TWA terminal at La Guardia. In the shadow cast by the neon light there, they stopped again for a longer, more tender embrace. They exchanged looks that conveyed emotions they were unable to verbalize yet.

"I'm so glad to be here," Drew said, his feeling investing the banal remark with special significance. The burdens of his experience in South Africa, Kraml's funeral, and the encounter with Madison fell away.

"I've been worried about you," Carol said simply. The minutes slipped by in the open parking garage, but the two lovers were oblivious to the cold. Finally, Carol disengaged herself and loaded Drew's bag into the small trunk of her Honda.

As they drove along the Long Island Expressway, Drew filled her in on his meeting that afternoon with Madison. It was after ten, so the traffic toward Manhattan flowed quickly.

Drew kept his eyes fixed on Carol's face as he talked, returning the smiles she flashed at him. He marveled at her beauty, as if meeting her for the first time. Of all the incredible events he had experienced in the past weeks, it seemed to him that falling in love with Carol was the most unexpected.

"Tell me what happened in South Africa," Carol said. Drew had been elliptical in describing his visit to the Kamfontein gold mine. He had not mentioned Van der Merwe's death at all. By the time he finished telling her the whole story, they were driving through the Midtown Tunnel. Carol's face looked pale in the harsh neon light. When she turned to look at Drew, there was fear in her eyes.

"What are you going to tell Halden?" she asked.

"Everything. There's no reason to hold anything back."

"Halden will use you," Carol said.

Drew pondered her statement. "What is he trying to do?" he asked finally.

"I think he is planning to sabotage the monetary system. I only have vague clues about how he'll do it, but I'm sure he'll use the gold hoax as a pretext for putting his plan into action."

"But he's the one who's done so much to keep the system going! How could he destroy his own work?"

"I don't know, I don't understand, but he's been doing too many things that don't add up. And I heard he went up to see Wagner over the weekend."

"You don't think Wagner would go along with any plot to undermine the system?"

"I don't know. Both of them have fought hard to keep it going, but I'm beginning to see that what counted in the fight is that it was theirs. They felt—feel—as if they have a special mission to do what's best for the country, but they think they are the only real judges of what that is."

"So if the situation seems desperate, they'll take it upon themselves to control the outcome?" Drew's question emerged uneasily as he thought through the implications of what Carol was saying.

He saw Carol nod. "That's it, I think."

"Is the situation desperate?"

"You know what's going to happen when you expose this hoax."

"It'll make what happened last month look like a Sunday picnic."

"Halden has some ideas about turning the panic into a complete stampede, I'm sure," Carol said. "It has something to do with the Latin American safety net, and maybe with the United States foreign debt."

"But those aren't directly linked to gold."

"No, but you know financial markets aren't rational. They're volatile. And gold is a symbol. No matter what any central bank president says, gold remains the reference point for any system of monetary value. You can't change thousands of years of human history that quickly."

Drew wrestled with the idea, although Carol's argument made sense to him. The news of the gold sabotage had panicked the entire financial market, even though gold had no official role in the world monetary system. Exposing the sabotage as a hoax would completely destabilize the markets. Any further unexpected shifts mounted by Halden would compound the disturbance.

"But I can't suppress the news," Drew protested aloud.

Carol heard the anguish of Drew's appeal. "No, of course you can't," she murmured, her lips at his ear. "You have to go ahead."

III

It was nearly 10 A.M. by the time Drew got into Halden's office. The New York Fed president had tried to squeeze in the journalist right after the nine o'clock staff meeting, but several phone calls from Washington had required immediate responses, so Drew sat in an outer office.

"Sorry to keep you waiting," Halden said cheerily as he rose to greet the journalist.

Drew studied Halden as they crossed his office to the sitting group. Carol had convinced him of Halden's intentions, but the

175

central banker seemed as much at ease and in control as at any other time Drew had seen him. The fact that Halden had not invited Carol to join their meeting this morning, however, even though she had been following gold, lent further credence to her suspicions.

"I appreciate the appointment at such short notice," Drew told Halden. "I know you're particularly busy; I wouldn't have asked unless it was urgent."

"So you said," Halden responded. "I'll admit it's a new one for me. I'm sure it's the first time a journalist ever called up to give me information."

Drew smiled at the irony. "I have evidence that the story about the gold mine sabotage in South Africa was a hoax," he said, becoming serious again. When Drew had information, he did not measure it out in small dollops but, like a wire story, led with the big event.

Halden's eyes lit up. He cleared his throat quickly. Drew watched him carefully.

"What kind of evidence?" Halden asked.

"For one thing, a letter from one of Philip Marcus's traders. He cracked the computer code in Zug and saw figures indicating that Marcus was channeling South Africa's full production into the market."

"Can I see the letter? Do you have it with you?"

"I brought a copy for you."

Halden was already jerking his glasses out of his front coat pocket. He took his time puzzling through Kraml's European handwriting. When he came to the figures, he whistled softly.

He took off his glasses with a quick movement and looked at Drew. "Was there something else?"

"I've seen a Rand mine in full operation."

Halden paused as he reflected exactly what that flat statement implied.

"Whoever thought financial journalism would require hazardous-duty pay?" he said with a grim chuckle. "Goddam. It almost makes sense. Can we talk to the fellow who wrote this letter?"

"No. He was killed a week ago. His car went off the road."

"Jesus!"

"You'll see that there seems to be collusion between South Africa and the Soviet Union." Drew told Halden about his earlier conversation with Kraml and the mysterious comings and goings at Marcus's place.

"Our famous spooks in Washington don't have a clue. At least, not anything I've heard, and I would've heard," Halden reflected. He put on his glasses to look over the letter again. "I'm glad you came to me. What are you going to do about this?"

"I've got to try to get some sort of statement from the South Africans and the Soviets; confront them with the notion, get a denial or some sort of response." He told Halden about his trip to South Africa and his talk with du Plessis.

"He looked me right in the eye and told me that at least half the country's capacity is out for months," Drew said.

Halden grunted. "That one could look you in the eye and tell you the moon was made of green cheese and reserved for whites only. I saw the story; it was helpful, or at least it seemed so at the time." He paused. "The mine you saw might have been one of the survivors. But the big Rand mines were supposed to be the hardest hit." He shook his head again. "Jesus, this is a bomb! Why did you come to me?"

"It seemed to me that the potential impact of this news could destabilize the markets, and I didn't want to take the responsibility all by myself." Drew looked straight at the Fed president.

"You sure as hell didn't hesitate to destabilize them a few weeks ago."

"I got the idea after our meeting in London that you might prefer to have some advance knowledge," the journalist explained. "Besides, this isn't breaking news, really; it's more like the negation of breaking news."

"What does Madison say?"

Drew hesitated. "He doesn't like it much."

"Won't back you up, huh?"

"He told me to get off the story."

"But you're not going to, are you?"

Drew shook his head.

"I see," Halden said.

The two men looked at each other. Drew had no idea whether his expression betrayed his knowledge of Halden's real attitude.

"Drew, I'm not going to interefere," Halden said to the younger man. "I'm not going to call on your patriotism, tell you you owe it to your country not to endanger its interests with this story. There's no doubt that if this is true, and if you break the story, the situation is going to get real hairy. As you know, there's a lot of other things coming to a boil as well, with the Latin Americans and that whole mess.

"But I respect your position. In fact, I think our positions are similar." Halden paused. "It comes down to integrity. I have the firm conviction—and working with Peter Wagner strengthened that; I know he feels the same way—that in the long run markets can function only if they keep their integrity. All this bullshit of papering over the gaps, maintaining fictions, might be expedient, even necessary in the short term, but in the long haul, things can keep on working only if the foundation is solid, if the structure is sound.

"Even if I wanted to, even if I *could*, what good would it do me to block this story? Sooner or later it's going to come out; not even Marcus with all his tricks can hide a thousand tons of gold!

"I'll tell you the truth, Drew. I think the structure is so rotten that it's only a question of time before it comes crashing down. I don't know if your gold story will do it—who knows? But I do know a market can't function on lies and fictions; not this one, not any."

Halden sat back and looked at his visitor. Drew was amazed at the central banker's frankness: if he had not already heard Carol's theory, Halden's long speech would have taken on a more noble, innocent meaning.

Drew cleared his throat. "It's a question of integrity for me too. My own conviction is that a journalist has a duty to the truth. It's not the journalist's role to assess the news—I mean, he has to sift through it, find the important things, verify their reliability—but he can't *judge* the news, decide whether it's good, for him or for society, if he reports it. His job is to deliver the news; there are other people—people like you—who have the responsibility for events."

A look of doubt passed quickly over Halden's face, but he recovered immediately. "That's why I said I think our positions are very similar."

There was a sudden embarrassment in the air. The atmosphere had grown intimate; both men had a sense of the importance of what they were saying to each other.

"Your talking to me helps me a lot, though," Halden said.

"I'm not sure when I can go with the story, but I have to do something fast," Drew said.

"This is a critical week—you know that—with this Latin American ultimatum hanging over the market."

Drew nodded. The two men looked at each other.

"All right, then, Drew, we'll leave it at that. You do your job and I'll do mine, and God help us all."

IV

Drew did not pay attention to the movie, nor did he sleep. The plane was only half full, so there was no one next to him. The cabin was dark except for the flickerings of the movie screen. Most of the passengers seemed to be sleeping, wrapped up in the thin airline blankets.

Drew felt exhausted but was too nervous to fall asleep. Carol had taken the afternoon off and they had spent a tender hour in her apartment before she drove him to JFK airport for his flight to London.

The journalist thought vaguely about adding up the number of miles he had flown in the past few days—Johannesburg to London, London to Zurich and back, London to Atlanta, Atlanta to New York, and now New York to London. He gave up the effort.

The meeting with Madison had been disagreeable, but it was his ambiguous encounter with Halden that upset Drew more. He felt very strongly that Carol had correctly analyzed the central banker's intentions, which meant that Drew was another pawn in Halden's strategy. His exposure of the gold hoax would give the Fed president the catalyst he needed to carry out his plan.

For Marcus, too, the journalist was a tool, an instrument. And for du Plessis and the Russians. He had been duped, and the treachery still rankled. But his discovery of the gold mine, and Van der Merwe's and Kraml's deaths, made his own chagrin less important.

One idea drummed at him insistently—he could refuse to expose the hoax. It would give Marcus and the South Africans more time before the market collapsed under the weight of its own contradictions, but it would foil Halden's plans.

Each time the idea came to mind, Drew rejected it. He repeated to himself the reasons for disclosing what he knew. He was a journalist; he had no right to keep secrets. He had no leverage, either, to compel any of the parties to change their behavior; the matter was much bigger than any single journalist. His only weapon was disclosure, and his previous mistake magnified his obligation to use it.

Still, the idea came back to him. He had no obligation to risk his life to see the mines in South Africa; he had no right to endanger Kraml's life by spying on Marcus; he could not arrogate the responsibility for ushering in a recession or even a new depression.

But Van der Merwe had been killed in the visit to the mine; Kraml was dead because he had helped Drew. Halden needed him to carry out his megalomaniac plan to sabotage the world monetary system, but that was the central banker's own responsibility and that of the officials above him.

The arguments twisted and turned inside Drew's head as the airliner crossed the Atlantic. The journalist saw that reason alone could not resolve the turmoil of his emotions. He resented the hoax, the attempts on his life; he seethed at the deaths of Kraml and Van der Merwe; but he feared the consequences of Halden's plan.

His feeling for Carol was a solace in this anguish. For all its comfort, though, his new bond to her could not remove his responsibility. Carol had been supportive, but she could not tell him what action was right or wrong. It was his decision alone.

Drew had called his office from Carol's apartment, instructing Tom to send identical telexes to the ambassadors of South Africa and the Soviet Union in London: HAVE NEW EVIDENCE REGARDING GOLD MINE SABOTAGE AND SITUATION IN GOLD MARKET. SEEK OFFICIAL COMMENT BEFORE PUBLICATION. PLEASE RESPOND SOONEST. DUMESNIL WCN.

Drew wanted to give the South Africans and the Russians until noon, just a few hours away, to respond. Then he would have to decide whether to break his story.

The movie was over. Drew slid up the window shade to see a faint glow of dawn ahead. The lights came on in the aircraft as the cabin crew prepared to serve breakfast. Drew shut his eyes and tried to blank out his troubled thoughts. Carol's image filled his mind. It helped him to know himself, to know what he would do.

Seventeen

I

The blazing December sun already portended summer, while the air held a slight velvety balminess to remind Michael Mijosa it was spring. The departure of a large part of the government for Cape Town meant a slacker pace on the grounds of the Union Buildings.

Mijosa was content, though his contentment had nothing to do with the weather or his work. The black gardener was glad that the hour for the big ALF offensive was near. None of them knew the exact timing, or the details of the whole plan. But Mijosa and thousands like him knew the objective: to destabilize the white government and cripple the economy that was the basis for its power.

This had been the objective of the Azanian Liberation Front since its creation a scant three years earlier. The radical splinter group of the African National Congress had grown quickly, enlisting clandestine support throughout South Africa from those dissatisfied with the slow progress of the ANC.

The group at first had conducted sporadic guerrilla attacks and sabotage in outlying white areas and occasionally against military installations. But only their increased supply of arms and explosives in the past year had enabled them to plan and execute larger operations. The training given to hard-core commando units abroad had been the means of making the ALF a serious threat to the highly trained and motivated white forces.

And so, with the technical and logistical assistance afforded by their foreign friends, ALF had increased its activity and begun plans for the big offensive.

Mijosa was pleased with his role. He commanded five other ALF clandestines in his unit, all working in the Foreign Ministry offices housed in the Union Buildings. Their ability to gather sensitive intelligence had enabled ALF to coordinate the offensive with their allies abroad.

As the government put its plan to manipulate the gold price into action, the ALF had its policy already in place. Rather than waste scarce resources in a futile effort to debunk the fake sabotage laid at their door, the ALF used it as a cover to accelerate their own plans. Their acquiescence in accepting the responsibility for an event that never took place was part of the elaborate deal with their allies to achieve ALF's own objectives.

Now they had been put on the alert. Mijosa's own role in the planned offensive was relatively minor; after all, he was a gardener with no particular combat skills. The heroes would be the commando units, coordinated for the first time in a nationwide offensive.

But Mijosa was content. His help had been vital in preparing the way, and now the day he had hoped for so long was near.

II

A telex awaited Drew when he came into the office Thursday morning after his overnight flight.

Drew read the brief message: MUST TALK TO YOU URGENTLY. WILL BE IN EUROPE WEDNESDAY. REQUEST MEETING. DU PLESSIS. At least one of the telexes he had asked Tom to send had brought results.

"He's already called this morning," Tom explained. "He

wouldn't leave a number, but he said he'd call back at ten." Drew looked at his watch, which said ten o'clock precisely.

The phone rang.

"You know what the telex means," Drew said in response to du Plessis's question. "I have proof, and it makes sense. I'm going to break the story." Drew's face was tight with concentration.

"Yes, we can meet. In Frankfurt? This afternoon?" Drew did a quick mental calculation. "All right. It will be four or so." Drew jotted down a street address. "No, no problem," he said. "See you there."

"He wants me to meet him at a banker's home in the Taunus," Drew said, calling out to Tom. The slotman looked at him blankly. "It's a wooded mountain range outside Frankfurt where all the posh suburbs are. I've got to run."

Drew woke Carol up in New York to tell her the news.

"Aren't you afraid it's a trap?" she asked, the concern in her voice clear over the telephone. "After all, it may be du Plessis behind these attempts on your life."

"He can hardly get a top German banker to conspire in my death," Drew said, with more confidence than he felt. He still had trouble connecting men like du Plessis and the bloodless world of high finance to brutality and violence, but the two attacks against him had shaken his comfortable presuppositions.

"Be careful," she said.

"Keep an eye on Halden for me. I'll call tonight when I'm back from Frankfurt."

Du Plessis had talked about discretion in arranging the meeting in the home of Hans-Peter Schmidt. The number-two man in one of Germany's biggest banks, Schmidt was the most famous goldbug in European banking circles and had made Deutsche Effektenbank the largest German player in the market. Traders called him Happy Hans for his unrelenting bullishness on gold. He had always preened himself on his good relationships with South African authorities and mining houses.

Königsberg in the Taunus was certainly discreet. The exclusive suburb had quiet roads winding through wooded estates and handsome mansions. As though to allay Drew's reservations, du Plessis had told him that Schmidt would be there. Surely, Drew said to himself, a banker of Schmidt's standing was a sufficient safe passage for the meeting.

By the time his taxi from the Rhein-Main Flughafen found

the Königsberg address, Drew was fairly relaxed. He had even slept part of the brief flight from London, as jet lag caught up with him.

It was Schmidt who met Drew at the door. Beaming, effusive, Happy Hans seemed anxious to justify his nickname. Du Plessis was installed in the formal sitting room used only to receive guests. The room exuded a tranquillity that further reassured the journalist.

"Thank you for making the trip," du Plessis said, neither curt nor gracious, just matter-of-fact. "You agree that it's important for us to talk." Drew declined Schmidt's offer of refreshment, and the banker quietly left the room.

The South African official and the journalist regarded each other for what seemed like a long time. Drew wondered whether Van der Merwe's body had been identified, whether du Plessis was aware of the incident at Kampfontein or suspected the journalist's direct knowledge of the hoax.

Drew took a deep breath. "As I've told you, I have information indicating that the gold mine sabotage announced by your government did not in fact take place and that South Africa's gold production has not been impaired."

"The sabotage was reported by your agency and then announced by our government," du Plessis interjected, still unruffled.

"I can't tell you the exact nature or source of my information, but it has come to me in circumstances that guarantee its authenticity," Drew continued, ignoring the remark. "I'm prepared to break the story on the basis of the information I have, but in the interest of fairness I wanted to offer you a chance to comment beforehand."

"Don't you think you'd look a little foolish running a story like that without any verification?" Du Plessis smiled a smile devoid of any feeling.

"Is your government prepared to allow independent verification of the mine sabotage?" Drew asked. He had his note pad ready.

Du Plessis studied the journalist again. "For the record, of course, I remind you of our national security considerations. Off the record—"

Drew interrupted. "I want to be clear that I consider this conversation and any other communication between us to be very much on the record."

"I think you'll see afterward that some things will remain

off the record," du Plessis said evenly. "I know what your information is; I know where it comes from and how you got it. I know about your trip to Atlanta and your talk with Mr. Madison, and about your trip to New York and your meeting with Mr. Halden. I know a lot about you, Mr. Dumesnil." Du Plessis's eyes burned with intensity. "You're all alone on this, and I don't think you can pull it off."

"Will you tell me what mines were damaged in the alleged sabotage, what the nature and extent of the damage was, and what the effect on overall gold production was?"

"Put aside your notebook, Mr. Dumesnil, and consider for a moment. Do you think the interests of the free world would be served by a one-party black dictatorship under Communist control in Africa's largest economy?"

"Do you have any agreement with the Soviet Union for marketing gold?"

"Don't you see that we have to maintain some measure of white control in South Africa in order to avoid the fate that has overtaken so many nations on our continent? I'll tell you something in confidence—*this* must remain off the record—our government is very near to announcing a major constitutional change, reorganizing the provinces and black nations into a confederation of autonomous cantons. This will enable us to preserve white enclaves, under white control, while giving blacks perfect freedom and independence to govern their own territories."

Drew had heard many variations of the cantonal solution when he was in South Africa, always from whites. Moderate black groups insisted on a multiracial unified state. They saw the canton proposal as a way of preserving the white hold on the country's mineral resources while fostering artificial divisions among the blacks.

"Mr. du Plessis, with due respect, I did not come here to talk to you about South African politics. As you pointed out at our last meeting, I am a financial journalist. My question is very specific: Was there or was there not a sabotage of South Africa's gold mines?"

Du Plessis did not answer. "Do you miss your drinking buddy, Hannes Kraml?" he asked. There was no mistaking the menace in his question, although his voice remained flat, uninflected.

Drew knew his face lost color. Outside the bay window behind du Plessis, the dull gold and rust colors of fallen autumn

185

leaves softened the landscape gray from an overcast sky. It was very quiet. Schmidt made no noise in whatever part of the three-story house he had retreated to; Drew had heard no car leave, so he trusted the banker was still home.

Drew regarded du Plessis steadily until he felt he could trust his voice. "Was there or was there not a sabotage of South Africa's gold mines?"

"You're a fool!" du Plessis hissed. For once his placid bureaucrat's face contorted in rage and contempt. The hatred and menace of his look was so incongruous with the pastel flower pattern of the English cotton covering the sofa he was sitting on that Drew nearly smiled. "For the record, Mr. Dumesnil, no comment."

"Will South Africa allow an independent inspection of the mine sites to verify the alleged sabotage?"

Du Plessis stood up. He had regained his composure. "I'm afraid any further conversation is pointless. I've conveyed to you the message I had for you. I'm not going to answer any of your questions."

Drew stood up as well. "Mr. du Plessis, I have personally seen Kampfontein in operation." The journalist had saved this revelation for the end and had the satisfaction of seeing du Plessis lose control once again, a passing moment of fear quickly suppressed. He made no further acknowledgment of Drew's disclosure.

"Mr. Schmidt's car will take you to the airport," the South African said curtly.

"I'd prefer to call a taxi."

"It takes forever to get them here. There's no need; his driver is waiting for you." Du Plessis held the front door open for him. "Goodbye, Mr. Dumesnil."

Drew saw a slight, deferential man in a gray suit holding open the back door of the blue Mercedes parked in the driveway. He went down the walk and got into the car.

III

The Mercedes had a gray leather interior and tinted windows. The armrest was down in the back seat, forming two comfortable armchairs.

The Frankfurt plates reassured Drew; there was no reason to think this was not in fact Schmidt's company car. But the clear menace in du Plessis's allusions made him uneasy.

He was watching closely, then, as the Mercedes approached the access to the Autobahn. The driver passed up the entrance leading southward to the airport and turned onto the highway going north.

"The airport's in the other direction," Drew said to the driver in German. There was no response. Drew suppressed his panic and repeated his remark in English.

At this, the driver nodded in assent. He turned slightly toward the back, keeping his eyes on the road. "Do not worry, Mr. Dumesnil, we are not going directly to the airport."

"Where are we going, then?" Drew heard his own voice sounding unnaturally shrill.

"Please do not worry. There is no danger."

The reassurance that there was no danger in a situation that should have none to begin with did not dampen Drew's fears.

"You're not Mr. Schmidt's driver," Drew said. The driver nodded his head in agreement. "Who *do* you work for? Mr. du Plessis?" The driver shook his head.

"Where are you taking me?"

"Please relax, Mr. Dumesnil." The driver remained calm, polite, even deferential. "I am not supposed to answer your questions, but only to reassure you that there is no danger."

The Mercedes held a steady speed of 180 kilometers an hour as the driver maneuvered his way along the Autobahn, flashing his lights at the laggards blocking the passing lane with an authority that brooked no opposition. Drew recognized the direction signs for the A3, connecting Frankfurt to Bonn, Cologne, and the western Ruhr cities. He resigned himself to his situation. There was no question at that speed of a physical struggle with the driver, let alone any heroics like jumping out of the moving car.

Scarcely an hour later, the driver took the exit marked for Bonn–Bad Godesberg, keeping on the highway that crossed the Rhine just below Bonn itself.

Bonn, styled the "provisional capital" after the postwar division of Germany and Berlin, became the permanent capital of West Germany once it was obvious that there would be no immediate reunification of the divided country. Beethoven's birthplace had no historical claim to be the seat of government; the city was disparagingly referred to as the "capital village."

Bonn made a brave effort nonetheless, extending itself along the Rhine by absorbing various suburbs, notably Bad Godesberg, which housed many of the embassies.

By the time Drew's driver had turned onto the B9—Bonn's main street—the journalist was wondering which diplomatic representation was their destination.

His question was answered when the Mercedes turned abruptly from a quiet side street into the gates of the Soviet Embassy.

The darkness of the garage disoriented Drew, who suppressed a resurgence of fear. He was fairly certain that the Soviets were allied with the South Africans, but he still could not really accept that American journalists could be murdered in Bonn embassies, despite du Plessis's threat.

In the garage, Drew was taken in charge by a portly man in a dark blue suit. His mystery driver disappeared without another word.

The new guide—or guard—led Drew down a deserted, carpeted corridor to a large office that may have been the ambassador's. The civilized surroundings allowed curiosity to overcome Drew's fears once again. Seated on the couch to one side was a man with craggy, irregular features, dressed in a dark woolen suit.

"Mr. Dumesnil: Abrassimov," the Russian said, rising to his feet. "Excuse the mystery. I can explain to you why it was necessary, but I apologize nonetheless."

Drew was trying to assimilate the news. He had never met Oleg Abrassimov, but he recognized the name immediately as that of the powerful vice-chairman and de facto chief executive of Vnesheconombank.

"I have been apprised of your telex to the Soviet embassy in London," Abrassimov said, as though reading the question in Drew's mind. "I wanted to talk to you anyway. By one of those odd coincidences, I happened to be in Germany today too."

Drew still did not know what to say as he accepted his host's invitation to sit in an armchair facing him across a coffee table with an exquisite inlay pattern.

"I presume your meeting with my friend Mr. du Plessis was unpleasant," Abrassimov kept on smoothly. "It's odd—despite their European heritage and their long alliance with the West, the Afrikaners seem to understand American attitudes less well than we do. But then, international diplomacy has never been their strong point."

"Do you have an agreement with du Plessis regarding gold sales?"

"Patience, my friend, I'm going to explain things to you. Would you care for a vodka?"

Without waiting for an answer, he poured two small glasses full from a bottle still misty from its removal from the freezer.

"Several months ago," Abrassimov recounted, "du Plessis contacted me and we met in London. As you know, our nations have not been on a friendly basis in the past. But South Africa was worried about the future.

"Du Plessis made a proposal to me about gold. South Africa was upset, gold was stagnant, and they depended on gold exports more than ever to keep their country going.

"We were unhappy with the gold price too, but it was less bothersome for us. We had many alternatives, including, as you know, increasingly favorable access to the Western credit markets, which didn't quite know what to do with their money.

"But who knows how long that will last? You don't need an avowed enemy of capitalism like myself to warn you of the dangers faced by the Western financial system; there are enough American professors and bankers who have been talking of little else for years."

Drew concentrated on his companion's explanation. The accumulated effect of jet lag and travel fatigue rendered his sense of the world outside himself tenuous. The richly decorated room was overheated; the vodka he had gratefully downed to quiet his nerves dulled his senses even further.

Abrassimov refilled the vodka glasses and continued. "So I talked to du Plessis about his plan. It is the plan you are aware of—to force the price of gold upward by simulating a sabotage of South Africa's mines and then to coordinate our sales of gold at the much higher price."

Abrassimov picked up a manila folder on the table in front of him and placed it before Drew.

"This is a copy of the protocol, which you may keep. I can offer no proof, but I assure you it is authentic."

Drew picked up the folder as in a dream. The typewritten

memorandum, in English, appeared to be about ten pages long; it was innocently titled *Protocol for an agreement on the marketing of precious metals between the Union of Soviet Socialist Republics and the Republic of South Africa.*

Drew felt dazed as he was leafing through the protocol. It was very explicit regarding both the disinformation and the deal with Marcus.

"Of course," Abrassimov resumed, "it took several weeks of meetings to gain the necessary agreement."

Drew interrupted the Russian. "Why are you giving me this? Why are you telling me all this?"

"Amazing, isn't it, that document. The South Africans have a fetish for legal form, even when they are lying and stealing." Abrassimov lit a cigarette. "Why am I telling you? Let me explain first why we went along with this agreement.

"The financial side *was* interesting. We calculated that gold would double or triple in value—which it did." The Russian leaned forward. "But it was the politics that decided us. We saw an opportunity to exploit the falling out between Washington and Pretoria, our first real chance to form an alliance with the white government."

Drew concentrated his energies on listening to the Russian. Abrassimov's explanation was plausible, but the journalist was not completely convinced.

"But aren't you double-crossing the South Africans by telling me all this?" Drew interjected.

"Am I? You won't be able to quote me or cite me as a source. I've given you a document that verifies what you already know; I'm satisfying your curiosity to some extent. No," Abrassimov continued, "such a hoax cannot last long. In the event, it was you who uncovered the information to expose it."

Abrassimov read the skepticism in Drew's face. "You are not satisfied. Think a moment of the position of South Africa when the hoax is exposed: the gold price plummets, the white government loses its last shred of credibility and legitimacy in the eyes of the West. Desperate for assistance, they turn to their new allies, their friends in the East, to preserve their grip on the country they think is theirs."

Drew's mind buzzed. Such a heady dose of Realpolitik was out of his league. Yet it made a crazy kind of sense.

"So you want me to help you take over South Africa?" The

question, so natural in the context of the nightmare he was living through, alarmed Drew as he asked it.

"You are not responsible for what happens in South Africa, Mr. Dumesnil. You are responsible only for doing your job well. If it were not you, it would be someone else who would break the news of the hoax."

"Is someone trying to kill me?" Drew asked suddenly.

Abrassimov was quiet. He crushed out his cigarette. "As I said, the Afrikaners have not much experience in international diplomacy. They asked their allies to help them ensure the success of the plan. In their eyes, that meant eliminating all possible sources of exposure."

Kraml? Van der Merwe? MacLean?

"The incidents involving you were carefully stage-managed. You were never in real danger, and you will not be unless the South Africans try to take matters in their own hands. But we have you under constant surveillance. We showed ourselves at times to alert you."

"But the Bulgarian really died," Drew said, half as statement, half as question.

"Our Bulgarian friends were distressed that you had succeeded in overcoming the agent they sent at our behest. They did not know, of course, that there was a third man who came to your rescue. The other deaths, too, as you know, were quite genuine, but absolutely necessary for us to retain the confidence of the Afrikaners."

Drew tried desperately to maintain his sense of reality. Abrassimov went on.

"Our mutual friend Mr. du Plessis thinks in fact that you have already met a fate much less congenial than sitting here drinking vodka with me. It's all, as you say, a bit over your head, I think," he said. "Do you have other questions?"

Dozens of questions buzzed in Drew's clouded mind. He needed time and rest to sort things out. The confrontation with du Plessis had wiped him out, while his conversation with Abrassimov was surrealistic.

"What happens next?" he asked.

Abrassimov shrugged. "We await events," he said noncommittally. "I'm afraid it's too late to return to London this evening, but I have booked you a room in the Königshof. The driver will take you there."

Eighteen

I

Carol looked at her watch again. Her computer screen shimmered with a spreadsheet of statistics that she found impossible to keep in focus. She stared at the watch. It was after four; Drew should be calling.

She stood and paced up and down the narrow office, holding her arms as if to keep off a chill. She turned abruptly and sat at her desk, quickly tapping a code on the keyboard of her Reuters monitor. The latest headlines flashed onto the screen. Nothing out of the routine.

The calm seemed sinister to her. The markets were quiet but hardly tranquil. Even in the bank, a surreal stillness reigned. Halden's uncharacteristic withdrawal had created a feeling of isolation among the staff. People avoided each other. Since Daniels's timid approach, Carol had had no contact with the trading staff except to exchange data.

She stood up again. She was worried about Drew. Du Plessis had no moral sense and would not hesitate to act against the journalist if he felt threatened. And Drew certainly threatened South Africa with his knowledge.

Carol understood Drew's sense of duty intuitively, even though its consequences were harder for her to accept. At the Fed, the highest value was to protect America's economic interest, and Carol had made that value her own. She could even sympathize with Halden's radical approach, because his motivation seemed to be sincere. But she could not understand Halden's willingness to take such great risks on his own authority.

Carol jumped when the phone rang. She grabbed for the receiver.

"Thank God it's you," she exclaimed when she heard Drew's voice.

"In Bonn?" she interjected as he told her where he was. She listened intently as Drew recounted his meeting with Abrassimov.

"You're sure the document is genuine?" she asked.

"It all fits."

"Do you want me to tell Halden?"

"No. I don't feel that he and I are on the same side anymore. He's taking too much responsibility into his own hands. Have you seen him doing anything unusual?"

"It's quiet here. Creepy."

Drew sighed. "I'll catch the eight o'clock plane to London tomorrow morning. I've got everything I need now to break the story."

Carol was silent a moment. "You have to follow your conscience."

"I'll call you when I'm in the office." Drew's voice was faint as he wished her good night.

Carol sat at her desk. She wondered whether she should call Roberts at the Federal Reserve Board or Johnson at Treasury to warn them about the gold story and Halden's plans. They both had known her since she had accompanied the U.S. delegation to the economic summit in Toronto.

But they would have to confront Halden with her revelations, and Carol felt certain he could make his own plausible explanation of events prevail. Nor was Carol convinced that she even had the right to use Drew's knowledge in that way.

She stood up suddenly and walked with quick steps to the

elevator. She came onto the tenth floor and went to Halden's office. This time, the Fed president was standing at his desk, poring over several open files.

He looked up when Carol knocked, but neither smiled nor said anything.

"What are you doing, Mark?" Carol was surprised at her own boldness.

Halden removed his glasses. "Come in and sit down." He lowered himself into his chair. Carol crossed the room and sat facing him across the desk.

Halden studied her face for a moment. "Of course, you're very bright," he said. "How much have you figured out?"

"I haven't figured out anything. I know you have collected certain types of information, and I think I know why. But I don't understand how you can do all this on your own. If you're planning to sabotage the world financial system, you've got to talk to Roberts, or Johnson, or even the President."

Halden expelled a long sigh. "I've spent many, many hours talking to those men," he said. "I can assure you, if I had the time now to talk to them, I would convince them that my way is the right one."

Carol frowned. "How can you be so sure?"

Halden glanced over the papers on his desk and wiped his face with his right hand. "I said I could convince them my way is the right one." He looked at her. "I didn't say I was sure it was."

Carol's face drained of color.

"It's a great risk to engineer the collapse of the financial system. There are so many unknowns. But I don't see what else can be done." Halden seemed to slump in his chair; he looked smaller and older to Carol. "We've been fighting a losing battle for years. I see no other way to regain the initiative."

Carol felt numb, as if anesthetized. She heard herself ask, "What are you going to do?"

Halden did not respond for some time. Finally, he asked her, "Is Dumesnil ready to break the gold story?"

Carol did not challenge Halden's inference that she would know Drew's plans, but she did not answer his question.

"He must be," Halden continued. "He won't sit on it, and I don't think he'll suppress it." Carol kept her face impassive.

"I'm going to stay here and monitor the wires tonight," Halden said. "You're welcome to stay with me."

"Mark"—Carol's voice was gentle—"I don't think you have the right to do what you're planning to do." Her tone became firmer. "I think you should call Washington."

Halden returned her gaze. His eyes squinted and he shook his head, smiling sadly. "Do? I'm going to watch for developments in the market. I'm going to react to those events in a way to ensure our long-term interests."

Carol stood and walked to the door. She turned back to face Halden. "I'll be back later this evening."

Halden smiled. Carol knew she had answered his question about Drew's intentions, but she knew as well that it no longer mattered.

II

"So what's going on?" Drew asked Tom as he came into the office. He was pasty and haggard, having come directly from the airport. He had managed to shave, however, with a throwaway razor from the hotel in Bonn.

Drew felt drained of energy. But he had awakened with a sense of purpose that forced him to draw on his reserves.

Tom peered into his bank of screens with concentration.

"Quiet, so far."

Drew grunted. "It's going to get a lot less quiet." He sat down at the rim, signed on to a terminal, and began to write his story. He referred to his notes, to Kraml's letter, to the protocol. He took his time with it; it was not an easy story to write.

At one point, Drew interrupted his concentration and punched out a number on the phone next to him. The phone rang several times in Carol's apartment in New York, but no one answered it. Drew felt a stab of anxiety but pushed the worry out of his mind. It was 4 A.M. in New York. Perhaps she was just sleeping through the phone's bell.

The newsroom was quiet, except for the patter of the keyboards. Bart came in and took his place on the rim.

Drew continued typing. Finally, he closed the file and stood up. "OK, Tom, you come over here and I'll take over the slot."

Drew automatically began pushing buttons as he stepped into the slot. The main monitor screen gave him twenty seconds to decide what to do with incoming stories: code them for direct feed on the wire, pass them to the rim for editing, or delete them.

Drew watched the items flickering across the monitor. He checked dollar and gold prices on the trading screen.

He called up his story on the right-hand screen. He coded it urgent priority and addressed it to all subscribers. He punched three keys and the story was gone. In just seconds, the world would know that the sabotage was a hoax.

"Tom, go look at my story coming up on the wire," Drew said to the young man, installed now at one of the rim terminals. "I'd advise you to keep in mind, if anybody asks you later, that I wrote it and sent it myself; that you never saw it before it was on the wire."

Tom obediently went to the printer which read back the WCN wire. He gasped as he saw the headline.

NEW EVIDENCE SUGGESTS SOUTH AFRICAN GOLD MINE
SABOTAGE A HOAX
by Andrew Dumesnil

LONDON (WCN)—Evidence made available to World Commodities News indicates that the reported sabotage of South Africa's gold mines was a hoax designed to manipulate the price of gold higher to benefit the two main producers of gold, South Africa and the Soviet Union.

Documents in the possession of WCN show that South Africa has continued and even increased its production of gold. They show further that the Soviet Union was aware of the scheme but agreed to market its gold in collusion with South Africa.

"No comment," was the response of Andreis du Plessis, director general of South Africa's Ministry of Finance, when apprised of WCN's findings. The South African official said last week that more than half the country's gold production had been damaged by the alleged sabotage.

In response to questions from WCN, Mr. du Plessis reiterated South Africa's rejection of any independent verification of the mine sabotage.

Officials of Vnesheconombank, the Soviet foreign affairs bank

responsible for gold trade, declined any comment for the record.
—MORE—

"My God, Drew," Tom said as he read, "do you know what this is going to do to the market?"

"I've told Madison and Halden. I can't hold it back," Drew responded. The second take came up.

GOLD MINE HOAX -2-

The announcement of the gold mine sabotage last month disrupted financial markets throughout the world and prompted central bank officials to halt all currency trading for two days. Major securities and commodities markets in the United States also closed down.

The price of gold has remained fairly steady since its sharp rise, but several experts have expressed their confusion at the amount of gold available in the market.

The documents in the possession of WCN indicate that South Africa and the Soviet Union continued to channel their full production into the market through Marcus Trading of Switzerland. Officials of Marcus Trading were not available for comment.

Drew's story sent the price of gold plummeting.

"The gold price has gone into free fall," he said. "Bart, get on to the London traders, get a reaction piece—tell them it's WCN calling; they'll pick up after this story. Tom, you answer the phone; I'm not available." All lines were lit up on the phone, which had been buzzing mercilessly but unheeded for several minutes.

"No response yet from South Africa," Drew said. A news blackout cut both ways; it would take some fancy footwork for Pretoria to issue its denial. But each minute the denial was not forthcoming would lend added credibility to the story.

Was it true? Was the sabotage a hoax? Drew was convinced of it, but he had been equally convinced at one point that the sabotage had occurred.

The market certainly accepted his report as the truth. Gold dipped under the thousand-dollar mark within twenty minutes.

Tom brought a telex to the slot. " 'Seaman's Savings Limited is closing for the rest of the day,' " Drew read aloud. "Write this up, Tom. Try to reach them if they are answering the phone. Call the Old Lady, find out if they knew about this. Will there be others?" The crusty old New England bank had become more daring in recent years. Their London subsidiary probably had gone long in the gold futures market, Drew figured.

"Oh, my God," he exclaimed, seeing the next item on the screen. He swallowed hard; Halden was making his move. "Look what's coming in from New York."

Drew coded the story and flashed a copy to Tom.

NEW YORK FED WITHDRAWS INTERBANK SAFETY NET

NEW YORK (USCN) — The New York Federal Reserve Bank issued a statement early this morning declaring it was withdrawing the unlimited guarantee for Latin American interbank deposits that it had implemented just two weeks ago.

"The intention of Latin American countries to follow through on their decision to suspend debt payments and repudiate part of their debt leave us no choice," Mark Halden, president of the New York Fed, said in a prepared statement. "We can no longer countenance or accept their failure to meet their financial engagements."

Tom whistled. "That means the Latin Americans don't have a pot to piss in."

"It will leave big holes in the accounts of a lot of banks who have money out to them—too big for some," Drew said. "Halden's acting like this is a preemptive strike, but how can he do it when the markets are already in an uproar?" Drew's voice was tight with stress.

" 'Hunter Bank closing London branch,' " Drew read aloud from the screen. "Call around and see what their exposure was in the interbank market." It was a bad sign; if Hunter was already experiencing a run in its London branch, a lot of banks were in for a hard ride.

The Fed's announcement arrested the fall in the gold price, as the market tried to figure out whether it was more urgent to get out of gold or get out of dollars.

"Yen is rising," Drew announced. European stock markets were posting strong gains.

"I can't get through to the Bank of England, but there's a telex coming over from them," Tom called over from the telex printer. "They're extending unlimited credit to U.K.-registered banks. They're reminding all foreign banks of their responsibility for branches in the United Kingdom."

Drew thought about Halden and what he really sought. The Fed president had simply reversed his stand on the safety net and yielded to the administration, which wanted to take a hard line with the Latin Americans. The difference was that Halden knew how dangerous this was to the U.S. banking system, while the administration seemed blind to the consequences.

Drew wondered as well about Abrassimov and his waiting for "events." Drew realized that one of the expected events was his own report of the hoax. Did Abrassimov anticipate the crash of the Western financial system?

Drew could see that his report unmasking the South African hoax would play into the hands of both Halden and Abrassimov. But he was not going to be deterred by that realization any more than by du Plessis's threats. As Abrassimov had said, Drew was not responsible for what happened in South Africa or for what happened with the markets. He was responsible for what happened in this newsroom.

The yen had gained 20 percent in an hour, reaching 150 to the dollar. A Tokyo dateline flashed onto the monitor. "MOF instructs Japanese banks to cease all yen exchange immediately," Drew said. The all-powerful Japanese Ministry of Finance reacted quickly.

" 'Rumors of a bank holiday in the United States.' " Drew read the next headline. Bank holidays stop runs—you cannot withdraw money if the bank is not open—but they don't stop bankruptcies.

The dollar was taking a beating. If the Big Board opened it would be overwhelmed by sell orders from foreigners anxious to liquidate dollar holdings.

"There's lots of demand for ECUs," Tom reported from his calls to currency traders. The European Currency Unit had been created in 1978 as a basket of the European currencies for official monetary cooperation. To the surprise of its creators, a private market in ECUs began to grow, as banks bundled together the component currencies and traded the ECU as a unit, in time deposits, credits, and bonds. By the late 1980s, it was gaining increasing recognition as a genuine pan-European currency.

"Carol Connors on line four," Bart called.

199

Drew picked up the receiver and cradled it on his shoulder to keep his hands free for the keyboard. As he listened, his face drained of color. He put down the phone and looked blankly across the rim at Tom.

III

Drew tapped his control keys like a robot as he tried to assimilate what Carol had told him. She had called from the Fed trading room; no wonder she had not answered the phone in her apartment.

Drew could hear voices shouting in the background. Carol had been brisk and businesslike, although Drew had detected the concern in her voice.

She had been right about Halden's intentions. But neither of them had anticipated the extent to which he was willing to go. Drew felt a pain in the pit of his stomach and a curious detachment from reality looking at the flickering monitors in front of him.

The headline from USCN flashed up on the screen just minutes later: U.S. SUSPENDS DEBT SERVICE TO FOREIGNERS. Six words to change the face of world finance forever.

The story followed:

WASHINGTON (USCN) — U.S. Treasury Secretary Donald Johnson announced that the United States Government was suspending service on all its debt securities held by foreigners, effective immediately.

"It is a measure we adopt with great reluctance," Mr. Johnson said in an extraordinary predawn announcement. "But we see no alternative in view of the breakdown in international credit resulting from the decision of Latin American countries to suspend their debt service and to repudiate part of their debt."

The measure affects Treasury bills, bonds and notes registered in foreign ownership, and all bearer notes, which can legally be owned only by foreigners.

The story seemed too sober and dry to contain the explosive message it did. By reneging on the more than one-hundred-billion-dollar debt owed to foreigners, the United States was definitively giving notice that the world monetary system—based on the U.S. dollar and the impeccable credit of the U.S. Government—no longer existed.

The failure of the United States to honor its debt was like Armageddon; it was the event signaling the end of the financial world. U.S. Government debt was the touchstone of the whole system of international credit, the top credit by definition. If the credit of the United States of America was not good, nobody's was.

Drew could picture the consternation in executive offices and trading rooms around the world as the message flashed across screens and spurted from printers. Central bank governors who held the bulk of their country's foreign exchange reserves in Treasury bills deposited with the New York Fed had to cope with the realization that these reserves were now worthless.

The measure represented the nadir of America's sense of responsibility with regard to the world monetary system. In accepting the stewardship of that system after the war, by making the dollar's link to gold the basis of the system, the United States had pledged to subordinate selfish national interests to the overall benefit of the world economy. Now it was announcing that national interest had ultimate priority. In order to protect its own banks, the United States was willing to scuttle the world monetary system.

Silence reigned in the newsroom, except for the ceaseless patter of the keyboard in the slot. Tom was looking pensively past his screen to the window on the far wall, where closed venetian blinds kept the light out. Bart kept his eyes on his screen. The untended phones stopped buzzing.

"Gold is quoted at two thousand," Drew said. The Fed shock had driven all the traders left in the market stampeding into bullion. The removal of the dollar as a reserve currency left gold alone as a reliable store of value. No matter how much there was after the hoax had been revealed, it was not enough to contain the hot money now desperate to get out of dollars.

Nobody wanted dollars now. Calling up the Morgenthorpe page on the trading screen, Drew saw that the British merchant bank was making its gold quotes in pounds sterling, at £700, which meant that the pound had already doubled in value against the dollar.

With no other alternative left, the market desperately was

trying to get out of dollars and into gold. The question of whether or not the mine sabotage had been a hoax was rapidly becoming moot. The market right now was ready to buy South Africa's full production for the next century.

The denial of the South African government finally came.

PRETORIA REJECTS HOAX CLAIM

PRETORIA (FPA) — The South African government dismissed Western news reports that the sabotage of its gold mines was an elaborate hoax. A communiqué branded the reports as "malevolent propaganda."

Although the official denial seemed almost irrelevant in the wake of subsequent events, Drew turned it around at urgent priority.

Nineteen

Ron Sinclair hated to get up this early. Four hours was just not enough sleep.

He forced his eyes open, but only the darkness of his small barracks room greeted him. Outside it remained quiet. Sinclair lay still several minutes, savoring the silence. The last men had regained the surface only at eleven-thirty, and it was midnight before he had collapsed in his cot bed. The noise of the machinery still pounded in his ears.

It could not go on like this, he reflected. The men would start making mistakes, expensive, dangerous mistakes. He found himself forgetting things—the details of the operation he had always prided himself on.

He threw aside the blanket and shuffled over to the sink. The low-wattage bulb above the mirror blinded him as he switched it on.

Sinclair was a big man with a balding head and thick black hair on his chest and arms. At forty-two, there was not a trace of gray, but his undershirt outlined a belly swollen by twenty-five years of steady drinking.

Ron Sinclair was manager of the Witsfontein mine, one of the largest and most profitable mines in South Africa. He had gotten his first mine twelve years ago and was assigned to the Far West Rand just last year. Conditions had been difficult then. Since the "sabotage," they had become nearly intolerable. The security restrictions and the ambitious production schedule created unbearable stress.

Sinclair had no assistant, which obliged him to personally oversee the mine when it was in operation. Now they were digging nearly eighteen hours a day to meet the production quotas assigned to them by Pretoria.

Sinclair squinted at his reflection in the mirror. He saw an unhealthy red through the slits of his eyes, surrounded by dark circles. A chalk-gray pallor gave his slack cheeks a ghoulish cast.

He rubbed his hand along his jaw. He could not go another day without shaving. He pawed around the sink until he found the lather. A runny cream came out of the nearly empty aerosol can. He smeared it thinly over the thick stubble and began pulling the dull razor down his cheek.

Suddenly the mirror flew down into the sink. Before he could think, Sinclair found himself flat on his back. Instinctively, he raised his hands to ward off the door that came crashing down on top of him. He heard a thunderous clap outside and choked as dust filled his lungs.

He scrambled out from under the door. Miraculously, his trousers were still hanging on the hook above his bed. He jerked them on as he stumbled through the gaping hole left where the door had been.

Outside was pandemonium. Someone had managed to switch on the floodlights, but the beams hardly penetrated the thick, roiling clouds of dust. Sinclair lost his balance and fell as another shock rocked the mining complex. A machine gun hammered to his right as Sinclair regained his feet. He ducked low and ran for the office, just twenty yards from his hut.

The building was still intact, affording some shelter from the dust. Tom Lacey, the chief engineer, was at the phone, holding a handkerchief over his mouth.

"What in the hell is going on?" Sinclair yelled.

Before Lacey could respond, the crash of shattering glass deafened the mine manager. The large window facing the mineheads disappeared. Glass shards lacerated Sinclair's exposed arms and chest as the blast knocked him down again. Repeated bursts of automatic fire followed the explosion.

Lacey came over to pull Sinclair to his feet. His arms and neck were slick with blood from the cuts.

"Phone's dead," Lacey yelled. Hundreds of voices shouting created a din further augmented by the machine-gun fire and the sound of heavy motors.

"Who are they shooting at?"

"Miners, trying to get away," Lacey shouted through his handkerchief. "We should get out of here."

"What the hell is going on?"

"It looks like the sabotage is for real this time," Lacey called back, lurching for the door. A muffled explosion from farther away caused a slight trembling in the hut.

"Where's the captain?" Sinclair yelled as he followed Lacey's dim figure outside.

An armored car wheezed to stop in front of the office as the two men emerged. "Hurry up, get in!" A uniformed figure at the wheel waved at them. They clambered into the empty vehicle, which promptly lumbered away. Captain Terry Limon, commander of the garrison force at Witsfontein, crouched bareheaded at the large steering wheel.

"They've gone and done it," he yelled to the two men behind him. The clumsy vehicle rolled blindly ahead as Limon steered for the camp entry from memory.

"Did you see them?" Sinclair leaned forward. Lacey was on the floor. The rattle of gunfire drowned out Limon's response. Sinclair could not see a thing.

How could they have done it? The fence, the garrison, the dogs—how could anyone have planted enough explosives to cause this much damage? The ALF sabotage was supposed to be a fairy tale. He had always reckoned that security made it impossible for any black terrorist to get that close to the mines. Or had it?

He sat back on the hard leather bench as the armored car ground along. The loss of blood made him lightheaded. He felt nauseated. The dust choked him.

He saw how it had been done. A chill shook him and he tightened into a crouch. In that case, he thought, there really is no hope. He lost consciousness.

Twenty

I

Drew punched the flashing light on the phone.

"It's Tony Edwards," a thin voice said.

Drew fumbled for a response, not recognizing the name.

"In Johannesburg."

Of course, the managing editor of the Sun.

"Thank you for your note about Van der Merwe. I was sorry to hear about him," the thin voice continued. Drew had given Cyril a short note about Van der Merwe's death, not specifying the circumstances, to deliver to the Sun.

Drew waited. The tension crackled over the transcontinental connection.

"ALF launched a nationwide offensive last night," Edwards said.

"There's been nothing on the wires."

"The government's trying to put a cap on it, but it's too big. We're putting out a special this morning. The publisher says the Ministry won't be able to stop us."

"What have they hit?" Drew felt a tingling at the back of his neck.

"The airports at Johannesburg and Cape Town, some power plants, the Sasol coal-gasification plants . . ."

Edwards paused. Drew's apprehension grew.

"Our reports are spotty, but they seem to have hit some of the gold mines."

Drew's mind reeled. He felt a sudden churning in his stomach. "The government just affirmed that the sabotage took place a month ago!"

"That's a crock of shit and you know it." Still thin and tinny on the phone, Edwards's voice lost its hesitancy. He talked in a quick, clipped stream. "The 'sabotage' a month ago was a hoax, you know that. But today it's happening for real. We've gotten calls from Carletonville, from Welkom. We had a call from Ron Sinclair, manager of Witsfontein—that's the big one on the Far West Rand—he says they've bombed the hell out of his mine."

Nausea welled up in Drew's throat. He could not respond.

"Sinclair says *white* miners planted the explosives—that's how ALF could get to the mines."

The precision of Edwards's explanation calmed Drew's incipient hysteria. It made sense. It removed one of the anomalies from the previous reports.

"Why would they do that?" Drew asked.

"Who knows what they've been promised, or by whom?" Edwards sounded indifferent.

Drew tried to picture the busy, banal newsroom in the Sun building, so like his own newsroom, like newsrooms all over the world. The special edition would come out in spite of the doomsday ambiance. Drew had sometimes fantasized, seeing himself putting news on the wire even during a nuclear war, up to the last possible minute.

"Why are you calling me?" Drew asked suddenly.

Edwards did not respond immediately, inarticulate once again. "I suppose for Tony's sake," he said, almost a whisper. "You must—"

The line went dead. Drew felt the blood drain suddenly from his head, he nearly swooned. He shook off the dizziness and slowly put down the phone.

Tom had returned to the slot. He peered intently at the mon-

207

itor screen, his hands tapping vigorously on the keyboards in front of him. Bart, too, was intensely preoccupied with his screen.

"Jesus, Drew, look at this!" Tom nearly cried for help.

Drew looked blankly over Tom's shoulder at the story on the monitor screen. The Johannesburg correspondent of the French Press Association had profited from the open lines used to disseminate Pretoria's denial of the hoax to transmit another report.

ALF CLAIMS NEW SABOTAGE OF SOUTH AFRICAN GOLD MINES

JOHANNESBURG (FPA) — Radio transmissions of the Azanian Liberation Front monitored here announced that ALF commando units had succeeded in sabotaging South Africa's major gold mines. The ALF radio denounced earlier reports of mine sabotage as a defamatory lie, but claimed that today's attack has truly crippled the country's gold production.

The mine sabotage appears to be part of a coordinated nationwide offensive. Sporadic reports of strategic commando raids have filtered through the news blackout since early this morning.

—MORE—

Drew numbly signaled to Tom to go back to the rim, taking the seat in the slot. He saw his hands playing across the keyboard, coding the story, as though they belonged to someone else. He pushed the execute button and sent off the item.

"Tom, see if you can get anybody to answer the phone at the banks," Drew said, in a voice that mildly surprised him by its normal tone. A high-pitched singing filled his ears. Other, stronger feelings fought for his attention, but he held them back. "Bart, you try to get through to the Bank of England for a comment."

The markets went quiet, as though the whirring, buzzing trading rooms and floors had been suddenly wiped out. A dizzying flurry of government communiqués from various capitals announced the cessation of foreign exchange trading, the closing of stock markets, bank holidays of unspecified duration. Washington, Tokyo, London, Paris, Bonn, Berne, Rome—time zones had become irrelevant. It was as if the entire globe had suddenly entered a new dimension of simultaneous perception. The age of instantaneous communication had brought an instantaneous crash.

"Holy shit," Tom whispered almost reverently. He held the telephone receiver in front of him, waiting in vain for bankers to answer their ringing phones, as he watched the monitor.

Drew saw the figures blur on the screens before him. He blinked and felt hot tears tracing down his cheeks. He breathed deeply, pushing the keys.

He felt giddy. He suppressed a sudden urge to laugh out loud. The full irony of the situation hit him. The double reversal in the gold market had whiplashed the financial system. Halden and du Plessis certainly had not counted on this.

Abrassimov had. Drew understood the Russian's ambiguity. He wondered if the Russian would really be pleased with the outcome of their machinations.

He wasn't sure that Halden or Abrassimov was getting what he had wanted. It didn't matter to him, anymore than du Plessis's defeat. Drew felt he had remained true to himself in spite of the confrontations with these men.

Halden, Abrassimov, du Plessis, Madison, Marcus—their faces flashed through Drew's mind. His stomach tightened. Each of these strong and powerful personalities had tested his resolve. He had stood up against them and done what his own sense of integrity demanded. He felt good about that.

He took another deep breath. The second take from South Africa came up on the monitor.

ALF CLAIMS NEW SABOTAGE -2-

Terrorists have apparently hit international airports in Johannesburg and Cape Town. The Sasol coal-conversion plants are reported crippled. Power plants throughout the country have been hit.

Reports filtering through indicate that major mines on the Rand, including the large mines in the West Rand area, have undergone extensive damage. Also, several mines in the Free State are reported damaged.

The government has denounced foreign intervention. But initial reports indicate that white blasting engineers have aided ALF, enabling the liberation group to carry out the coordinated sabotage.

Drew coded the story and sent it off.

II

Marcus lit his cigar with a slight flourish. He leaned back to watch the screen.

It had worked! In spite of himself, Marcus broke into a huge grin. My God, how it had worked!

He had sensed something in the Russian. Oh, he was a crafty fox, but Marcus had detected the touch of falseness in the old man. Abrassimov knew all along about the sabotage plans.

Midas, Croesus! Marcus exulted in his victory. His timing had been impeccable. Thank God for that damned nosy journalist. The encounter with him had given Marcus the clue for the timing.

If the Russians were going to act, it could not be too long after the hoax was revealed, or the gold price would collapse. Seeing that the journalist was near to disclosing the hoax, Marcus knew he had to move.

He had moved fast. He had unwound his short positions, even taking a slight loss. Then he had simply gone long in bullion. How easy! He had bought thousands of ounces of bullion from his two favorite clients, Midas and Croesus, the two leading producers! And on credit! He now owned billions of dollars of gold and his creditors were bankrupt.

Marcus's head swam. He had been astonished at Halden's actions. It was a coherent plan serving an insane goal. It was not in the interest of the United States to sabotage a financial system that enshrined its hegemony on the world's money. Why Halden or anyone else would think it was baffled Marcus.

But he did not mind. He had never put much stock in monetary instruments anway. Gold, oil, minerals, property—these were the things that counted. These were the things he owned.

He puffed madly on his cigar. Blacky would join him shortly, once the dealers had been carefully instructed in what they were supposed to do. Nothing! Let the world get itself sorted out; then everyone would come to Marcus, bidding for his gold.

Marcus savored his triumph. He smoked his cigar and happily watched his screen.

Twenty-One

Drew was watching Dan Rather when Carol came home.

"So the conference will be held at the château of Rambouillet," he said, relieving her of the folders she clutched to her chest.

Carol gave him a quick hug and heaved her bulging satchel onto the kitchen table, sighing heavily.

"Yes, in three weeks. Keynes had three years to get ready for Bretton Woods. I have a feeling I'll be working late tonight."

"Carol Maynard Keynes," Drew said. "It has a nice ring to it."

"How were your interviews?"

"Nothing earth-shattering. One thing that strikes me, though, in all these talks I'm having, is the undercurrent of relief."

Carol raised a skeptical eyebrow. "You don't think you're projecting?"

"No, it's there, all right. It's as though everyone had been under a terrible strain and is just happy to be rid of it."

"We're not rid of it yet, I'm afraid," Carol said, extricating files from the tightly packed briefcase.

"How does it look?" Drew asked.

211

"Halden made a major miscalculation. You see it already in the choice of Rambouillet for the monetary conference. Halden thought the United States, as the dominant economic power, would be able to dictate the terms of a new monetary system, as it did in Bretton Woods at the end of World War Two.

"It's true, the U.S. still has the biggest national economy, but Europe, with its single market policy, is actually a bigger economic unit, and Japan, with its Asian market, is an equal party too. And this time, given the circumstances of the collapse, it's as though we lost the war."

"So the Europeans and Japanese will be dictating the terms?"

"Let's just say that the initiative is really not ours. Wagner made that very clear in his briefing today."

"How is he holding up?"

"Holding up? He's never looked better; he loves every minute of it." Carol succeeded in emptying the case and set it aside, sorting the files into separate stacks. "I've been wondering just how innocent his role was. You remember Halden went up to see him the week of the Crash."

Drew heard the capital C on Crash and winced in spite of himself. Usually, now, it was referred to as the Gold Crash, although Drew felt it should be called the Fed Crash. To spare each other's feelings, Drew and Carol simply referred to the Crash.

"He certainly wasted no time in answering his country's appeal for help."

"He's running the New York Fed like he never left it, and he'll be the head of the U.S. delegation to the monetary conference."

"Any news of Halden?" Drew asked in a gentler voice.

"He's still incommunicado on Long Island. But you don't hear any more talk of charges or grand juries. After all, he got general authorizations ahead of time for crisis action that could justify everything he did."

Drew was reflective. "He was too clever in the end."

Carol picked up a folder and opened it.

"Good luck," Drew said to her, returning to his seat in the living room. He found Channel 13 and listened to Adam Smith explaining to investors the complicated formula for evaluating stocks until the markets reopened.

It had been just over a month since the Crash. The markets

212

remained closed through December and the holiday period. A fairly active gray market had sprung up, with the brokerage houses effecting sizable trades among institutional investors. Private individuals had been generally blocked from liquidating or trading their stocks, but the authorities now promised to begin limited trading by the end of January.

The Fed, effectively directed by Wagner from New York, had kept the domestic economy flush enough to head off a deflationary spiral that would have ushered in a depression like that of the 1930s. The only real hardship, becoming more apparent as inventories ran down, was the unavailability of foreign goods. Even the impact of that was surprisingly mild; it was Japan that was running the greater danger of recession, with the United States no longer able to buy Japanese products. Tokyo was even talking of a Marshall Plan for America until the monetary conference restored convertibility of the dollar.

Drew had been in the States for three weeks and separated from Carol for only one of those days, when she had to cut short their Christmas holiday in Iowa to rush back to the Fed for meetings. She was the third-ranking economist in the U.S. delegation, after the Treasury expert and a Harvard professor who had been drafted into service.

Drew had been commissioned by *Commentator* magazine to write a story on the upcoming monetary conference, now scheduled for the beginning of February in Rambouillet, outside Paris. The Europeans had insisted on a European site, and the French won out because of their long insistence on a new world monetary system.

Drew's interviews in Europe and in the United States indicated a lot of uncertainty and worry about the future, but also this undercurrent of relief. The worst had happened and life continued.

Drew's own feelings were ambivalent. He knew that in the long run the overhaul of the monetary system had to be made, but he regretted the manner of the old system's passing. He was ashamed still of having been duped by the gold hoax, and remorse for the deaths of Kraml and Van der Merwe haunted him.

He could rationalize that all of them were caught up in events and machinations beyond their control. He knew, too, that his decision to follow through with exposing the hoax had given him

213

a new strength of character. That partly effaced his chagrin at being fooled. But it did not bring the two dead men back to life.

Drew felt a sudden intimation of warmth and then Carol was on his lap, embracing him with a kiss.

"How much do you think the New Dollar should be worth?"

"That's easy. One ECU, the good old European currency unit."

"That is the easy part. But how many old dollars does it take in exchange for a New Dollar?"

Drew shrugged. Prices had been frozen in the United States to avoid hyperinflation like that which ravaged Germany twice in two decades after the currency collapsed. But Drew had been astonished by how many dollars he was able to purchase in black market trading with the sterling he had brought with him from London.

"The big question is gold or no gold," he said finally. "There doesn't seem to be any way around it. Every other possible anchor that was in use depended on the dollar and the U.S. economy. Neither the Europeans nor the Japanese will accept that; nor do they want their currencies to be the sole reserves either."

Drew hesitated to be drawn into a discussion of monetary reserves. He had a journalist's working knowledge of how they functioned, but the economists' view of central bank reserves was as subtle and impenetrable to him as scholastic theology.

"Doesn't the situation in South Africa influence what role gold will have?" he asked.

"Yes and no," Carol answered, smiling at herself for her easy slide into the traditional posture of economists. "The damage from the ALF offensive, the prospect of protracted guerrilla warfare, the operation of some Orange Free State mines by ALF—all that will make the supply of gold uncertain.

"But," she said with emphasis, "demand is virtually infinite—gold is literally priceless." The gold fixing still took place in London, but the current price of £5,000 on ounce meant nothing, for practically no gold was for sale. "And the Russians have told the Europeans discreetly that, although they will not attend the monetary conference or participate immediately in the new system, they will manage their gold sales in a way not to disrupt whatever role is established for gold."

"How very considerate of them." Drew said it lightly, but he was unable to keep an edge of hardness out of his voice.

"Is Abrassimov going to talk to you for your article?"

"He had better, or I'll unmask him," Drew joked. Although the journalist himself had been the subject of many stories and interviews in the aftermath of the Crash, he had not divulged the sources of the information that enabled him to break the hoax story. In the context of the U.S. action and the real sabotage of the ALF offensive, the exposure of the hoax had become a minor event.

But Drew knew that the effect was not minor. More than the impact of the story itself on the horrific day of the Crash, the exposure of the hoax bolstered the credibility of all news reporting. Drew's story had demonstrated the tenaciousness of the truth.

"By the way, I'm fairly certain *Commentator* is going to offer me a job," Drew said to Carol as she rose to return to her files. He had not waited for any reaction from Madison, but telexed his resignation from WCN on the day of the Crash itself. *Commentator*, a highly regarded British monthly, had called him the following week with his freelance assignment.

"In London?"

"I'd be the 'roving economics correspondent.' " He paused. "It probably doesn't matter where I hang my hat when I'm not roving."

Carol smiled at him. "Maybe we should start looking for a bigger apartment."